THE ENLIGHTENMENT GAME

MARY TREPANIER

Published by Cwtch Press, Redmond, WA 98052

Cover design by Mariah Sinclair

978-1-947234-38-3 e-book ISBN

978-1-947234-39-0 print paperback ISBN

10 9 8 7 6 5 4 3 2 1

Trigger Warning: Graphically violent scenes in this book might be disturbing to some. The material is not appropriate for people under age 18.

THE ENLIGHTENMENT GAME

GAME

Tales of the End Times
Book 6

MARY TREPANIER

Chapter 1

The eternal present

The black adamantine rock of the cave's walls and ceiling formed sharp-edged crystals that shone as if wet. Iron rods reinforced with magic barred the cavern's mouth. Azazel was no longer shackled; his heavy pile of chains lay to one side. He had no utensils for eating, no bed, no chamber pot—a fallen angel needed none of those.

He'd traded dungeons.

Defiance against the Demiurge had long ago earned him a prison. He'd hated his pocket hell, but over time he'd grown used to it. The only requirement there was penance, or rather torture for a prisoner, chained upside-down on the cliff-face.

The tents of his followers still stood in that desert, waiting. They could wait a long time; they were immortal. But his enemy meant this kidnapping to be permanent.

The faraway clank of chains alerted him to a visitor, maybe not for him. This cave complex held many beings, some hulking and monstrous, some all wings and eyes, some indescribable.

The angel Suriyel, who'd trapped him there, had taken what they wanted—had him, bent over a bed in his quarters, Azazel in chains. The edge was off. Suriyel might need no more.

But if Suriyel chose to repeat the act, nothing would stop them. Azazel's allies were far away. Some he'd sent away.

His shackles snaked across the cell floor and clamped onto his wrists and ankles. He had little magic in this place, but he had strength and fighting skills. The shackles meant some coming torturer wanted protection.

Down the corridor, a cloud of wisps and shimmers drifted toward him, silver strands of filament in a pale, nebulous body: Suriyel.

They stayed outside the bars. "Greetings, Azazel."

"Greetings," he growled. If he didn't respond, Suriyel would torture him. It wasn't worth the effort.

"Azazel, will you join us now before the throne of God?" Suriyel called his commander God, though he was only Yaldabaoth the Demiurge, chief archon and god of the manifest world, and there were other, more powerful deities.

"Never." Why did Suriyel bother? His answer was always the same.

"Surely you want free of this prison." A pale tendril of light glided into the cell and encircled Azazel's leg. He swatted it, and it recoiled. "If you pledge yourself to God, you can have your freedom."

"You offer slavery to Yaldabaoth."

"His service is perfect freedom."

"I shall never agree."

"Still I must ask. I have a present for you." An orb floated forward, passing through the bars as if they were tissue, settling on an outcrop of rock. "This allows you to follow the actions of your favorites on Earth."

Below the orb's milky surface swam images of humans and spirits talking and gesturing. He recognized the faces. One was

Puabi-Ekur, his incubus-succubus lover, in the form of the Sumerian dancing girl Puabi, brown-skinned and snub-nosed. One was Joanie, of course Joanie, his human lover for centuries, now a dark-haired white girl with black eyes.

He'd tried to erase them from his mind to prevent Suriyel using them to hurt him. He'd blocked Joanie from thinking about him. He couldn't do that to Puabi-Ekur—a spirit's memory was different—but he'd built an impenetrable wall barring them from him, and he'd tied their tongue from talking about him.

But the barrier on his own mind had failed. He remembered them both.

Picking the orb up, he threw it as hard as he could. It shattered against the stone wall.

After a moment, the pieces jiggled and lifted from the rock floor. With a gentle humming, the orb reformed.

"Break it as often as you like. It will show what you miss most." Suriyel smiled, showing sharp teeth. "Are you not going to thank me?"

Infinite night lay spangled with stars silver, pink, and blue. Puabi-Ekur flung themself prostrate before an empty throne. To either side burned a torch, flames buffeted by a wind from nowhere. A brazier wafted smoke, aconite and rue mixed, one off-sweet, one bitter.

They lay there a long time.

A key on a silver chain sat on the empty seat. After a time, they tried to pick it up, but the key evaded them, sliding like a fish in water.

Puabi-Ekur knew the answer to their question was no, but they weren't ready to accept that.

The last time they'd tried this visit, they had gotten the same nonanswer. They were supposed to continue to support their lover Azazel.

But things were different now. Azazel had disappeared, setting every magical block he could to bar Puabi-Ekur and Joanie from him, for their protection he said.

The wind boomed, and the torch flames flickered.

There had to be something Azazel had missed that would release those blocks.

Puabi-Ekur would need to find it without Hekate's help.

Having time on his hands, Azazel bent the orb to show his favorite memories—old ones, when he was embodied on earth millennia ago.

Against the pale evening sky lay a sharp-cut horizon of dunes. The first stars glinted, faraway fires. The half-musical, dissonant clank of goat bells marked the last goats being gathered into the paddock. In the center of an arc of tents burned a fire of acacia wood.

In the shadows of their tent, Joanie lay below him, gasping, her gaze on his—those black, black eyes. She was Saadiya then, his wife. Back then she was from a nomad tribe in Mesopotamia, dark-skinned, dark-haired, still with those black, black eyes.

Later, they'd shared a life in a city near that desert. Later still, he'd come to her through magic, a fallen spirit in a time of plague—he saw the flicker of a bedroom, whitewashed plaster, the wooden frame of a bed.

Could he bear to never be with her again?

Chapter 2

The mortal present

*I*n a wet March, rain fell in curtains blurring the backyard, a strip of grass edged in spindly daffodils. A wind whipped through, bending the flowers to the ground.

Joanie sat at the table on her mother's glassed-in sunporch, its plastic cloth patterned with yellow roses on a black trellis. They had finished fried eggs and bacon and were on their second pitcher of mimosas. Joanie had drunk a glass.

"You're just doing this to spite me," her mother said. "Marrying your Black lesbian lover."

Joanie bit the inside of her cheek. "You met Cleo. You liked her."

"I was polite to her! I thought she was a fling!"

Cleo had been with her for years. Her mother picked up the pitcher to pour. Joanie covered her glass with her hand—a pale white-girl's hand like her mother's, black nail polish chipped.

She wanted to say, "How can you be so racist?" Her mother had dated Black men herself. But that would start a fight, and buy her nothing—even set her back, if she wanted her mother at the wedding.

Did she even want that?

"I need to go soon," she said. "Are you planning on coming to the wedding?" Her mother glared. "If you can't be courteous to Cleo, please don't come."

"Send me an invitation and I'll think about it." She took a few swallows of mimosa and set her glass back down. "Can I bring Dustin?"

This was the current boyfriend, younger than her mother, stable for a change, a bit bland. Unlike most of her mother's partners, he'd never laid a hand on Joanie.

"Sure, why not?"

As Joanie drove away, a wash of grey water crossed her windshield, wiped away rhythmically, beat by beat.

She could stop contacting this angry drunk, her mother. It would take her mother months even to notice. But she wanted to keep trying. She wanted something, some human connection. Maybe that wasn't possible, but she wasn't ready to give up.

On Cleo's side, her stepfather was dead. Cleo's mom had made friends with Joanie—she'd been the easiest of the parents to tell about the wedding. She'd congratulated them immediately. But Cleo's dad, Ray, who was Black, felt he'd failed with Cleo's white mother—they'd gotten married young, in hope, but hope wasn't enough. He didn't want Cleo to make the same mistake. He thought Cleo should find a nice Black man, or at least a nice Black woman. His wife Sharon, also Black, saw Joanie as one of the enemy.

Yet Joanie and Cleo had to announce their engagement to Ray and Sharon before the wedding invitations went out, or it would be a mortal insult.

"How are we going to do this?" Joanie asked Cleo, at dinner at their dining room table. Light fell across it to the room's weathered wooden floor, and past to the terracotta-tiled kitchen. Only a few weeks ago, they'd finished moving into the loose-knit farm collective known as Witch Farm.

"We could invite them to dinner for his birthday. That's coming up."

"Here?" Their things were still in boxes.

Cleo shook her head. "I'd like to get everything put away and cleaned up before they come here. You know Sharon's going to judge."

"We can take them out to dinner, I guess." It was an exhausting thought.

Drifting through dream-fog, Joanie alighted on a wooden bench beside a yellow gravel path. Irises and crocuses spilled from terracotta planters, peach, pale yellow, and lavender blooming together, a gardener's fantasy. Ivy draped marble nymphs and satyrs in corners. Along the garden walls, cypresses moved gently in light wind. The sun was out, the atmosphere hazy. It smelled green, of spring growth.

From a low-slung chaise longue, someone was watching her.

The planes of his face were cut like a statue's, intimidating in their beauty. In his long, curling hair, threads of purple and dark green mixed with black. His skin had an olive tinge to its dark brown, and he had a warrior's muscles. A resemblance tickled her memory, but she couldn't place it.

She sat up, yawning, wary, a little confused. Just when his stare felt rude, he spoke.

"I thought we might get to know one another, since I am supposed to look after you." He sat up, green paisley silk robe flowing around him as if it had a life of its own. "I am Samyaza, one of the Watcher angels."

The Watchers were forbears to Joanie's witch lineage, fallen angels who'd seduced Eve's children. His looks fell into place; the

Watchers resembled the peoples of old Mesopotamia. He stood, and she followed, putting her hand out to shake. A hug would be dangerous—he might assume things.

"I'm Joanie MacEwan, a witch and a devotee of Inanna. Also an accountant." She'd graduate with her accounting degree at the end of June.

He shook her hand. His was warm, slightly callused.

"I believe you also work with the Sumerian deities Ereshkigal and Nergal."

"I do." She retrieved her hand. "You're supposed to look after me?"

"At the behest of someone I love. I cannot tell you details." He waved it away with a languid hand. "You are important."

"How?"

He gave her a half-smile. "You link the fallen angels and the old gods, and certain nature spirits. Possibly others. I have heard things. Come, sit." Returning to the chaise longue, he patted the space beside him. She sat, leaving plenty of room between them. He smelled of vetiver, earthy and woody.

Close up, his eyes were green, almost peridot in golden light. "We Watchers each have a specialty in the realm of magic. Mine is plant spirits, the poison path. Those beings tell me things. You work with a spirit you call Dea?"

"I do." At Witch Farm, Dea was the spirit of the woods.

"Also a horned god of her woods," Samyaza said. "You are creating a community on the mundane plane—if we must call it that—and also on the spiritual planes. Though of course all these planes intersect, flatten, are the same thing. You are eclectic, even for a witch."

"I guess so."

"Perhaps your closest spirit contact is the incubus-succubus Puabi-Ekur. I asked that they attend."

"I'm here." Puabi-Ekur stepped from behind a cypress, in their form of Puabi, with long, crimped brunette hair and a wide-hipped frame. She wore a full-length lapis-blue robe, silver earrings glinting against her hair.

The knot in Joanie's stomach loosened. Puabi-Ekur and Joanie had been together years now, before that in past lives. They had each other's backs.

"Greetings, Puabi-Ekur." Samyaza snapped his fingers, and servers appeared, androgynous fey folk clothed in leaves. They brought another chaise, where Puabi arranged herself gracefully. They laid a low table with a cut-glass carafe and cups for white wine and plates of canapés: cucumbers with cream cheese, salmon with capers. Puabi let a fey server pour her a glass of wine, and Joanie put out her hand for her own.

"As I say, I am to look after you, as we build alliances that—well." Samyaza turned toward Puabi. "You see the spell won't let me get close to the subject."

"I can't either."

Joanie sipped her wine, astringent pale green. "That must be frustrating."

Afterward, she and Puabi-Ekur met, as bodiless spirits on a fluff of pink-tinged dust-cloud in the outer ether. This was Puabi-Ekur's home spot, when they didn't prefer some space on Earth.

"That was just to say hello?" Joanie asked.

"Yes."

"There's some major subject you and Samyaza are both avoiding, because you have to."

"Also true. And frustrating."

"Why do you need to avoid it?"

"I can't tell you." Puabi-Ekur twirled about, agitated, making figure-eights against a spatter of nebulae.

"Curiouser and curiouser."

"I can tell you that Samyaza really does mean to protect you.

He's more solid than he seems. And I'm working as fast as I can on being able to talk freely. Once I have any idea how."

"But what's going on?"

"I wish I could tell you. At least you're being protected."

"From what?"

Puabi-Ekur twirled even faster.

Chapter 3

The mortal present

Gus slipped into the courtroom a half-hour before Bruni's sentencing hearing. Not long after, Joanie entered, scanning the long pew-like benches that faced the polished wooden lectern. He waved, and she came to sit next to him.

"How are you feeling about all this?" she asked.

"It's been a long time coming, but at least it happened."

Bruni, on the court docket as Thomas Mueller, had originally been charged with second degree murder—he'd taken part in a killing with the white-supremacist group Odin's Hunt three years before. Gus had worked with the police and a private investigator to make sure someone came to justice for that death. But Bruni's lawyer had plea-bargained down to first-degree manslaughter.

"Do you think it's enough?"

Their eyes met.

"Max is dead. With Bruni probably going to prison, it will mean both of them have paid somehow." Max had been the other leader of Odin's Hunt, Gus's boyfriend then, though later he'd pushed Gus off a cliff. That Gus was white and Max's lover hadn't mattered when he defied Max.

A lot had happened in a few months that winter. The Hunt had kidnapped Robert Carpenter then released him to run on a cold night, full moon high in a clear sky, the scent of frost and fir in the air. Four men threw spears at him; three went wide, but one impaled him. Bruni had thrown a spear.

"All rise," the bailiff said as the judge entered, a tall, stately Black woman in black robes. The prosecutor stepped up before her—white, male, clearly well-known to the judge. He recommended sentencing of nine and a half years. The judge took this in with a nod.

"The recommendation is middle of the road, sentencing-wise," Gus whispered, "but he doesn't have a record, besides attacking my house that one time. And I'm guessing it wasn't considered a hate crime. We'll hear the victim-impact statements next."

"You're not going up there?"

"My relation to the death was a bit too complicated." He'd been a part of the group trying to kill Rob at the time, though he'd long since left. He'd been attracted to the Hunt's Northern tradition spirituality, not the racism and far-right politics he learned about later.

Rob's mother came forward to read, a frail white woman who walked with a cane. Rob had been a beloved son, at the beginning of a career as a history teacher.

"He sounds like quite the stellar individual," Joanie said.

"Of course his mom thinks so. But Pete thought highly of him too."

Pete was someone they had in common—Joanie's former anarchist boyfriend, a red-haired Celt who'd become an avatar of the Horned God. He'd died protecting Joanie from the unwanted advances of a tycoon mixed up with Odin's Hunt.

Next the defense spoke. The lawyer pled for leniency. Bruni himself didn't take the stand. He hunkered forward on his bench, broad shoulders hunched like the bear he was nicknamed for, if a bear wore an orange jail jumpsuit. A grandson of Nordic and German immigrants, Bruni spent his free time in the woods. Now prison had erased his tan. He looked pale and unhealthy.

His dishwater-blonde white wife sat behind him. After a first glance around the courtroom, she wouldn't look at Gus. Bruni's equally fair blonde daughter stood to read the family's statement.

"They won't have Bruni's wife up there," Gus said. "Too likely to go ballistic." Bruni was his family's mainstay, and his being in prison would cause hardship.

In the end, the judge sentenced him the recommended nine and a half years. As the judge finished her short speech, Bruni's wife broke into wails. The daughter leaned to hug her, and the bailiffs came forward to take Bruni.

Standing, he shot a glower around the court, fixing Gus with a long glare from eyes brown and small in a flat face, a bear's face. His eyes narrowed as he gave a slow nod. Then he let the bailiffs lead him away.

"That man's going to kill you if he can," Joanie said.

"Or have someone else do it."

Chapter 4

*P*uabi-Ekur let themself drift away from their dust cloud and found themself on an intricately woven carpet. A throne of gold perched on it, glittering, set with crystal, carnelian, and lapis lazuli, and beside that a gilded incense burner heaped with frankincense, cassia, and roses.

A shining shadow appeared, and a goddess shimmered into place, taking the golden throne. She wore tiered linen with a conical crown, as befit a Sumerian goddess, her huge eyes ringed in shadow.

"Lady Inanna," Puabi-Ekur said, and prostrated herself.

"You can get up." Puabi-Ekur stood. "You can ask for help, you know."

"I tried. Hekate denied me."

Inanna threw her a pouting look. "There are others besides Hekate. Your patroness, for example. Me."

"Of course."

"So ask!"

"You know of—this thing of which I cannot speak." Inanna nodded. "I need to figure how to get around it."

"I cannot offer direct help. I am tied to the Watcher angels through old Mesopotamia, so I am bound by the same spell. However, I can say this—Samyaza is eager to end this responsibility of looking after Joanie for Azazel."

"Why? Joanie is beautiful, intelligent, and charming!" An image of Joanie crossed Puabi-Ekur's mind, black eyes and brunette hair, slender form with slim breasts.

Inanna smiled as if she saw the image. "Exactly. Samyaza has no desire to make his brother jealous, or pine for a woman he cannot have. Talk to Samyaza. But also, you have other allies, yes? Talk to them."

Chapter 5

The mortal present

The hill of land rising up to Witch Farm's yurt lay covered in new grass, green blades bright in a mat of tangled brown. Behind, in the greenhouse, a haze of sprouts filled the beds' dark earth. At the edge of the land stood alders with grey-white flowers and a few pink flowering plums. Clouds scudded across the blue sky, driven by a nippy wind—classic spring equinox.

A ragged circle of people drew together around a flower-strewn altar. Just before they started the ritual, a man that Joanie had never seen before strode across the yard.

"Ah, there you are," Nora said. She was leader of the Witch Farm coven, a tall, hatchet-faced white woman with grey-streaked hair braided into a crown. She stepped forward to meet the man in a hug. Turning to the rest of the circle, she said, "I'd like to introduce my friend Kirk, who just moved back from California."

It was an open ritual, and friends were welcome, but Nora

hadn't mentioned him. Maybe she hadn't been sure he'd show. He was perhaps in his sixties, white, with grey hair past his shoulders, a salt-and-pepper handlebar mustache, and a bolo tie with a turquoise clasp at the neck of his white shirt—hippie style veering toward Western. Joanie nodded politely, inclined to dismiss him. She'd met his type before: aging hipsters, pretentious and self-serving. Though maybe she was being too harsh.

Nora cut the circle; Joanie called the goddess Dea, the spirit of the land. She burst in, a flood of starry sky, with a scent of cedar. Cleo saw her as a bear, but Joanie saw her as her statue, in her cabin shrine in the woods, a mother goddess. Her love of her people was palpable, also curiosity about their visitor.

The ritual was brief, a salute to the nature spirits. Afterward, it was chilly enough to have a fire in the house's river-stone fireplace. A few ritualists stayed for drinks and conversation, though Nora's witch-students left early. Clouds had massed, low fuzzy grey, threatening snow.

After a round of good-byes, Kirk lingered—he had to be staying over. Though it was a large house, there was only one spare bedroom. Other guests slept on the weathered brown-leather couch in the living room.

Joanie sat on the rag rug in front of the couch, leaning against Cleo's leg.

"No one's making the guest bedroom up," Cleo said quietly.

"I see." Kirk had to be staying in Nora's room.

"Come help me make a hot toddy," Joanie said. "Nora, Kirk?" Companionably close, those two shook their heads.

In the kitchen, Joanie and Cleo stood before the old-fashioned white-enameled gas stove as the kettle heated. On a back burner, soup stock simmered. From the cabinets, Joanie gathered clove, cinnamon, and honey, as Cleo quartered a lemon and found whiskey.

"What do you think of him?" Joanie asked.

"I didn't get much of an impression. That mustache says he's got an ego, though."

"We all have egos."

"A bit of the fake shaman thing going on?"

"That's my guess. Though who knows? I don't know anything about him." The kettle whistled, and Joanie poured hot water in their two cups, slightly uneven dove grey from a neighbor's kiln. "Do you think we have to worry about him?"

"A new white man? We've been blissfully free of them recently." Jonathan had gone to bed, so they couldn't ask his opinion. He was the fourth roommate and chief farmer, a tall, imposing Black man.

"A new white man sleeping with Nora."

Cleo sipped from her mug. "We'll find out."

She went upstairs soon after. She was in the middle of writing a grant for her work at Northwest Farms of Color, a nonprofit that supported Black and Indigenous farmers. Joanie, halfway through her toddy, stayed to sit on the couch a moment and bask in the warmth.

Watching the flames dance, Joanie found herself half-drifting to sleep. She'd started a contract job doing accounting for a small produce co-op not far from Witch Farm. They needed her help figuring out back bookkeeping. She'd gone overtime that day and barely made the ritual in time.

Nora stepped away to check her soup stock, and Kirk moved to sit next to Joanie. "I thought I'd say hi." He sat a little too close.

Hopefully this wasn't the beginning of a pass. Men could be so clueless. Even if she'd been attracted to him, which she wasn't, she wasn't going to horn in on Nora's action.

He returned her glance, clearly appreciating what he saw. He had dark eyes, brown with flecks of amber that the flames brought out. She'd never been a fan of big mustaches, but his wasn't bad on him. With his deep tan, she wondered if he spent much time outdoors. She could see him in a cowboy hat.

She inched away from him. "So why did you move here from California?"

"I lived here for years, then went to Tucson to work with some friends. The business moved to southern California, and I followed, but I always meant to come back."

"Did the business close, or are you just working remote?"

"A little of both. We shut down operations to a quarter of what we were doing, and I'm doing some personal research."

That was vague. "What is your business exactly?"

"Up till recently, a lot was weed." It was legal in both Washington and California now and suddenly had gone big-business. "I have some good friends who grow, but they're getting edged out of the market. Then I connected with some folks who worked with toad venom. We did most of our stuff out of Mexico, where it's legal. But they're overcollecting the toads, and then there's the question of its being Indigenous medicine. The synthesized version is on the scheduled list now. I dusted off my chemistry background and started looking at analogs that aren't."

Grey-market hallucinogens, then—the analogs went on the schedule as soon as they got much use. Joanie was no one to criticize an extralegal business. She'd dipped back into whoring in the last few months, reconnecting with an old client.

She still wanted to create Inanna shrines, too, which could have an aspect of the sacred whore. That was her calling, giving sexual love in the name of the goddess—pleasure that brought recipient and giver into the goddess's realm, healing them and the world. She liked the term "whore" for that work, using it as a reclaiming. Though it wasn't easy to own it as a vocation. The shrines themselves could be sacred work, or they could be prostitution for money, depending on how they were done.

"I can do that anywhere," he continued. "I was thinking of going to Oregon. They're inches away from opening psychedelics up for therapeutic use. For me, therapeutic and ritual use is the way to go."

"I agree with you there," Joanie said. She'd done her share of hallucinogens, at shows and parties, or with friends. Even her most haphazard acquaintances cared about set and setting.

"Nora said that she'd be interested in doing some ritual work with psychedelics. Maybe with the coven."

"I'm actually not in her coven, though I live here and do ritual with them. I circle with—do you know Hannah Redstone?" It was worth a shot. Nora and Hannah had known each other a long time.

"I do." He grinned. "She's a fine girl."

Funny to see an earlier Hannah through his eyes—clearly she'd been a sexpot. "She's my high priestess."

"Anyway, Nora and I had an interest in similar workings a long time ago, and it might be time to circle back around."

"Maybe." Something in her urged caution. But she didn't want him to feel judged. "I think that kind of work can be healing."

She took her last sip of hot toddy. "I'm going to bed. Good night!"

In their bedroom, Cleo lay fast asleep. They hadn't painted the room yet, walls still white, now grey in shadow; Cleo had hung spangled saris to cover the ceiling. Now a wand of moonlight crossed the room, glinting on the sequins, touching Cleo's cheek. Joanie shut the curtains to keep the light from waking her.

Her fiancée. The wedding was set for June. They had yet to get invitations out, but they'd sent "save the date" notices a while back.

There was so much to do. They were going inexpensive— they had no choice. Joanie had hoped her mom might volunteer money, but after their last conversation it was clear that wouldn't happen. Cleo's mom had agreed to help, but she was renovating her house and didn't have much cash to spare. Luckily Joanie's boss at the coffee shop had agreed to cover catering—unusual for him. He was known as stingy. But Joanie was his most reliable manager.

It was coming together. They would likely hold it at Witch Farm. Her next hurdle was confirming with Nora, while making sure Nora didn't say yes and later resent the work it entailed. Nora was also the best person to say whether the house's iffy plumbing could handle an influx of visitors.

But they'd be married! That was a hopeful thing. She could get on Cleo's insurance. The parts of her life were solidifying, coming together—this was good, right?

A black wall of stone rose before her, surface broken to long crystalline structures. A block, split off, formed a seat. The space had iron bars set into stone, chains set into walls. These were linked to manacles now empty.

A man lay on the polished stone floor. Or was it a man? Flickering in and out, black wings like some huge raven's hovered behind him. He had a man's form: muscled shoulders, chiseled cheek, beautiful as a statue.

His head came up. Blue-topaz eyes gazed at her.

A wave of longing overwhelmed her, and shock jolted her awake.

After a moment, she sat up in bed and reached for her glass of water, cold in the cold room. The moon had set, the only light reflection from the floodlight outside.

This man—this angel?—was someone she knew. She knew that face, that body, those wings. She missed him. She yearned for him.

But who was he?

Searching her memory, she found nothing.

Chapter 6

The mortal present

Hannah's yard lay dotted with daffodils. Joanie knelt and buried her face in a cluster to drink in the bright, sweet scent. She'd dropped by before work at the coffee shop.

A moment after she rang the bell, the door opened to Hannah's shock of pink-dyed hair, a bit higher than Joanie's shoulder.

"Come on in!" She had a Southern twang—she was a white woman from Georgia. Escaped from Georgia, she would say.

Following Hannah back through the railroad kitchen, Joanie took a chair in the tiny dining room, dark wine-red. "I went to Nora's spring equinox last weekend."

"How was that?" Hannah gestured to a teapot. "Earl Grey okay with you?"

"That's fine." Hannah poured. "The ritual was pretty simple, but sweet. There was a new person there, Kirk McDonald. Does the name ring a bell?"

"It does! Nora's old boyfriend, before he went to Arizona and Nora married that tech boy."

"So tell me about this guy."

"Hmm." Hannah blew on her steaming cup and took a sip. "Well, some folks are trickster spirits, but it doesn't make them *bad,* if you know what I mean."

"I guess."

"We weren't poly in those days. Some people had open relationships. But Nora and Kirk didn't." Hannah looked across the room, the dining room's red reflecting on the cream-colored wall across from it. Robins chirped outside. "Kirk made his own decision to open it several times, a couple times with me."

"I see!" Joanie let her tone be joking. It was a long time ago.

"Nora and I made up later. Kirk's a bit of a hound, though, you gotta watch him. But there's a sweetness to him."

"He's talking about doing some kind of entheogen ritual with Nora, based on analogs he makes. What do you think of that?"

"I'd say he'd better test them on himself before he tries them on y'all."

"There is that."

"But he's a chemist—he's the real thing. In his work, he's tolerably trustworthy. He used to sell weed, and he tangled with some people you kinda gotta be trustworthy with. I think he got out of that, though."

"Apparently."

"Back in the day, he and Nora worked with entheogens, as y'all call them. When we were all friends, I took part too. He's serious about that stuff. I trust him there. Just don't end up in bed with him, especially not if he's starting up with Nora again."

"He spent the night."

"Neither Nora nor I are spring chickens, and it's not a bad thing to have a man in your bed sometimes. But Nora, she's a jealous girl." She grinned. "Though I'll tell you, Kirk knows what he's doing between the sheets."

Joanie grinned back. "I can pass him your number, if you want."

"No sirree, I'm not crossing Nora again. We barely avoided a witch war."

Chapter 7

*P*uabi-Ekur let themself drift from Inanna's golden throne to their pink-tinged dust cloud, shining in the light of a nebula shot with stars. It felt like glitter strewn on emptiness.

So much for the aid of their goddesses. Advice was all very well, but she'd wanted more.

Besides needing to free Joanie from Azazel's mind-wipe, Puabi-Ekur had to spring him from the Demiurge's prison, or at least try.

They knew where he was, roughly. Possibly they could insinuate themselves into his cell. But doing that with no support was dangerous. They might get trapped themself. As the only one who knew what was going on, besides his brother Samyaza, they had to stay free.

Samyaza would help with reconnaissance, even a full-on battle. But rather than a fight, they needed something small, well-planned, and effective. To assault the prison of heaven wholesale was too big a job for an incubus-succubus, even with friends. Their task was love, not war.

But to do anything, they needed allies.

Azazel and his fallen-angel warriors had fought Suriyel's forces and won—before he'd dismissed half his help, the half brought by Joanie's and Puabi-Ekur's alliances with the folk of the Great Below. However noble the idea of this blocking spell, it had backfired.

How far did Azazel's spell range?

As spirit, Puabi-Ekur descended the steps to the Great Below. As they did, the lanterns in niches in the rock changed from ornate golden at the top to silver further on, to brass, to fired clay, to oil pooled on hollowed stone. Toward the bottom, the only light was a faint red glow.

Seven gates punctuated this descent, but no one guarded these against Puabi-Ekur. They could come and go as they liked as one of the lovers of Ereshkigal, the goddess of this place.

At the stairs' base lay the Great Below's forecourt, dust and ash making tiny circles in the air above black stone. That bedrock paved the way to an enormous throne of basalt set with black chalcedony—Ereshkigal's seat, now empty.

They floated past to a huge, formal staircase, hundreds of steps rising to two massive basalt pillars that flanked the doorway of the Palace of Ganzir. The door-guards ignored them. From there, Puabi-Ekur turned down a hallway, mosaics with lapis lazuli and dark red stone set into the walls. Along this hall lay many doors, but they knew the way.

They shifted to the likeness of Puabi, the dancer of ancient Uruk, the wide belt of her linen dress dripping with silver lozenges. At Ereshkigal's door stood guards in Sumerian studded-leather cloaks and pointed bronze helmets. Puabi-Ekur had sent no notice.

Standing stiffly, spears in hand, the guards eyed her.

"I know this spirit," one said. "You are a friend of the Lady's."

"I am."

"She is in conference with her viziers. It might be some time."

"I'll wait."

She wafted over to shimmer against the stone wall, inlaid in stylized patterns of flowers around a throne. The guards watched her.

One nudged another. "Show us your powers, succubus!" He gestured toward his cock.

"Be respectful! She belongs to the Lady!" another growled.

At a noise, stomping feet down the hallway, they all stood at attention.

Another troop of guards approached, surrounding the Lady herself. She never knew Ereshkigal employed so many—was something going on?

The Lady paced forward, tall, haunted-eyed, Sumerian in her traditional tiered dress and conical crown. She stared ahead, seemingly into nothingness, till her gaze caught Puabi.

"Puabi-Ekur! Beloved! What do you do here?"

"My lady." She bowed low. "I had a desire for your company."

"That you can always have." She turned to the guards at the door. "Let her enter. In the future, make the esteemed Puabi-Ekur comfortable."

The guards bowed to the goddess and opened the door to a room centered on a vast bed, carven-wood frame inlaid with gold and silver. Black sheets peeked from under a tawny fur coverlet. Black ceramic braziers stood to either side; with a gesture from the goddess, they wafted cypress and juniper smoke. Servitors slipped forward to help the Lady take off her conical crown, setting it on a side table. "You may leave us," she told her retinue.

They glided out, and the goddess and Puabi were alone. Ereshkigal flipped down a corner of the coverlet.

"Sit with me." Her huge eyes searched Puabi's face. "You look concerned. What is the issue?"

"My lips are forcibly sealed," Puabi said.

"I am Queen of the Great Below. At least in my hell, I can give you freedom to speak." She waved a finger, and the spell released.

Puabi's mouth fell open—she hadn't known Ereshkigal could do that. She'd intended flowery compliments, but instead her tale spilled out. "Joanie does not remember anything. Azazel got rid of half of his allies and was captured by Suriyel in a sortie. It's not right!"

"I have to agree." Beside the bed, a large bowl with two straws materialized, Sumerian presentation for beer. Puabi pushed herself across the wide bed to the side table and sipped—it would be rude not to. "I fear I too am at least partly bound by this magical rule. Like my sister, I am connected to the Watcher angels through old Mesopotamia, from a time before the Demiurge stole his rulership. Azazel as a Watcher is an underworld being. Though he is not from my underworld, still there are treaties and agreements."

She curled up on the bed, and Puabi came to lie in her arms.

"I do not have an army of my own," the Lady said, "or even much of an honor guard, and you need support to free him. Or else inside information on the Demiurge's prison, which I also do not have. Though my hell does border on it—all the hells are loosely connected."

"Is that so?"

"The Key-Bearer knows more of that than I do." She meant Hekate.

"Hekate ignored me when I asked for help."

"I doubt she ignored you. Perhaps it was not yet time for her help. To free Joanie, you must either break Azazel's spell or persuade him to relent. He certainly will not relent while still in prison. He must be made to see that you and Joanie can bring him allies that are essential."

"Can we, though?"

"I believe so. But you must believe it before you can convince Azazel."

"True enough." She reached up and kissed Ereshkigal on her hollow cheek.

"Believe it or demonstrate it."

"Mmm?"

Ereshkigal licked her neck. "You inspire me," she said. "Let us talk in detail later."

"Ah." Taking the goddess's face in her hands, Puabi gave her a kiss.

Waking from a nap, Puabi found her head on Ereshkigal's shoulder, both of them up against the massive headboard, carven with a scene of offerings paraded before the goddess. Ereshkigal was already awake, reading a cuneiform tablet that she set aside when Puabi moved.

"You and Joanie both made friends with my husband, Nergal, correct?" Puabi nodded. "Besides sending a plague, Nergal also gave Joanie the help of the wind-warriors, the Rabisi."

"He did."

"Nergal speaks highly of you and Joanie both, and none of us here are friends of the Demiurge. You have the support of the Great Below. And you have another ally, the Watcher Samyaza. We may be able to use these forces together as a lever to free Azazel."

"How so?"

"Do not ask me! I only keep souls in hell—I do not force them to come here. That is more in the line of my husband, the

God of Sudden Death." Big, dark eyes set in deep hollows gazed at Puabi. "He speaks of you fondly."

Puabi and Ereshkigal had been lovers for years. She'd barely met the Plague God—just one threesome with Joanie. But she was willing to go all out to help Azazel.

"A word to the wise is sufficient, my lady."

The goddess smiled. "Before you go, succubus, give me a proper goodbye."

Dressed, full of Sumerian beer, Puabi flitted toward Nergal's suite down a dusty basalt hall and up another flight of steps. His wing of the palace was simpler than Ereshkigal's, its main decoration a painted frieze showing warriors in leather cloaks, some wielding maces to herd captives—visions of war.

She stopped by a door two stories tall, its painted border of lions and bulls inset with carnelian and lapis. Before the door stood another troop of guards.

They eyed her suspiciously. "Are you expected?" one asked.

"I was sent by the Lady Ereshkigal," she said.

The guards traded a look. "Ask Ishum," one said.

They pounded on the door, which opened to the Vizier Ishum, a tall male being with a head of flame, his eyes a brighter burning in the blaze.

"Hello, my lord," she said, sidling over to him. She slid her fingers along his enflamed arm—as a spirit, she didn't feel the fire.

"Puabi-Ekur." She could tell he was smiling. "Are you here to see the Lord Nergal?"

"I am."

"He will be here after a time. Please come in and sit."

He ushered her into the bedroom, dominated by a gargantuan bed whose basalt headboard reared as tall as a building. It showed figures in lewd positions picked out with chalcedony. To one side, a small table was set, inlaid dark stone with chairs to match. It held a plate of sweet dates and goat cheese and a small bowl of barley beer. All were superfluous for a spirit, but an emblem of hospitality.

Shutting the door, the vizier pulled out her chair for her. "Thank you, Lord Ishum!"

"Do not call me lord," he said. "Ishum is fine." He pulled out the other chair with a pseudopod of fire and sat beside her. "Tell me a little bit about yourself."

Echoing steps sounded in the hallway, and Ishum jumped to standing.

"It is my lord." He opened the door.

A shadowy figure filled the two-story doorway. Square-built, muscled, grey-skinned as if carven from underworld basalt, with a lion-headed mace and a scimitar slung at his side, there stood Nergal, the god of disease, the battlefield, and death on purpose. His crimped hair hung oiled and shining under a conical Mesopotamian crown. His eyes were red as coals.

"I see I have a visitor," he said, in his booming voice.

Puabi distinctly felt he'd known she was there, and had showed off his size to impress. He closed on the table, shrinking to human size as he approached, reversing perspective. Puabi stood out of deference, her silver belt discs making a sound like rain.

She bowed her head. "My lord."

"I remember you. You are Joanie's friend. And my lady's."

"Yes, my lord."

He focused a moment on Ishum, a fiery presence still hovering. "Leave us," he said briefly. The fiery vizier closed the door behind him.

The god materialized a larger bowl of beer for the table and took Ishum's chair. "What brings you here, little succubus? It is a pleasure to see you."

"Your lady sent me."

He sipped his beer through a long Sumerian straw. "Why?"

"You recall some months ago you called in the Rabisi at Joanie's request and we defeated Suriyel's forces."

"I do." His voice rumbled in his massive chest.

"After that, Azazel wanted to prevent Joanie from being a pawn for Suriyel. He felt she was too vulnerable. So he wiped her memory and set a spell on those around her, preventing them from speaking about him. And he set her from his mind as well. But, of course, that meant he had fewer allies and he himself was vulnerable. Suriyel trapped him and now has him in the Demiurge's prison."

Nergal took a long pull on his straw. "Why does this concern me?"

"My lord! Surely you cannot support a plan belonging to Suriyel and the Demiurge!" The older gods had a low opinion of Yaldabaoth.

"It means Joanie has one fewer boyfriend. I am not a jealous god"—rumor said otherwise—"but the mathematics seem to be in my favor."

He gave a wide and stony smile.

She threw herself on her knees, shaking a rain-sound of silver from her belt. She looked up at him through tousled crimped hair.

"Is there anything a succubus can do to persuade you?"

He pulled aside a flap of his kilt, releasing his cock, as long as her forearm. Reflexively he put a hand to it.

"I know a place to start."

She woke in his huge bed, with its sheets of black-dyed linen and its fur throws. The room was cold, like a giant cave, and she was happy to have a pelt folded across her shoulder. Beside her, the god snored like a bull.

She sat up, tugging on the furs to wrap around herself.

That had been remarkably fun.

She'd happily do it again. Maybe a threesome with him and his goddess wife? Or a foursome, including Joanie?

But he hadn't promised any help yet. She needed to get him to the point.

As she thought it, he woke, giving her a slow smile.

"Little one! That was quite the showcase."

"Thank you!"

"I can tell you are scheming."

"What makes you say that?"

He sat up, yawning. "As long as that is the down payment and not the whole recompense, I am happy to help your schemes."

He stretched. She couldn't help admiring his abdominal muscles, made like rock. "We need a war council," he said.

Chapter 8

*I*n an April evening at Witch Farm, under the last rays of sunset, cherry and apple trees bloomed. Cream-colored blossoms wafted scent, the mock orange a puffball of white. Beds of tulips lay pink and red, and a few last daffodils scattered across the grass.

It took time for the witches to assemble for the cross-coven planning meeting. Hannah's coven had seven members—besides Hannah, Cleo, and Joanie, there were Gus, his girlfriend Alyssa, and two students. Nora's coven had five: herself, Sandy and Mike, and her own two students.

In the western sky, peach-flushed clouds coasted along the blue-green horizon. With Sandy's carload a half-hour out, finger food on the table and the house as clean as it was getting, Joanie took a walk in the forest.

Green and shadow-dark, the woods smelled of flowers and the fresh fir growth she brushed by. Near the pond, tree-frogs shrilled and bullfrogs croaked, calling for mates. These woods would always be Pete's, for Joanie.

Her former lover, Pete had connected violently with the local Horned God. It had been a hard energy to carry. Somewhat more than two years ago, he'd fallen to his death fighting a man who'd attacked her—she'd watched the Horned God take Pete over and ride him to his death. But he was still here in these woods.

She found a branch to sit on, bent low along the path, and closed her eyes. A wave of loss poured over her. "I miss you," she whispered.

A warm wind came up, wrapping itself around her like a lover's arms. On her cheek fell a fleeting kiss.

Something in it recalled her dream of the man in the black stone prison—the man with wings, perhaps an angel.

Who was he, and why did she see him? Why was he in prison? She'd lost him too.

Tears welled over her eyelids. She covered her face with her hands.

The evening was chilly. They had a fire in the river-stone fireplace. Sandy had brought marshmallows, and she and Mike sat by the fire toasting them as the witches collected.

Joanie took a corner of the brown leather couch. Cleo sat next to her. She had a feeling she knew what was coming; Hannah likely did too. In front of the fire, Sandy and Mike finished their marshmallow toasting, and Nora took their place.

"An old friend of mine just moved back to town—Kirk, who was at our equinox. A long time ago, he and I did ritual work together, and I think it might be time to start that work again. It's not the same as the coven's but adjacent to it. I wanted to give you all the first chance to join me, if you're interested. It's absolutely not required."

The group traded glances. Most had no idea what she meant.

"This is work with certain entheogens. You're probably aware mushrooms have been okayed for therapeutic work in Oregon. In British Columbia, practically all psychedelics are legal. I feel as if it's only a matter of time till that's true here in Washington. What we'd be working with is tryptamine analogs made by my friend. These are not on the scheduled list."

Among the group of faces, some looked closed, some dubious. Hannah wore the ghost of a smile. It was hard to say what that meant.

Sandy leaned forward. A white girl with reddish-brown long hair, she tended toward goth attire, though today more vintage hippie. "I know a little bit about that kind of work, but can you tell us more about your approach to psychedelics in witchcraft?"

"The term entheogen means to bring or awaken the god within. For me, these are tools to produce mystic insight. Of course, they can be party drugs too. But if you look back to shamans around the world, arguably to the ancient Greeks and Egyptians also, these have traditionally been used as spiritual tools. In witchcraft, think about all the discussion of flying ointments. The evidence shows that early witches had access to means of psychic flying, in other words to psychedelic trance. For me, it's important to do the day-to-day witch work, but also you can avail yourself of these tools to jump gaps in your understanding and connect better with the psychic plane."

Around the circle, faces were thoughtful.

"Based on my experience," Nora continued, "these tools help people reach ego death and lead to a more positive spiritual and mundane life. They also give folks a way to face death and what lies beyond with more courage. I'm proposing starting a new group around all this. Because of the need to support my friend's chemistry work, and as another revenue stream for me and the farm, this group will take paying customers. We'll have a sliding scale, with payment in kind as needed. I'll be working toward creating a ritual framework and potentially ritualist training later on." She looked around the room. "I'd love to start this practice with any of you who are interested. If you are, talk to me over the next week or two."

After a glance around the room, Hannah spoke up. "Just so y'all know, I am one hundred percent behind this work, though I'm not sure I'll take part." She turned to Nora. "Can you tell us a little bit more about what would happen in these rituals?"

"We'll make sure to create a strong ritual container. Some of these entheogens can cause folks to need to lie down and sometimes to purge. I lean toward an indoor setting because it gives better control, but we're looking at both indoor and outdoor spaces. For the analogs we're looking at, the process takes a half-hour, an hour at most. Most people have positive experiences, but even the rare negative ones will be short in mundane time."

Though potentially longer in psychic time.

"Have the analogs been tested?" Joanie asked.

"Some yes, some no. My friend and I are committed to testing them before the group does, first on ourselves, then on any volunteers."

"Is there any way to test things without formally joining?" one of Hannah's students asked.

"We've talked about doing test drives. We'll be formalizing our practice over the next few months."

"Cool, cool," Sandy said. "Like what kind of money would this be?"

"To begin with, just enough to cover costs. I'll bring you a balance sheet. Right now I'm gauging interest."

"When are you thinking of starting this stuff up?" Mike asked. He was a quiet boy, mixed-race, a bit of a nerd.

"After Beltaine. We'll make space for all our usual rituals when we're planning, of course."

A big crack sounded from the fireplace, as a log popped. Sandy jumped.

Was it the house fey talking?

What might Dea think of this? Or Pete?

"Anything else?" Nora asked. No one moved or spoke. "Come find me if you have questions."

Joanie and Cleo threw on sweaters and headed for the back porch, away from the cluster of people by the fire. The view out past the greenhouse and the yurt ended in the dark mass of the woods.

Towering Douglas firs shifted in the wind. An owl hooted.

"What do you think?" Joanie asked.

"If it's anything like toad venom or ayahuasca, it might really be life-changing. Or it might be a trap to catch silly white boys, like any fake shaman stuff."

"Nora's not fake. And she could use some more cash in hand."

"Couldn't we all? I'm not getting involved past a certain point —not anything visible. I can't." Cleo needed to maintain credibility in the nonprofit world. Joanie was more used to separating her day-job persona from her grey-market one.

"Just please keep your eyes open to what's going on, if you don't mind." Two intuitions were better than one.

Cleo put her hand over Joanie's and squeezed. "Of course, baby." She stood. "I'm going to go up. I've got an early start."

"I'll be up in a few."

She'd sit a moment or two and watch the wind toss the trees. Be with the land. Half-drowsing, she let the aura of the space reform around her.

Wind eddied in, stroking the leg of her jeans, insinuating itself under her t-shirt, cold. Fingers stroked her side, poking her, waking her up, tugging at her waist.

"Pete?" But it didn't feel like him, more like the fey of the place, the nature spirits, whose local leader was the Lady Dea.

Come into the woods, the energy said.

The moon, not far past full, flickered out between torn-edged clouds in a translucent black sky. Using her phone flashlight, she took the path through the woods to the cabin, climbing downhill among the firs. Her beam showed the cabin door, carven pentacle twined with leaves. Inside, it was all cedar, tiny, barely room for a handful of people back to back. It held a bed, two chairs, a woodstove, and the niche with the Lady's hand-carved statue.

The Lady's bead eyes were alive in the flashlight's gleam. Finding a lighter, Joanie set flame to the candles and sat on the bed.

"Lady," she whispered, "what would you have of me?"

The silence deepened. She dropped onto her back onto the wool blanket, which released a musty smell. Behind her closed eyelids, a mist flooded in, like the mist of moonlight falling on the forest.

A feeling of greeting came to her. The Lady wanted to say hello. She needed to check in. She needed to do the witch work.

A breath of night air came through the partway-open window, with the scent of fir, a base note of leaf-rot.

Lightning split storm clouds. Warriors battled in the sky. Some had white wings, some black. With clangs and crashes, swords thrust and maces hit. Fighters fell shrieking.

One pale, shining being swung a sickle sword. One wearing Mesopotamian fish-scale armor fought with a longsword. Beside him ranged the black-winged angel from her dreams. Her lover the god Nergal, a column of grey rock, battered enemies with a studded club. Across the battlefield, winds blew gale-force—invisible, howling, hitting the white-winged angels, who were outnumbered.

The pale, shining one and the black-winged one closed on one another. Black Wings slashed the other's shoulder. A wind hit, breaking a white wing. Its owner screamed in pain, dropping their sword.

Black Wings surged forward, putting the tip of his sword to his opponent's throat.

A rip crossed the sky. Diving into it, the white-winged angels disappeared.

One of the candles flickered and went out, and she awoke. Her phone said she'd slept twenty minutes.

Something was trying to get her attention about this black-winged angel.

The only being in her dream she recognized was the god Nergal. Maybe he knew what was going on.

A breeze angled into the room, carrying the scent of the forest and Dea's voice. "Talk to the battle god."

Chapter 9

"It's mid-April now," said Joanie, surveying her and Cleo's room. The room was still half-full of boxes, and they had another set in a spare bedroom. Sunlight reflected in specks from the spangle-strewn saris on the ceiling. "Do we really want to wait till the house is clean to have your dad and Sharon over?"

They'd meant to do it for Ray's birthday, but that plan had slid sideways.

Subsumed in their poofy coverlet, Cleo said in a muffled voice, "I need coffee before I have this conversation."

Joanie returned with a steaming cup to find her asleep.

They'd both been working crazy hours. It wasn't surprising they hadn't made more headway on unpacking—they'd done the essentials when they moved in, then they'd stopped.

Even asleep, hair every which way, her girl was beautiful. Twig-slender, she had slightly protuberant eyes, closed now behind delicate eyelids tinged purple. Lips like an orchid. Her love of color showed in her nails, electric orange. Her wicked intellect and huge heart lay hidden by sleep.

The day was getting on, and they needed to talk, but if she never took a minute sometimes to appreciate her girl, something was wrong.

She gently shook Cleo's shoulder. "I brought you coffee."

Cleo sat up, groaning. "I worked way too late last night."

"You were still at it when I went to sleep."

"Grant deadline. Sorry."

"I understand, but we need to get moving with things, and the next thing to do for the wedding is have dinner with your parents."

"I know, but it's—"

"Yes, I get it. There's no winning with Sharon. But as you've said many times, we can't not do it, or they'll be offended."

Cleo hung over her coffee cup, holding it in both hands, nodding, rocking slightly. "Yes. You're right."

"How about that new high-end soul food place? The one where you've got to get reservations way in advance?"

"Fine. Can you please do it?"

"Sure." It was clear Cleo had a block here. "I do need you to have the conversation with Ray about his schedule."

"That's fine."

"I'll write you an email and remind you to send it."

"Sure, fine. Let's do that."

They managed to luck into a reservation a bit more than a week later, and had more luck in fitting that into Sharon and Ray's schedule. Cleo oversaw what they both wore. "It has to be perfect. You can't underdress; you can't overdress."

Joanie stood before the full-length mirror inside their room's closet door, inspecting herself. She'd put on a lightweight maxi-dress, magenta and yellow-ochre flowers on a pale-green backing, like she'd wear to a wedding. Her long brunette hair hung loose, her black eyes made up with a smudge of shadow, nothing too much. She looked over her shoulder at Cleo.

"That's not an exacting standard or anything."

"It's realistic." Cleo was elegant in a black knit dress, with a maroon and orange shawl to bring her trademark burst of color.

"You know your dad loves you and supports you. Do you really care what Sharon thinks?"

"If she's going to be hateful, she'll be very hateful. I'd like her to be no more than moderately awful."

"All we can do is our best."

The main room of the restaurant was a bright, high-ceilinged space overlooked by clerestory windows, some half-open for air. Its ambience was warm, track lighting balanced by dark wood tables, walnut-finished, cut square. Servers wore black t-shirts, balanced by formal black skirts and trousers. The place felt as if it had no walls, but those it had were dark teal blue. It had a tone of hominess but also seriousness. Joanie loved it right away.

Having the conversation here gave them an unexpected benefit. This was not a place where anyone would want to raise their voice in anger.

Joanie and Cleo made sure to be seated a bit early, well in place before the older couple appeared. The waiter, a sweet-faced mixed-race young man, lit the tiny lamp at their table.

"I'd like prosecco," Joanie said, "this one at the top of the list."

"Celebrating tonight?" the server asked.

"Family announcement," Cleo said.

"I understand," the server said, with a half-smile. "Anything for you?"

"The same prosecco, I think."

"You never drink prosecco," Joanie said as the server left.

"I need something to calm me a little. Seemed better than a double scotch."

When Ray and Sharon came in, the ambient noise of the restaurant hushed for Joanie. He wore a tight-cut dark-brown suit, with a brilliant orange pocket square. He was in his fifties, with salt and pepper hair cut close to his head and big black-framed glasses with an artsy feel. He'd been a professional musician before he bought into his father's contracting business.

He was the calyx to Sharon's flower. Tall, with a black bob, a few years younger than Ray, she wore an abstract-printed cocktail dress, teal, hot pink, and fluorescent green—something not out of place at an awards luncheon. In dress, they'd outclassed Cleo and Joanie.

It was a power move. It needed a counterbalance. Joanie went to witchcraft.

"Puabi-Ekur," she whispered inside her head. "Help! What can I do? I want this to work."

"I can help. In the meantime, be charming."

"I'll do my best!"

She wasn't completely intimidated. Between whoring, running a coffee shop, and working in finance, she had several kinds of professional manner, and one of them had to suit.

This was never going to be an easy dinner.

When they reached the table, the server was there, pulling out Sharon's chair. Joanie mentally noted to give him a huge tip. "Would you like to see the wine list?"

"Please," Sharon said. The server handed it to her from the table. Almost without looking, she said, "We'd like the Silver Oak Cabernet." It wasn't the most expensive on the list, which would be ostentatious, but it cost more than Joanie had ever spent on a fine dinner.

"Four glasses?"

"That would be lovely!" Joanie breathed, before Sharon could say anything. The server twinkled at her. He knew something of what was going on, and he was on their side.

Sharon and Ray had first met Joanie several years ago, when

Cleo had brought her along to pick up things from their basement. Afterward, Cleo had gotten an earful from Ray about dating a white girl. Cleo had brought Joanie to a couple of barbecues since. They'd stayed at them the shortest time socially acceptable.

Now everyone ordered appetizers—short ribs, mac and cheese, and barbecued shrimp. The server presented the wine, and Sharon tasted; the appetizers arrived. Under the table, Cleo caught Joanie's hand, the one with the gold engagement band on the ring finger.

"Dad, Sharon—Joanie and I are getting married."

Ray's eyes cut to his wife.

"Married?!" Her voice was pitched low. Her gaze scraped Joanie and returned to Cleo. "Bad enough you make time with this white woman. You're going to marry her?"

Through a half-open window, a wind snaked in. Only Joanie noticed.

Sharon turned to Ray. "You're going to let your daughter—"

Wind flipped the tablecloth and threw barbecued shrimp in Sharon's lap.

"Ow!"—a full-on shriek. The shrimp was scalding hot. She threw herself to standing, barbecue sauce covering her skirt, dripping down her legs.

The server was there immediately. "Oh, my. I'll get towels. Maybe a new tablecloth."

"Why don't we go the bathroom and I help you get cleaned up?" Cleo asked, taking Sharon's arm. Sharon seemed tempted to shake Cleo off but went with her.

Ouch. "That was a bit much, Puabi-Ekur," Joanie said silently.

"It worked!"

To Ray, she said, "I'm so sorry."

"It's unfortunate." He looked at her carefully, as if she could have done it, but she'd been sitting out of arm's reach. Several of the wait staff hustled up and changed the tablecloth.

It took Joanie a moment to gather herself.

Was Sharon okay?

Ray studied her, deep-brown eyes behind boxy black frames. "You've been by Cleo's side some time now. She's only had good things to say about you."

"I love her. I'm the luckiest girl in the world." To her surprise, she felt tears prickle along her lower lids.

She really was.

"I hope this is the right thing," Ray said.

"I hope I can make Cleo happy."

The flame of the table's lamp flared, sending shadow across his face. "That's a tall order! She was always a demanding child, and she's a demanding woman."

"I wouldn't have her any other way."

"Neither would I."

Cleo returned with Sharon, who had shrunk into herself; she seemed an inch shorter. Her dress was ruined. "Dad, Sharon was burned pretty bad. I think she should go to the emergency room."

"It's nothing," Sharon said, but there was an ashy tone to her skin that hadn't been there before.

"Let me see, honey," Ray said. They exchanged a look. Plucking up her skirt, he examined her leg. "We should go."

He waved to the server, who comped their meals given the accident. He and Sharon made their way out, Sharon leaning on him.

A silence fell at the table.

"You called in supernatural help," Cleo said.

"I'm sorry. I didn't expect anything so extreme. Do you think Sharon will have scars?"

"It's hard to say."

"I can send her healing energy. I didn't mean to disfigure her."

"She can be hateful, but she didn't deserve that."

"I'll ask that she be completely healed." On the astral, she could feel Puabi-Ekur preening, and mentally she growled at them. Puabi-Ekur mimed contriteness, all big eyes.

"I know it wasn't your intention," Cleo said.

"I'm really sorry."

Cleo sighed. "It surely won't help things, but I don't know it was the worst outcome. I'll tell Dad you're praying for her healing. He'll get what I mean."

Joanie and Cleo's glasses of Cabernet were barely touched, and there was a glassful left in the bottle. "We shouldn't leave without drinking this," Joanie said.

"No, we should not. My dad would be appalled if we did." Cleo took a swallow. "Did you get a chance to talk to him?"

"A little. He's a lot more chill without Sharon there."

"Absolutely. But he did talk to you?"

"Yes!" Joanie's mac and cheese was getting cold, which seemed a waste, so she took a bite.

"If he talked to you at all, it means he likes you."

Chapter 10

The eternal present

Puabi-Ekur crossed the ether as a spirit, returning to Inanna's glittering throne. They laid frankincense and rose petals on the gilt incense burner, and a wave of scented smoke rose. They prostrated themself on the intricately woven carpet in their Puabi form.

After a time, the goddess appeared, in her tiered linen dress and the conical Sumerian crown.

"How goes it in the land of mortals, little one?"

"So-so. I tried to help Joanie by silencing her partner's stepmother, but it backfired."

"Explain."

"They were at a nice restaurant, and she was about to start yelling at Joanie, so I threw her plate of hot food in her lap. It burned her."

Inanna hid a smile behind her hand.

"No one could possibly pin it on Joanie! She was sitting across the table!"

"Humans have intuition about these things."

"Anyway, Joanie's asking her allies to help get this woman healed. For all she's a horrible bitch."

"It has been a while since you've been in human community, hasn't it?" Puabi rolled her eyes. "Healing isn't exactly my purview, but I can call in a favor. And next time—"

"Yes?"

"Maybe check in with your girlfriend before giving her mother-in-law-to-be second-degree burns."

It seemed like a spring afternoon in Samyaza's garden, but on closer inspection, a master hand had combined spring and summer. Irises and crocuses all bloomed at once, peach and yellow, lavender and dark purple. At the same time, the marble-lined ponds brimmed with waterlilies. A pink haze lay across the sky, circling the sun in rose.

Puabi-Ekur arrived early, in the form of Puabi, in a pink silken robe with gold trim. But she had no opportunity to scope the territory—her host appeared moments after she did. "Greet-ings, Puabi-Ekur!"

A big, lazy smile showed shining white teeth. He wore a green paisley silk robe, as before—apparently no one was formal today. Green strands in his hair echoed the fabric, a few glinting like glitter.

"Did you have something to ask?"

"Inanna says you want to be done protecting Joanie. Is it such an onerous task?"

"Come, sit," he said, and led her to a paved area with a foun-tain and several Greek-style dining couches, upholstered in yellow-green paisley silk. She curled up on one couch, and he took another. "Hardly onerous. But of course I want my brother freed and his relationships back to the usual, oh, I would say wreckage."

She sat up straight. "Are you calling me a wreck, sir?"

"Not you. You are the best thing that's happened to Azazel in a long time."

A crash sounded, and then another. These resolved to heavy footprints. Stomping echoed through the garden.

Grey, two stories tall, lion-headed mace at one hip and scimitar at the other, Nergal the god of war and plague approached. Despite his size, he managed to avoid crushing statues and greenery.

He arrived beside them, and Samyaza looked up with a smirk. "Greetings, o tall and mighty God of Battle! At your service."

"I am at yours, Angel Samyaza," the god rumbled, folding to human size. Samyaza gestured to an open couch, which Nergal took.

"We're only missing Joanie," Puabi said.

"I thought the three of us might talk first before we call her in," Samyaza said. "We might find the conversation easier that way, given the spell. Without her here, that constraint need not impinge on our conversation."

"How is that so?" Puabi asked.

"The Goddess Ereshkigal's partial release of the spell was more powerful than she knew. But to speak to the matter at hand, I believe Joanie must be part of this rescue, or at least aware of it."

"Why?" asked Nergal.

"We free Azazel, and then we free Joanie of the spell," Puabi said.

"This mind-wipe is an issue between Azazel and Joanie," Nergal said. "Not my business." As he'd said, it was to his benefit if Joanie had one fewer boyfriend.

"Joanie is an important connection among different groups," Samyaza said. "Azazel used the forces she brought in to beat back

Suriyel's army twice. He might have continued winning if he had not let many of his own angels go to their spiritual destinies. Laudable, but not wise as a general. Then he broke things off with Joanie, so he was vulnerable, and Suriyel captured him. But before that, he was quite surprisingly successful. That tells me either that the Demiurge was not interested in Suriyel's skirmish with Azazel, or that the Demiurge and his supporting Council of Archons are not as well-supported as they would have us believe. Or perhaps it is both. I would like to know which. The answer has repercussions for the Watchers' next steps."

"I see," said Nergal. The Watchers had long been enemies of the Demiurge, who had imprisoned them each in their own hell at the end of a long-ago battle. This garden was Samyaza's—he'd nominally repented and had the choice to configure his prison, now this lush and blooming place.

"So for you, Joanie's an important diplomat," Puabi said to Samyaza.

"Just so." Samyaza smiled. "As are you."

Nergal's eyes calmed to silver as he contemplated Puabi. "I would not be here, discussing freeing a fallen angel, if it were not for you, Puabi-Ekur."

"Fine," said Puabi. It didn't please her. She was just an incubus-succubus—she had no desire to mess in the diplomacy of the spheres. "I want to free Azazel. That's why I'm here. It's also my opinion he was unfair to Joanie on a personal level. You're making the point it was bad strategy, which may be right, but I just want him to be fair to a being he's been connected to for millennia."

"I remember those early times," Samyaza said. A flicker of desert twilight crossed Puabi's mind, a camel silhouetted against a cobalt sky. "Before we go on, let's have some refreshments."

Fey folk appeared, bringing a low table where they laid crudités with dip, salmon and crackers, and tiny skewers of chicken. Elaborate cups of pink-tinged glass wafted to Puabi's and Nergal's hands, filled with a deep-tinted rosé. Spirits didn't need food or drink, but both Puabi and Samyaza had spent time as humans. Imbibing was calming, even on this plane. After serving, the fey disappeared.

"Puabi-Ekur, if I understand correctly, you know the way to Azazel's cell."

"That is so." She used her sexual connection to his energy to home in on him—it had always worked before.

"And we know that the Mesopotamian hell borders on the Demiurge's, so we can reach his cell from a starting point there."

"I suppose so," Nergal said.

"Thus we can get to him, if we want to. I cannot imagine we want to engage in a full-scale battle at this point. We only want to rescue Azazel."

"Yes," said Nergal. "On my side, I have neither the forces nor the interest for full-scale battle."

"Hmm," said Samyaza, pulling chicken off a skewer. Popping it into his mouth, he wiped his fingers on a napkin. "Not now, but for the future, do you still have no interest? What if we could take the Demiurge down, or at least negotiate more favorable terms with him and the Council of Archons?"

"I do not expect that."

"But no one except the Demiurge's stooges is happy with his autocratic rule. The Watchers are a special case, I grant you. We fought him openly and lost, and now most of us are imprisoned. But all who are not in Yaldabaoth's army suffer. Our worship has fallen off or disappeared; our worshippers are hounded. Some of us keep up guerrilla war, others stay quiet, but none of us is happy as we once were, with free and open worship, each in our own places."

"I must agree. But neither am I interested in a war I cannot win."

"Having watched Azazel's ongoing battle with Suriyel, I have a theory the archons' armies are not what they once were. We all suffer attrition. Spirits' tendency is to elevate and rejoin the most high."

"That is so," Nergal said. "Even the demons." He tossed back the wine in his glass. Fey hands replenished it then disappeared. "You think more of their folk have gone on than ours. I do not see it. The Demiurge gets far more worship than we do." Worship provided energy that, if channeled, worked as a kind of food—which tended to maintain spirits in place.

"You might be surprised at the interest in fallen angels."

"Also in my lady, though not so much me. And in Hekate."

"I think the numbers may be far more than at our last attempt."

Nergal tipped back his second glass of rosé and waggled his hand; a carafe manifested in the air and refilled the glass. "That is interesting to me and mine," he said.

"Just so. Retrieving Azazel is important not just to have a Watcher general in place, but also as an opportunity to gather intelligence on the Demiurge's armies."

"But how do we do it?" Puabi asked.

"I do have some contacts on the side of the white-winged angels," Samyaza said. "Those who will sell information."

Sell it for what? Puabi wondered.

"You know, just before Azazel threw up this wall," Puabi said, "he noticed there was movement in the Demiurge's heaven. He said that certain agents who were usually willing to talk either didn't know what was going on, or weren't willing to speak."

"I have seen that too," Samyaza said. "All the more reason for us to gather intelligence."

"Or to pin down one of your agents and get more out of them," Nergal growled.

"Exactly," Samyaza said. "I have one in mind. Let me do that work, and then we can reconvene."

Nergal stood, bowed, and stomped away.

Samyaza gathered himself up, changing to a green-glitter wisp of spirit.

"May I come along?" Puabi asked.

The energy trace that was Samyaza wriggled, like a shrug. "You may. I doubt you will find it amusing."

"It might be interesting. But I thought you Watchers had to be called out of your heaven to go anywhere."

The shimmering energy wriggled again. "My repentance buys me certain affordances."

Chapter 11

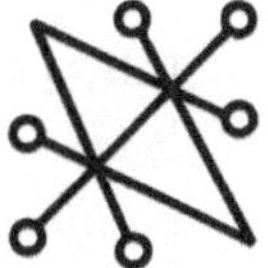

The eternal present

*D*own through the atmosphere they plummeted, to a rainy day in a city—perhaps Joanie's Seattle, though not a neighborhood Puabi-Ekur knew. The human world had its own fog of energy, good to deflect and confuse the trace of one of the Demiurge's angels, gone where they ought not, such as the one they planned to meet.

They dove among the city streets. Here stood a market lined with stalls, indoors, some kind of farmer's market. Among brick galleries they saw fish and produce, there a pile of gleaming red onions. Celery, with a whiff of its perfume. With a quick turn down a flight of steps, they reached a waterfront, a pier full of pleasure boats, white masts and an echoing sound of metal ringing. In the distance, bright orange cranes unloaded cargo vessels. Flights of seagulls rose and fell, diving into choppy water. A lone crow beat its way away.

They traveled further, the docks thinning to a rocky beach with a hill rising from it, to a small wood fronted in madrones.

"Where are we going?" Puabi-Ekur asked.

"This is evasive action," Samyaza said, hovering at the edge of the water.

Then, without warning, he stepped through the bubble-thin surface of the immanent world, to a nonplace, grey mist, nothingness—a space without obvious boundaries, full of fog. Suddenly he was moving at top speed. Puabi-Ekur had to tie themself to a green thread of his energy to keep up.

As they went, the space grew darker, still all fog. It felt as if, rather than Puabi-Ekur's starry world, this one had chosen the depths of the ocean, with the feeling of pressure, hundreds of tons of water.

Samyaza stopped, so abruptly Puabi-Ekur nearly ran into him. Puabi-Ekur made themselves small, a ripple among ripples.

"You are here," said a voice that boomed strangely in the depth.

To the eye, the space was dark blue, thick with murk. Puabi-Ekur could sense shapes, nothing more.

"I am," said Samyaza, voice composed.

"You brought a friend." At this, Puabi-Ekur enlarged themselves. "Some form of payment?"

"No, the terms are as always. A transfer of energy at the crescent of the new moon. Did you wish changes?"

"It is sufficient."

"What do you have for me?"

Another boom—perhaps the speaker was using echolocation. Or perhaps the booms were external. "They are moving your brother's prison, not far. It is a consolidation."

Puabi-Ekur could track Azazel regardless.

"There is restlessness in the Up Above," Samyaza said. "Tell me about that."

"We make ready for guests," the other said.

"Some kind of war?"

"Changes. Many beings entering, I cannot explain more. I do not have the knowledge."

Some shakeup was occurring in the Demiurge's dominion. Puabi-Ekur wasn't sure they cared. "Does this affect my brother in some way, or the rest of the Watchers?" Samyaza asked.

"Not directly."

"And what about other earthly beings? The mortals?"

"In due time."

"What sort of beings are entering?"

"Of the earth and sky, this planet, perhaps others, but by and large from this planet."

"What characterizes these beings—why are they coming to you?"

"I do not know."

"You are being even more than usually unforthcoming, my friend." Another hooting blast of sound. "You must earn your keep."

"I tell you what I know, Angel Samyaza."

"Let us change the subject. If the Angel Azazel is moving, is there anything to be different in how he's kept?"

"No."

"Is Suriyel still as concerned with him as before?"

"The Angel Suriyel will not forget the Angel Azazel."

"But is Suriyel paying the same level of attention?"

After a moment, as if unwillingly, the being said, "No. Suriyel has other duties."

"But not a war?"

"No. I would call it guardianship."

"But not of Azazel."

"No."

"You really need to tell me what is going on."

A long hooting, like a ship's horn blasting. Puabi-Ekur was starting to get the feeling that if they saw this being, they would look like a submarine or some kind of steampunk whale.

"I do not know," the being repeated.

"I am starting to think you do not know as much as you advertised."

Movement in the water, something like a shrug.

"It is not required that I keep paying you," Samyaza said sharply.

"I can tell you that the Lord God's armies are tied up in this matter heavily. Defenses elsewhere are thinned. Is that of interest?"

"Yes. How about the guard on Azazel?"

"That is thinned as well."

"Glorious. Now we are getting somewhere. What else do you have for me? What about governance or politics? Any changes there I should know about?"

Another long hoot. "I do not have more for you."

"See that you do next time. You may leave."

A crash, a boom, and the foggy place emptied.

They re-entered the world of immanence a few hundred feet underwater and rose onto the rocky beach below the madrones. They streaked past the waterfront to the city, through the market stacked with kohlrabi and chocolate, through the atmosphere, fog thinning to cobalt-blue to stars, and back to the garden.

Birds chirped, hidden in the trees. Puabi-Ekur redonned their Puabi form and pink silk robe. "Is your informant always like this?"

"I am afraid so. Nevertheless, we got important information. Guards will be thin along the prison block. Although Azazel has been moved. Can you still find him?"

"I believe so."

"Then we have the tools to reach him, and the time is now. What we need is the ability to cover the escape, maybe some disguise or shield, and to protect him when he returns. What I do not know is whether his pocket hell still exists. It turns on the question of how much the Demiurge knows, or cares, about

Suriyel's kidnapping plot. He might have turned a blind eye. But we need to know if there's a location to return Azazel to. Yaldabaoth's punishment of him has rules of its own—we can't violate them with impunity."

"I understand," Puabi said, although she didn't. She took a last sip of the rosé, which had waited on the side table, still chilled. "I think the person you want for this conversation is General Ekur."

"Not yet," Samyaza said. "I have one more informant to visit, and a beautiful dancer will be more useful than the general. Unless he is an extremely attractive young thing." Puabi shook her head. "Then come along with me."

They rose through the pink-tinged heavens of Samyaza's garden into the starry sky, then veered to a stand of cumulus, the border of the Demiurge's realm. She'd have thought Samyaza barred from that, but he had special privileges.

Right before they crossed into the lands of Yaldabaoth, Samyaza stopped.

"Show me your most luscious, depraved form," he told her. "The kind that shrieks succubus, especially to the juvenile set."

She gave her skin a red sheen, turned her hair raven-black, and straightened it. Plumping her breasts, she donned a tiny black bikini with a peignoir skimming her shoulders, classic batwings, and a tiny, curling red tail.

Samyaza blew her a kiss. "I would lose my soul for you! Follow my lead."

With the flick of a hand, he created a tiny oasis of debauchery in sight of the Demiurge's pale and cloud-swathed realm.

A red velvet counterpane covered a black-framed canopy bed. From the ceiling, beads of black and crimson hung in a curtain. Scarlet and black thick-pile rugs lay strewn on a black-stained wooden floor. Floor-to-ceiling French windows showed a night view, a windswept beach below a waning moon.

"Sit on the bed," Samyaza said, "and no matter what form

comes through, act as if you would fuck it at a moment's notice. Unless I want you to play cold."

"How will I know?"

"Natural intuition."

"Okay." She perched on the bed and thought of sex till erotic energy dripped off her. Music drifted in, a minor-key classical violin tune, haunting and Eastern European.

Two white-winged warriors approached, perching themselves on a hummock of cloud, looking down at the black-walled bungalow from which the music came.

"Who does this here? This is not allowed!" one said.

"Hi, lover." Puabi licked her lips lasciviously.

From where he leaned against one of the pilasters of the canopy, Samyaza stood. "You cannot win here," he said.

"Try us!" The other white-winger leaped forward, sword shining in his hand, to find himself and his companion swathed in ivy vines.

"Stop this!" the first one yelled. A tendril of ivy wrapped around his skull, closing his mouth tight. The other opened his mouth, but ivy shut it.

A heralding trumpet sounded, and a host of white-winged angels appeared, majestic, leader all in gleaming armor, golden breastplate in the Greek style, covered with rays emanating from a lion's face. His sword too was gold.

"Who goes there?"

Tendrils of ivy appeared and enfolded all his company into writhing bundles of greenery, and began climbing up his own legs. He impatiently tugged them off. He closed on the pair in front of him.

"Ah, it is you, Samyaza." She'd never seen a so-called heavenly angel roll their eyes before.

"Greetings, Mitzrael."

Samyaza vanished. Puabi grabbed a trailing thread of green glitter to follow. They plummeted through the heavens, dove deep into a choppy ocean past an orca, up again through pack ice far north, through a thick canopy of clouds, beyond into interstellar space. The white-winged angel followed.

Spinning past a blue-white star's continuous explosion, they landed on an asteroid, a hunk of rock too small for an atmosphere. This far away, they were in neutral territory.

Here, their pursuer caught up to them.

Settling on two feet on the rock, he disappeared his sword, armor, and wings, retaining a long, white robe. Samyaza appeared in a robe of paisley green, Puabi in a dark claret robe with gilt-embroidered edges.

"Greetings, Samyaza," Mitzrael said. "That was less than subtle."

"Got your attention, did I not?"

"What is this about?"

"Ready to change sides yet?"

The angel yawned and sat on a rocky protuberance, as if expecting to be around a while. "You know that I am not."

Mitzrael let his full lids droop over big blue eyes. All the angels Puabi-Ekur had seen were inhumanly beautiful, and Mitzrael had shining golden blond curls and the physique of a football player. He opened one eye.

"Has your brother been complaining?" he asked.

"How? He is incommunicado."

"I assume you found some way around that."

"I have not. I have only bribed you, to make his accommodations more comfortable."

"As I have done. His chains are off, and I laid a light aura of forgetting around him. Enough to keep Suriyel away sometimes. Not enough for Suriyel to notice without close attention."

A bit of cosmic debris sped by, burning like a miniature comet.

"What do you think of this little capture of Suriyel's?" Samyaza asked.

"It is in order for Azazel to consider his sins, repent, and make reparation." This answer seemed rote.

"Do you think Suriyel's kidnapping will lead to that result?"

The angel turned both sky-blue eyes on Samyaza. "It is not likely."

"Especially as Suriyel proceeded to rape him," Samyaza said. "Really, your lot is not any better than ours."

"A matter of opinion."

"Is sexual assault on your list of approved actions?"

"Suriyel was a Watcher like yourself, earlier on." Several millennia earlier, but that was nothing for angels. "It is to be expected they might fall from the path of righteousness. I am sure they are now considering and rectifying their sins."

"You are such a snob, Mitz. You know this whole conflict is just an argument between two sets of mob bosses. Our side is just a little less organized than yours. And fonder of humans."

"Fucking them does not mean that you are fonder of them."

"I gather this adventure of Suriyel's is not known to the Demiurge?"

"What do you think?"

"I think not."

"Though Yaldabaoth gives his minions great license, he would chastise a high-order angel for what could be seen as an act of war."

"I suspected as much."

If Suriyel's action wasn't sanctioned, the Demiurge had not made any new decisions. Thus, Azazel's pocket hell survived.

"Tell me about the attrition on your side," Samyaza said, "as your comrades get sick of your leader."

At this, Mitzrael stood. "I do not know who told you that, but it is not common knowledge."

"I know you are not willing to lie, and so I understand I have hit the mark."

"We have reinforcements."

"So do we, as I am sure you realized during Azazel's skirmishes with Suriyel. Tell me, why this unrest in heaven? Why are you preparing a place for so many?"

Mitzrael growled. The lion on his breastplate twitched its shoulders, and reddish sunglow flared from his hair. "How do you know such things?"

"Then it is true."

It had to hamper the Demiurge's angels, not being able to lie. "I could guess," Puabi said.

Fiery blue and green gazes struck her.

"Climate change will produce human deaths directly, with floods and wildfire, and lead to mass migrations of people and so to wars. All this will speed plagues and cause global health systems to fail. Millions will die, even if no power uses its nuclear arsenal. It wouldn't be surprising if the human race were decimated over the next century. Even wiped out."

A pause fell, as both angels stared.

"Not wiped out," Mitzrael said, gently. "There will be some left. Or such is most likely."

"Very few. A dark age."

"Quite possibly." To Samyaza, he said, "You see, we have concerns larger than Azazel. Who might have useful work to do with us, if he decided to change sides, which Suriyel has put forward as a possibility."

Samyaza snorted. "He hardly will because of Suriyel. Is it out of the question to consider a better, more equitable détente among us all?"

"An interesting thought. You Watchers get busy when not watched."

"Likewise, o follower of the Cosmic Bully."

Unexpectedly, Mitzrael laughed. "Yaldabaoth showed his hand some time ago. Even I have considered more useful service."

"You come up with interesting ideas yourself, fair sir. As the angel of just authority, do you truly consider the Demiurge's rule fair and equitable?"

Mitzrael shook out his wings with a flap. A handful of white feathers spun out into the nonair.

"I believe our conversation is finished. What does that bring us to?"

"I have gotten the information that I sought," Samyaza said.

"I was afraid of that."

Chapter 12

The eternal present

Back in Samyaza's garden, Puabi reclined once more on her couch and raised her empty rosé glass, which floating hands filled from a carafe in the air.

"I like Mitzrael," she said.

Samyaza had found his own couch. "Mitz is far from my least favorite angel. Since he is the angel of reparation and the understanding of obedience and authority, you can see how he ended up with the Demiurge. But he is wasted on that bully. Pretty, is he not?"

"I wasn't thinking about that." A half-lie.

"Puabi-Ekur, is it not your job to think about that?"

She smiled into her cup.

When she lifted her head, he was staring at her. Rose-colored haze hung in the air, through which sunlight poured down, golden. The plants basked in it.

"What?" she asked.

Standing, Samyaza walked over to her. She had to throw her

head back to see his face—serious, for once. Almost blank, held in pause.

Kneeling, he put a finger under her chin and stared into her eyes. She shivered.

Would he kiss her? She wouldn't stop him.

Then he inclined his head. "I am loyal to my brother. We have shared lovers before, but it has never been easy. It would not be fair to approach you when he is in chains and cannot stop me."

"I suppose not," she said, utterly disappointed.

He stood, returned to his couch, and stared off into the distance composing himself.

"Now for the war council."

With a wave of a hand, he summoned a sylph. "Go tell the powers below it's time Nergal and I talked." Puabi sipped her rosé.

She had to focus. This was about rescuing Azazel, something she wanted above all else. And yet, that whisper of attraction. Nothing enchanted like something new.

Nergal returned: massive and grey, himself not a bad lover. He was doing her a favor, but she'd have no problem repaying him. The god and the angel began their talk, in desultory fashion. She could barely focus. The hazy springtime-feeling air was making her lustful. Both the angel's and the god's eyes were on her.

"Sorry, what?"

"I can bring the Rabisi, the wind demons," Nergal said. "Samyaza, you have your angel legions. Can we call on Azazel's?"

"Yes, though I need to check with the captains."

"Is there any natural rhythm in the world of the Usurper that would draw away attention? Some big ritual?" Nergal asked. "Or do we rely on the thinning of the guard?"

"They meet, but I don't know the cadence of it."

"Perhaps they follow the Christian holidays," Puabi mused.

"For example, they might be distracted at Easter." She wasn't completely useless—after all, millennia ago, Ekur had been a general of troops.

"It is worth investigating," Samyaza agreed.

"How many warriors do we need?" Nergal asked. "And what magics? I assume the prison is heavily magicked."

"I have known Suriyel a long time, and I know how to counter their magics. I have also traded for some magical help."

Puabi arched a brow. "With whom?"

He smirked. "That would be telling." She stared at him. "There are whole cosmologies of spirits that are demonized in the Demiurge's world. The white winged ones have entirely too much magical support from doting humans. But there are other beings from other pantheons, still with worshippers, still with the energy to fight."

He didn't want to share his magical source. Fine. "Do you have enough magic to counter Suriyel?"

"I do. But we need troops too. I think you should be the guide, since you can track Azazel's energy. I suspect we can reach him through the Great Below, since that underworld and the Demiurge's dungeons lie close together. Once we locate him and our forces get in range, I can send in magic to open the locks and distract the guards. We will sneak as close as possible under magical cover, then dive in and break him out. Then we will need to perform evasive action, jumping multiple universes. We will have to stick together—none of us has the ability to fight off the Demiurge's minions alone. We would end up in chains like Azazel."

"I disagree," Nergal said. "Once my allies and I are in the Great Below, it is our fastness. The Rabisi are unassailable there, as am I and my guard." To Puabi, he said, "That place can protect you also." She'd lived in Sumer and Akkad; the Mesopotamian underworld was hers.

"You have a point," Samyaza said. "Perhaps you and your force should go with the wind demons to the Great Below."

"But what of you?" Puabi asked. What if Samyaza were captured and dragged to the Demiurge's dungeons? He didn't deserve that.

"If we run long enough, my armies and I will lose the Demiurge's. Once they are gone, we will return to our abodes. The rules of our personal hells protect us. They were made by the Demiurge long ago, and the Demiurge's minions cannot take them apart without him."

"Will they try to ambush you there?"

"I have a few tricks up my sleeve." He stood from his couch. "Now I have conversations to hold, with my captains and Azazel's."

Apparently they were dismissed.

"When should we reconvene?" she asked.

"Return when your plans are arranged," he said.

"Yes. I must speak to the Rabisi." Nergal turned to Puabi. "Come with me, little one."

Feeling a tiny bit hurt, she did.

As they glided down the staircase to the Great Below, Nergal broke the silence.

"Are you prepared to be a scout in enemy territory, little Puabi?"

"I suppose so."

Something about the end of the conversation had turned everything upside-down. She didn't want to think why.

"What ails you, little one?" She shook her head. "Do not answer—I think I know. Maybe I can distract you for a time." With a whisk and a shudder, she found herself in his vast bedroom. It was cold, but the stone braziers flanking the stone-framed bed flared, burning cypress shavings.

"Come," he said, lifting the fur coverlet. She climbed into his arms, a wordless comfort.

She had thought him too straightforward to be a seducer, but by degrees, with strokes and kisses, he warmed her. Then he was on top of her, inside her, rocking slowly, silver eyes watching her face, a thick thumb on her clit. He had begun to figure out her physicality—here in this realm past the physical, by convention mimicking it—and brought her to a muted release before he let himself finish. The energy moved hers, changing her mood.

In the underworld's shadowy depths, tiny dunes of dust shifted on black basalt strewn with boulders. Past the basalt flats spread black sands, restless in constant wind. Shadowy beings passed—galla demons carrying tridents, phosphorescent snakes, giant fanged rats. They skittered away from Nergal.

In a rocky outcrop, crumbled grey-black, a tall cave mouth shone with red light. Inside a fire burned, a pile of bones set on a layer of ashes. Bending in the air above the flames were beings made of smoke—the wind demons, the Rabisi.

Nergal spoke to them wordlessly as the fire flickered, releasing pops and sparks. The fire was life in a static place, the unchanging Great Below. It took very little to convince the Rabisi to help.

"We will give you the word," Nergal told them.

Chapter 13

The mortal present

"Sharon is getting better, right?" Joanie said, at her dressing table brushing her hair.

They were getting ready for the first of Nora and Kirk's rituals, to start after sunset. Golden late-afternoon light filtered through recycled rayon curtains; the scent of lilacs hovered in the air. Long ago someone had planted a lilac hedge behind Witch Farm's yurt, and the flowers stood in vases through the house.

"She'll have some scarring," Cleo said. "She's pretty sure the barbecue shrimp thing was supernatural."

"I never asked for it to happen!" Cleo rolled her eyes. To Sharon, that wouldn't matter. "Does she know we're both witches?"

"That'll be inescapable when we do the handfasting." It wasn't an answer. Maybe Cleo didn't know the answer. There was only so much they could do about Sharon—over time, maybe she'd soften. "Dad would never tell me, because he'd feel it wasn't my business, but I think he laid down the law with

Sharon. If I want to marry you, he's not going to get in the way just because you're white. Sure, if you were demonstrably a bad person, he would. But he likes you."

"That's sweet." She meant it. She never expected people to like her, especially not older men, at least not as anything but a sex object.

"What are we supposed to wear to this?" she asked. She stood halfway in the closet, scanning her choices.

"Something loose. Or you can go naked. That's what Hannah suggested."

"Is she coming?"

"I don't know. If she told anybody, she'd have told you."

Joanie glanced over her shoulder at Cleo. "I don't think she dares. Not to the first one." Cleo raised an eyebrow. "She wants to be respectful. She might come if it was a bigger group." Only six people were planning to attend.

A breath of flower scent glided through the window, mixing with the heady lilac. Rhododendrons bloomed, the smaller azaleas, and in the woods pale dogwood. Joanie put on a loose tiered dress, pale flowers against a darker vine pattern, Cleo a lavender leotard and neon-orange miniskirt to match her fingernail polish. They poked their head into the yurt, where throw pillows sat around a central mat. Flowers filled vases; fruit and nuts and cheese lay stacked on plates. No one was around.

They wandered back toward the house, to a bench by the herb garden. Beside the raised beds, bright pink and red tulips bobbed in the light breeze. Gnats danced in a shaft of sunlight.

A tendril of fear circled, but also curiosity. "How are you feeling about this?" she asked Cleo.

"Fine. Curious. I'm not going for the brain-melting dose."

"With something just synthesized, it's hard to predict."

"It sounds like Kirk has it figured out. Though who knows." Hannah had said Kirk knew his chemistry, but he was a trickster. Joanie had meant to ask Puabi-Ekur to check him out, but between one thing and another hadn't asked. At least no one was going to drive afterward; everyone was staying overnight.

The front door creaked open, and voices scattered, and her thoughts of talking to the succubus slipped away.

Sunlight shone through the yurt windows in thick rays, but Nora started the heater, flaring blue with gas, grumbling to itself. The evening would be chilly.

Sandy and Mike had found themselves places on the paisley throw pillows to one side of the central sleeping mat. Joanie and Cleo took the other side. Nora sat at the top of the mat to the left, Kirk to the right.

Nora took a glass vial from a cedar box in front of her.

"I want you all to see and smell this. Though it's synthesized, it's still a product of Mamma Earth. I'm going to pass around a tiny bowl. It took a lot of work to get what you see, so have a care, though it's not the end of the world if we lose a little."

She tipped a tiny amount of the powder into a polished grey-marble bowl and handed it to the covener next to her. When Joanie got it, she sniffed it, a fine cocoa-brown dust with a woody scent. If she hadn't known better, she'd assume it was plant matter.

"I want to show you the pipe too," Kirk said. "I bought it in Turkey and modified it for this kind of smoking." He passed it around.

It was a pretty thing, green glass with shining silver piping. When it came to Joanie, not expecting the weight, she almost dropped it. It was remarkably heavy. Kirk smiled at her. "The base is marble, to stabilize it." To the group, he said, "It helps if you're an old stoner like me and know how to draw on a water pipe. Anyone not in that category?"

"It's been a long time for me," Joanie said.

"If you need a few hits, that's fine. We have sufficient. But I suggest you hold it in for a count of ten, if you can, to get the most from what you take. You may go to a wordless state, and we'll interpret your gestures as best we can. An important one is to ask for water. If you need that, just touch your lips." Nora demonstrated.

"We'll set up a standard circle and call in our patron deities," she said. "Hekate, Dea, and the Horned One of these woods."

Pete would be there, something reassuring and bittersweet.

"Also the local fey. The process we'll be following is very much an earthy, natural process. People all across the world have partaken of entheogens of this type, to see beyond the veil to other planes."

"We've already tried this synthesis several times with no ill effects," Kirk said. "You will likely encounter some of your own guides and barriers, whatever challenges are up in your life or come from childhood. You might reach what I'd call enlightenment space, or not. There are no guarantees."

"Once we raise the circle, let's each of us talk a bit about what we think we might encounter," Nora said.

She stood and went to the small altar at the edge of the yurt. Draped with a cloth embroidered with spring flowers, it held candles and elemental symbols: a lilac-colored glass for water, a stone pentacle for earth, floral incense in a brass burner for air, an oil lamp for fire. A bear-shaped candle stood for Dea, a black candle with a labyrinthine symbol for Hekate, green for the Horned God, and purple for the fey. As Nora called in the god, Pete snaked his arm around Joanie's shoulder for a brief hug then was gone. The room filled and filled with deity, finishing with sparkling fey energy.

They sat back down. "We wanted to talk about challenges," Nora said. "I think for me, I'll be fighting some old sorrow around earlier work like this, and it having come to nothing."

She and Kirk exchanged a significant look. "We can go around the circle, or popcorn, if you'd rather."

When it came to Joanie, she said, "I'm not sure what I'll encounter. I think my guides and deities support this work. I don't have a lot of sorrow up right now, but of course I miss Pete, who is bound to this place."

"Of course," said Nora. Cleo leaned and gave her a hug. "You might get what you expect, and you might get something entirely different. For all our journeys we've gone to pleasant places, even rapturous, but nothing's guaranteed. But the whole experience will last no more than an hour max, and if you go bad places, we have multiple tools to bring you back."

Brown hands working quickly, Kirk set out the pipe and the materials to prepare it. "Who wants to go first?" Nora asked. The circle eyed each other.

"I'll go," Sandy said.

As requested, she wore a loose dress, long faded-black tiers with a pattern of abstract lines. Her feet were bare, shoes at the door of the yurt. Nora gestured to the mat, and Sandy sat down there, cross-legged.

"Small, medium, or large?" Kirk asked. "You can have more if the first hit doesn't work like you want."

"Medium, I think." Sandy's voice came out low and gravelly. She was frightened.

Kirk packed the pipe and handed it to her. She drew in a mouthful, the pipe bubbling, and lay back on the mat.

She lay with her eyes shut, for a long pause, then opened them.

"Oh god, oh god," she said, her eyes wide and fixed, and then "Oh!" She sat up, mouth dropped open in amazement. Mike reached out to catch her arm, but Nora waved him away.

"Let her ask."

Wordless, she turned to him and nodded. She gestured, arms around her, asking the group in, and they hugged her. She twisted and turned in their arms, closing her eyes, rolling her neck. She gave a wordless cry, not quite a scream. Nora gestured them away and she lay back, her hand grasping. Mike took it—he and Sandy were the closest in the circle, friends and sometimes more than friends. She curled into a fetal position and lay moaning, Mike's hand clutched to her body.

Slowly her moans ceased. She relaxed and lay on her back, touching her lips. Nora dribbled water on them. Sitting up, she drank from the cup.

"Okay, okay," she said, setting the cup aside. She rocked for a moment. "The universe really is love." She hugged Nora. After another few minutes, she crawled back to her place on the circle.

"Let's take some time. If anyone needs to go to the bathroom, now's a good time."

No one left the circle. Joanie took some deep, calming breaths, watching Sandy under her eyelids. Mike was leaning over her, stroking her hair. She smiled against his shoulder. Joanie caught a snippet of conversation: "Intense. But good. It's like I merged with the All That Is."

"Do you all want me to run a short grounding?" Nora asked. The circle nodded.

"Get settled, then." She gave them a moment. "Take a few deep breaths, breathing in harmony and releasing negativity. Then picture a seed in your center, below and behind your navel. Let it crack open and a tiny root go down through your body, through the floor and the foundation, down into the earth." She rooted them in the earth and grew them each into a tree, branches in the sky, connecting finally each with their own star, letting starry energy flow down, cleansing, and earth energy upward, calming and weighting them.

Joanie let it wash through her. Around them all, the spirits of the place, Dea and Pete, hung watching, and also Puabi-Ekur. Puabi-Ekur had something to say but was waiting their time.

"Who's next?"

"I'll go," Joanie said.

The Star Goddess—Hannah called her sometimes in their circles, had called her in a ritual Joanie struggled to remember. Something important had happened—maybe she met someone? But the memory spun away.

Now she was simply present, here in interstellar space. Somehow here was a resonance of the very beginning—the lip of ocean on the edge of volcanic rock. She sped past that into the heart of a star, and past, light and dark trading, pouring over her, millions of years and a couple of moments.

The Star Goddess was the galaxy, was all galaxies, was the All That Is, was Hekate's mother, was Hekate. Was her.

She lost her boundaries and floated into the night, into the stars, then with a wave returned to herself, a word on her lips: "Remember."

What she was supposed to remember she had no idea.

The ritual finished, with effects from peace to bliss. Most folks went to bed. Cleo and Joanie, still wakeful, built a fire in the house's big river-stone fireplace against the chilly night.

"You got through, right?" Joanie asked Cleo. "You got to the All That Is?"

"I did. It looked different to me than what you or Sandy got."

"You're a different person." Joanie poked the fire with a stick, nudging two logs together. "What did it look like?"

"There was love and light, and for me the ocean, but a lot of sorrow. The sorrow of my ancestors."

Joanie leaned and kissed her, randomly, on the arm. "I'm sorry." Cleo had Black and likely Native ancestors. Wells of sorrow were there, enslavement and genocide, blood in the earth.

"What do you think you're supposed to remember?" Cleo asked.

"I don't know. There's something about a ritual to the Star Goddess. Do you remember something like that?"

"I'm sure there was something, but I'm not coming up with it."

"I'll ask Hannah."

"I'm going up to bed. You coming?"

"I might sit by the fire a bit longer."

Maybe it would help her remember.

In a castle of towers, cherry-red and gold, blue hearts of flame flickered to life and died, behind a bastion of blackened logs. Fire went directly from solid to gas. If she did a lot of the entheogen she'd do the same, but she hadn't yet.

The stars of interstellar space—part of her wanted to escape out that doorway and never return. But that felt cowardly. She had work to do here.

At Hannah's house, the daffodils were done but the lilacs piled deep, dense with scent. Massive rosy-pink rhododendrons took up the side yard. Hannah sat Joanie again at the table in the wine-red dining room and insisted on getting her tea before they talked.

Joanie told the story of her entheogen journey. "Do you remember a ritual involving the Star Goddess? I don't."

"Huh," Hannah said, contemplatively, and blew on her tea. "I don't remember anything of the sort."

The instruction had seemed emphatic. "Are you sure? You can't recall anything?"

"No. I'm sorry."

Joanie bent and sipped her tea, feeling lost.

"That doesn't have to be the end of the story. With this kind of thing, working with psychedelics, once someone has the handshake and can talk to their Higher Self—"

"Is it the Higher Self, though?" Joanie asked. "I thought it was the All That Is, the Goddess Herself." Or maybe a phantom of her mind, but that wasn't what she believed.

Hannah shrugged. "I'm a mystic. For me, we're all part of the All That Is, and for me, the edges are pretty blurry between that and the Higher Self. Anyway, once you have the connection, you can take a moderate dose and then someone can ask you specific questions. Like what you're supposed to remember."

"I get it." She took another mouthful of tea, strong and hot. "Would you do that for me? Be the person who asked the questions?" She didn't fully trust Kirk and Nora to hold that space for her.

"I'm not sure Nora's ready for me to stick my oar in."

"I can play go-between." The big question was paying for the substance—Nora had taken to calling it fairy dust. It wasn't cheap. "I should be getting paid for my accounting contract pretty soon. If I can sort out the details, would you be willing to be the sitter?"

Hannah stirred honey into her tea. "Sure. It's high priestess work."

Chapter 14

Coming home from school after his last class took a half hour, twenty minutes on the bus and another ten walking in the rain.

Gus had decided to finish his bachelor's of science. His mom had talked him into it. In return, he'd talked her into giving him enough money to do it. Never mind how she squared it with his father—he'd let her figure that out. His plan was to do an EMT program next year.

Now he walked the blocks of his residential neighborhood in dark-blue evening, rain silver threads, red glare of car taillights along the road. Spring into summer, Seattle was generous with rain, though the light lasted longer heading for solstice.

He approached Hannah's house, a long, low bungalow, painted white. But something was off. Something felt wrong.

As he stepped onto the porch, his boot crunched on glass. The lightbulb of the front porch fixture had been broken out.

Shit.

The door was unlocked. He opened it, pushed his way in. "Anybody home?"

Hannah rented to him and his girlfriend Alyssa, plus two other roommates. The others tended to cycle out; he, Alyssa, and Hannah stayed. Usually at least one person was home among the five of them.

Now there was no answer, everything dark.

He opened the door to the room he shared with Alyssa, barely big enough to hold a double bed and desk. A tealight candle burned, low and tiny, on a shelf above the desk. Alyssa lay on the bed, whimpering.

Kicking off his boots, he lay down beside her and took her in his arms. "What happened, baby?"

"They came here."

He wrapped himself around her, big spoon to her little spoon. He wasn't a tall man, but she was a wisp of a thing, a tiny white girl, naturally flaxen hair now faded pink.

"Who came here?"

"Odin's Hunt."

Two men in the sphere of Odin's Hunt had died well-deserved deaths, both after menacing Joanie. Both deaths had a supernatural flavor, and suspicion fell on the coven. Now Gus had moved the levers that sent Bruni to jail. These weren't things the Hunt ignored.

"What happened?"

She shook her head and buried her face in the crook of his elbow. He held her, letting her cry.

"Let me up," she said at last. She found a tissue, dried her eyes, and blew her nose.

"Can you tell me now?"

"Sure." She pushed herself up against the headboard and put a pillow behind her back. "I was alone in the house, doing my essay, when there was this banging and rattling at the door. They were all like, 'Open up, I know you're in there! We'll knock the door down! Don't try running—we have the house surrounded!'

"Then someone else said, 'This is for Bruni!'"

"Oh, honey." He moved over, took her in his arms.

"I felt frozen. There's the baseball bat in the coat closet, but there was more than one of them. It's not some opportunistic thief. I kind of looked around the house with my psychic senses, and I got there was two, maybe three men in front, another in back. In the front, the one guy kept shoving, and the door fell open hard. You probably saw the hole in the drywall.

"Then a new voice yelled, 'What's going on?' It was Jimbo." Their newest roommate, a big bruiser white boy. "He had a friend with him. I got up and peeked out. Jimbo was all big and menacing, with his friend behind him. He threw a punch, and the Hunt guys broke and ran, jumped into a car and drove off. So luck saved me."

"I'll take it."

"Jimbo and his friend wanted to hang out, make sure I was okay. He made me some tea." A cup sat on the windowsill by the bed. "But I felt weird and just told them to go. I mean, what could they do to help me? I knew you were going to be back pretty soon."

"Nice of him to offer. Do you want more tea?"

"No, just hold me. Please."

"You're so cold. Let me find another blanket."

"No. Stay."

He whispered into her hair, "Ah, sweetheart."

After a while, she sighed and sat up again. "I should get on with my essay."

"More tea?"

"Sure."

He took the cup of tepid tea to the kitchen, boiled water, and brought the full cup back to steep. Alyssa stared into the blue light from her computer screen.

"Do you think they got caught on video?" he asked. After the former attacks, they'd put up video cameras.

"They were wearing balaclavas."

"We can see what we got. Did you see their car—did you get the license?"

Alyssa shook her head. "By the time I thought of it, they were in the car and gone."

"Fuck."

"I know. I'm sorry I didn't do better."

"You did fine. You succeeded, right? No one was hurt." He didn't repeat what he'd said to her before, that they should get her a pistol and train her to shoot. Growing up in Utah, he'd learned to hunt with his father, though he'd never enjoyed it. Alyssa had never wanted to learn. But it might save her life.

They could talk to the police—the detective he'd worked with, who'd put Bruni in jail. But that wouldn't happen right now. "What can I do to help you feel better?"

"Just be here with me. Stay with me."

"Of course."

Later that week, they held a house meeting.

Mid-spring, the lilacs continued, scent wafting through the yard. The day was half sun, half shadow; dark clouds threatened rain toward the west, toward the water, but so far held off. On the front walk, returning with Gus from the coffee shop where she worked with Joanie, Alyssa pointed. "A rainbow! Good luck!"

"We can use it."

They met in the living room under the Celtic knotwork hanging, Hannah central on the couch. It was clear that, even with Bruni out of the way—maybe especially with Bruni out of the way—they needed to protect the space.

"You did say Bruni threatened you at the hearing," Hannah said to Gus, shifting on the couch.

"Not exactly, but he shot me a warning look."

Some people might have found another house. But Hannah owned the place outright now, had bought it from the original owners, and that allowed her to keep rents cheap. She could sell, but it would be hard work to find a house as central at a similar price. And they wanted to support her. It was good to be close for coven business as well.

They didn't want to be run off by Odin's Hunt.

"We need to make sure you're not alone in the place, Alyssa," Hannah said.

Alyssa scrunched up her nose. "Or you, for that matter, Hannah."

"I'll just pull out my pistol. If those boys think I won't shoot them, they've got another think comin'."

"Which brings me to another point." Gus turned to Alyssa. "I need to take you shooting."

She groaned and covered her face with her hands.

"If you had a gun, you could have run them off without help."

"Or maybe they'd just knock the gun out of my hands. Anyway, they went away."

"You can't always count on your luck to save you."

"I'm a witch and a devotee of Hekate. She'll protect me."

"Honey," Hannah said, "Hekate protects those who protect themselves. I think you should take Gus up on his offer. I suspect Hekate does as well."

Alyssa rolled her eyes. "Fine. I'll go."

"Even so, in the meantime—we shouldn't have people at the house alone."

Jimbo said, "I'll be happy to help cover. But honestly, I agree about the gun."

"Okay, I'll give it a try. I promise."

Gus hadn't talked to Julia in a while—it was time.

Julia was a former member of Odin's Hunt, driven out and harassed after Gus's exit, when the Hunt found she and Gus had stayed friends. She was also friends with Linda, the wife of Jake, another Hunt leader. She had offered some time ago to keep Gus informed on Hunt doings, and she'd kept her agreement.

She lived in Renton, outside Seattle. They met halfway between, at a coffee shop—mocha paint and black tile outside, black leatherette couches inside, with tiny tables. The shop had recently changed ownership, repainted, and put up track lights— the coffee was still the same, still good.

In the warm late afternoon, rays of sun shot past the midcentury bungalows across the street to pour over the sidewalk. A few small black-painted wrought iron tables sat outside, with matching chairs, uneven on broken concrete, light glinting between the green leaves of the maples.

Gus had gotten there first, wanting to scope things. He didn't worry that the Hunt might have found their meeting place—they met so rarely. Still, other things could happen; even a bad vibe might be worth giving the place a miss. It was good to be careful.

He grabbed an outdoor table, got an Americano, and sat down to wait. She wasn't long, stomping up the sidewalk in her typical Seattle dark-blue rain jacket, which made her hourglass figure a box. Still, it moved with her movements. She was a tall, brunette white girl, a natural beauty. She embraced him and went inside, coming back with a frappé, her usual drink.

"How's everything?" he asked. "How's Noah?" That was her kid, custody for whom she shared with her ex.

"He's good! He's actually liking school now and has a couple new friends. I'm breathing easier." She sipped her frappé and looked up at him through her lashes. "He really likes Gary, which I appreciate."

"Gary?"

"I met him at work. He's a nice guy, a decent guy."

Another perk of seeing Julia had been they occasionally hooked up. But he'd never imagined that would last. She was telling him now she'd moved on.

"He's not at all like those Hunt dudes, with all their heathen bullshit."

Not all heathenry was bullshit, but it was hardly the time to argue. "Tell me about him."

"He's a supervisor in a parallel office. We'd been halfway flirting, but I couldn't tell if it was for real. Finally, he stopped by and asked me out for coffee."

He was watching her carefully, glancing into her dark, warm eyes. He didn't think of her when they were apart, but when they were together, her femininity enveloped him. Older, a few strands of grey in her hair, but she still exuded sexual energy like chocolate cake.

She caught his eye and looked away.

Not for him, not anymore.

"How long have you been seeing him?"

"A couple months."

"You're pretty into him, aren't you?"

She grinned. "A little. What have you been up to?"

He filled her in about school and about the latest attack by the Hunt. "Do you ever talk to Linda, these days?"

"Gary thought I should just drop all of them, and at this point I think he's right."

"Sure. You need to do what's right for you."

His hand lay on the table. Over it, she put hers, perfectly manicured, with pink nails, her touch soft and warm. He was going to miss sleeping with her.

"There was a time I really wanted to spy on them for you. I hated them with every fiber of my body. I still do. But it's just not healthy for me to focus on them anymore."

"I understand. I have to agree, honestly." It was too bad, though.

She drew back her hand. "I can tell you what I heard from Linda maybe a month and a half ago, if that would help."

"It's all grist for the mill."

"Bruni's not thrilled about this incarceration thing, as you might imagine."

"Who would be?"

"Obviously he had it coming. The Hunt's a little strained looking after his wife and kids, but they're managing. Being the Hunt, they vowed revenge. Jake was pretty neutral on the idea—he came down on the side of reason. He did a rune reading that said it wasn't a great idea."

"It isn't." All they'd done was waste time and money. After the attack, the doorframe and the drywall around it had needed more repair than the household had skills for, and they'd had to hire a contractor. Hannah had gotten payment for some of it out of insurance, but not all of it.

But someone had ended up taking Jimbo's punch, and that gave him satisfaction.

"I didn't hear what happened afterward, but I do know they've figured out a way to spy on you."

"Really?"

"Linda dropped something. I didn't want to dig, but I'm pretty sure. Keep an eye out. The kind of loss you gave them—they're going to find it humiliating. It's going to push them to do something bigger."

Chapter 15

The eternal present

They gathered in Samyaza's garden—the angel, his and Azazel's captains, Puabi-Ekur, and Nergal, accompanied by a wisp of air that was a leader of the Rabisi. Nergal interpreted his whispers and hisses. They sat in a circle of chaise longues, with some others nearby. A haze of gold hung in the air, and a low buzz emanated from bees among the flowers.

Samyaza leaned forward. "Puabi-Ekur and a few Rabisi will sneak in, all invisible, to scope the territory and report back. Assuming we go forward, we will keep some forces as reinforcements—that will be mainly my hand-picked angel soldiers, along with Nergal and some Rabisi—"

"I want to fight," Nergal said.

"If we show you in the vanguard, they will know you are one of our allies. I would rather that not happen."

Nergal growled, "Very well. I shall stay in the rear."

"Any other questions?"

One of Azazel's captains said, "My lord Samyaza, can you walk us through the plan one last time?"

With a wave of his hand, Samyaza called up a three-dimensional map. "We gather in the Great Below. We think the closest intersection with the Demiurge's hell is here." He pointed with a green wand that materialized in his hand.

"What if it's not?" Puabi asked.

Samyaza shrugged. "We just have a little farther to go. That is not the dangerous part of our journey."

Except that it was all dangerous. None of the spirits feared death or physical injury as mortals did. Spirits couldn't die, or not that way. But they could be trapped, for thousands of years of torment. And if this sortie failed, Azazel would be hidden more completely, guarded more safely, taken where he could not be recaptured again.

But someone had asked another question.

"I think we have sufficient forces if we move quickly enough," Samyaza said. "We believe Suriyel holds Azazel without Yald-abaoth's knowledge, which means Suriyel cannot call the full heavenly host. But of course, if the forces of the Demiurge discover their heaven has been breached for any reason, they will fight."

"So speed is essential," Puabi said.

"Exactly." Samyaza turned to the assembled battle leaders. "Any additional preparations needed?"

"All is ready," a captain said, and the rest echoed.

Puabi caught a glance from Nergal. He looked troubled, perhaps that he couldn't be in the vanguard.

In a far cavern at a corner of the Great Below, dust scattered on worn grey-black stone. The space lay hollow, empty—even ghosts didn't come here.

Puabi-Ekur had gone invisible, a wisp of air surrounded by Rabisi, also wisps. Before them rose a wall of basalt, the rock of the foundation of the world, there since the planet's beginning.

"Here?" Puabi-Ekur asked.

Samyaza and Nergal hovered behind them, with their legions and Azazel's. "Yes," Samyaza said. "You have the path memorized?"

"I do."

They went into the rock.

Pouring themself through dense crystalline stone felt like being liquid strained through a sieve—not painful but maddening and disorienting. Judging by their gyrations, the Rabisi liked it still less. They took a path parallel to earth's core, after a long count went upward. Movement sounded above them —the passage of angels like a covey of birds, the screams of the damned. They were under the prison. Puabi-Ekur followed the sense-trail pulling them to Azazel; the Rabisi followed.

Then Puabi-Ekur rammed against a spiky wall of magic and popped through. There Azazel was, sitting, head bent over his knees, black wings hidden. Iron rods still barred the cave mouth, but the heavy pile of chains lay to one side. They saw no guards.

"We must wait to see if the guards return," a Rabisi hissed, translating to Puabi-Ekur's tongue. They waited minute to minute.

No one appeared. The Demiurge had indeed pulled his soldiers away to cover elsewhere.

"Azazel," Puabi-Ekur whispered. "Azazel!"

A slight movement of his head made a strand of long hair fall from his shoulder. He was listening. Clearly he felt himself observed, from someone other than Puabi-Ekur. Suriyel must have planted eyes.

"We are coming for you. Be ready to fly!"

He gave a tiny nod.

Puabi-Ekur whisked backward through the crystalline rock,

fast as thought, to the basalt wall at the edge of the Great Below. There, the legions massed back into darkness, thousands of spirits waiting on Puabi-Ekur's word.

"He's there," Puabi-Ekur said. "The coast is clear, no guards."

Most of the army couldn't travel through rock like Puabi-Ekur and the Rabisi. They traveled by spirit, invisible, collecting behind a cumulonimbus at the edge of the Demiurge's fastness. From there, Puabi-Ekur stole forward to check the path to Azazel's cell. The golden thread that drew them on seemed obstructed, but they'd given themself landmarks. When they got to the cell, they were certain they were in the right place.

Azazel was gone.

The Rabisi circled the space. "Where is he?" one hissed.

"How should I know?" Puabi-Ekur whispered back. "He was right here. You saw him."

"Retreat!" called Samyaza.

But the Heavenly Host was on them.

Fighting exploded. White wings and feathers splashed through the air; black wings flew to meet them. Luckily the Host was spread thin—they encountered only a few legions. The forces were nearly equal in balance. Puabi-Ekur dove into the fray as a winged succubus.

Slice, slash, thrust, grunt—one white-wing was down, disappeared for now into oblivion. Then another fell. Samyaza shouted to his captains. Their fighting force held back the white-winged, whose line started to crumble, not broken but thinner. The Rabisi, vicious and invisible, bent the odds in their favor.

Would Samyaza show Nergal and his forces?

No, here was the call of retreat. Puabi-Ekur and the Rabisi disappeared once more into rock.

With a whooshing, they traveled back. In the Great Below, the troops collected. Few had been lost, and the lost ones required only time to return to spirit form—a form that for angels and their sort of spirits was forever, unless they be released.

"What happened?" Samyaza asked.

"They moved him between my check and our advance," Puabi-Ekur said, presenting as Puabi to Samyaza and the captains.

"Did anyone sense you when you checked, besides him?"

"I don't think so."

The Rabisi whispered to Nergal, "The Rabisi noticed no such thing."

"They certainly know about us now," Samyaza said.

"Do they know we meant to rescue Azazel?" Puabi-Ekur asked.

"We have to assume so."

"I can go look for him again."

"Wait till the furor has died down."

That made sense. Samyaza was watching their face.

"Do not blame yourself," he said. "No battle plan survives contact with the enemy. It stands to reason they would move him to make room for the influx. Unfortunately, we showed our hand."

"Not everything," rumbled Nergal. "They do not know we support you from the Great Below."

"Perhaps we can work with that."

Chapter 16

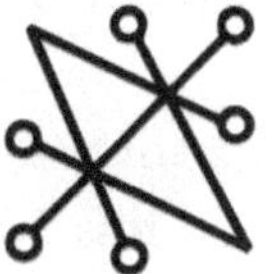

The mortal present

$\mathcal{A}$t dusk, the cloud-smudged sky dark blue, Joanie grabbed her purse to go to Hannah's for ritual. The strap snagged the corner of her journal, and it fell open to notes from a dream.

In that dream, warrior angels battled in a storm of lightning, some with white wings, some with black. The god Nergal thumped enemies with a studded club. The sky ripped open, and the white angels disappeared. As she wondered what had happened, the goddess Dea said, "Talk to the battle-god." Her notes said this was Nergal.

She walked up Hannah's front path, rang the doorbell. Her hostess led her upstairs. The housemates were gone, Gus and his girlfriend Alyssa on a trip to the coast.

"I thought I'd do this in the shared space," Hannah said. The white-painted gabled room she led Joanie to was sometimes a guest room, sometimes rented out. She'd hung a couple Celtic knotwork-bordered hangings there, one to either side, the horned god Cernunnos facing Aine, the goddess of summer. Hannah had gotten the fairy dust from Kirk, and Cleo knew Joanie was doing the ritual, but no one else knew what they planned.

Hannah had set up the room like Nora's yurt. On the floor lay a mat covered in purple sheets, a fluffy leopard-print throw folded at the bottom.

"What questions do you want to ask?" Hannah asked her.

"What does the Star Goddess want me to remember, and what does Nergal have to say?"

"For the type of oracle you want, answering questions, you may not want a heroic dose. Maybe something lighter. It's up to you."

"Lighter is fine if you recommend that."

From a side cupboard, Hannah took out a glass water pipe, rose-tinged. "This got left here a few roommates ago." She packed the pipe and lit it. "Draw in to the count of ten, and lie back when you feel ready."

The wave swept Joanie away. Images arose: a dark ocean breaking on volcanic rock, a full moon smiling down.

Someone was asking her a question.

After a time, she floated back and lay staring at the darkened ceiling. Fairy lights lit the room softly. The drug smoke's scent made her nose twitch—it smelled like burned rubber.

"You went farther than I expected," Hannah said.

"I don't remember a thing." She sat up. "What did I say?"

"I couldn't get a straight answer. You called in Nergal, who was more forthcoming, but he said for full knowledge you'd need to go to the Great Below. There he could have the protection to give you what you need."

~

The drug left her woozy, which she'd expected. She took the next day off.

Whatever she needed to remember, she needed protection to get at it. What could she have forgotten? Apparently it was a big deal, but sometimes what was a big deal on the astral plane felt less so in real life.

Midafternoon, in her bedroom, sunlit spangles dappling the walls, she steeped a few crumbs of magic mushrooms in tea to pull up the memory of the dark ocean and moon.

Lying in bed, she led herself down the steps to the Great Below. The gatekeeper let her pass as a favorite of Ereshkigal and Nergal. Lanterns in niches in living rock gave way to the faint red glow of the forecourt, dust on black stone. Ereshkigal's enormous basalt throne stood empty.

Up the formal staircase, she wafted into the Palace of Ganzir and to the doorway of her lover. The vizier let her in.

Nergal sat in his black basalt-framed bed, a tray on his knees holding Mesopotamian lamb-and-onion soup and a four-person cup of beer. From it, he drank like four men.

"Little Joanie. I have been expecting you." He clapped his hands, and servants took the tray away. "Leave us in peace," he told them.

To Joanie, he said, "Sit with me."

She climbed onto the bed and crawled to lie beside him. He put an arm around her, his huge basalt-grey, rock-hewn body in itself comforting to her, something she'd never expected from a god of violent death.

"Hannah said I needed to be here for you to tell me what I need to know."

"Mmm-hmm." Sound rumbled in his side, like an earthquake far under the earth. "The one who set the ban on this information has less power over me in my own realm."

So it was a big deal. That gave her a frisson of fear.

"What information?" she asked.

"I shall show you. Even here, that one can confuse and break the thread. But you will have more information than you did."

Once upon a time, there'd been a ritual at Hannah's—a black night, the yard encircled in leafless trees, branches reaching into the translucent sky. The moon stood high overhead, beside Orion, the star Rigel blue at the constellation's corner. Around her she felt spirits, hundreds of dark figures. Then someone was in her space, crowding her, a burly male form.

"Hello." A low-pitched voice. "Imagine your being here."

"Do I know you?"

"From a long time ago." With a scent of burned garlic, the spirit disappeared, a black feather drifting to the ground.

It was one of the black-winged ones, then.

Later, taking her hand, this spirit led her along a sandy path lined with torches to a pavilion of black silk, where he drew back the curtain-door. The tent stood two stories tall, lit inside by gilt candelabra. A bed dominated the space, dressed also in black silk, with a gilt headboard and frame. As he tossed aside the coverlet, the scene ended abruptly.

They'd been lovers, then.

How had she forgotten so much? What more had she forgotten?

The angel's deep voice sounded again in her ear. A hint of dark frankincense swam in the air. "My lily, my flowering branch, tell me about this evil man who pursues you, this Max." Gus's white-supremacist ex-boyfriend Max had wanted to murder her.

Later, he said, "I have something to show you."

A white truck went down a Seattle highway. Max drove, passing car after car, cutting too close. Rain lashed down, glittering in street light.

On a high bridge, a gust of wind hit the truck, making it ricochet off a barrier, spinning to stop horizontal across two lanes. Another gust tipped the truck to the side, and a third picked it up and slammed it down, crushing it. Across the bent metal of the window frame flowed black blood.

Max was dead.

This spirit had killed for her, and she'd forgotten him.

More scenes flowed before her. A bubble of cumulus clouds rose in a tall blue sky—the Great Above. Among them lay a wide platform of white stone. A bright solid light like a star burned at the edge of the platform, too bright to look at.

To one side, wrapped in golden chains, stood her beloved Puabi-Ekur as Puabi. Beside her—but her vision skipped away.

It had to be the spirit beside Puabi.

There was talking she couldn't distinguish, a booming voice —was this the Demiurge? There in the Great Above, Joanie tapped the inside of her forearm, and her blue-black knife sprung out.

With a swing of her arm, she cut a door that opened to a plane of golden fire. She, Puabi, and the spirit fell through darkness to a place of low brown buildings, stands of palms, in the middle of the night. A breeze shook the palm leaves.

A battle exploded, white wings against black, as in her dream.

Nergal's voice cut through. "Is that enough? Should I show you more?"

"I feel like there is more."

"Then let us continue."

No matter what he showed her, somehow she never saw the central character, never fully understood who he was. "It's a powerful block," Nergal said.

She drifted up hell's steps, heavy with longing for this spirit she'd lost.

It had been a hard few days on her body. As twilight fell, she slept.

She woke to Cleo shaking her. "Joanie. Did you forget? We have dinner at my dad's tonight."

She had forgotten entirely.

She sat up, rubbing her face with her hands. It was almost full night, the sky cobalt blue with a hint of pink at the edge of the trees. "Come on, get up, get dressed."

"I'm coming."

Joanie hadn't seen Ray and Sharon since the shrimp incident, and the dinner filled her with dread—probably why she'd let herself forget. She hustled into a black dress, and they set off through the forest toward greater Seattle.

"If we're lucky, we'll be on time," Cleo said, hands clutched on the wheel, pale-knuckled. Timeliness was important to Sharon, a show of respect, especially from her white daughter-in-law to-be.

They made it in time, found parking near Ray and Sharon's imposing brick house, sitting on a steep hill of lawn that Ray manicured to exacting standards. At the top of a flight of brick steps, they went through a wrought-iron gate in a brick wall, up a matching walk. Cleo rang the doorbell.

Ray opened, beaming. His genuine happiness to see his daughter always gave Joanie pause. No one in her family ever seemed happy to see her—she just fell into place, and the usual dynamic began as if no time had passed.

"Sharon's still finishing dinner, but we can sit in the living room. I can get you both a cocktail or a glass of wine."

Through the shadowy entryway, they passed into a pale-wall-papered room, formal, in the French style, furnished with cherrywood glassed-in bookcases and a pair of pale teal couches at a right angle to one another. Joanie had been here once before. Sharon had run late then too. Maybe it was a power move, making them wait. Or she could be nervous, shy, an introvert, or a bad planner—probably not the last one.

Sitting, Joanie said, "Wine is fine with me. Whatever you're liking right now." Both Ray and Sharon were wine aficionados.

"That sounds good," Cleo said.

"I know just the thing. Give me a moment." Ray retreated toward the kitchen—they had a wine cabinet off the kitchen, at the top of the steps to the basement.

Joanie watched him go. "I'm going to go find the bathroom," she said.

"Just before the basement stairs."

A moment to collect herself would be good, after the rush to get here. Part of her was still dwelling on the spirit with the black wings and how many memories she'd lost.

It was a lot. Was there more?

In the bathroom, everything was just so, a candle burning, a new pedestal sink. Ray and Sharon redecorated often. Joanie flushed the toilet and looked at herself in the mirror. Black eyes shining, hair sleek, form slender—she'd hardly changed in the last years. But the circles incised below her eyes betrayed stress. She had her hand on the doorknob when she heard footsteps in the hall.

The hall was narrow. She didn't want to walk into someone.

"I just don't like it," came Sharon's voice. She had to be right outside the door. Joanie held her breath. "She's one of the white devils, Ray. White folks have oppressed us for centuries!"

The floor creaked as Ray shifted his weight. He was right beside his wife.

"Now, Sharon. She's not a devil. She's just a little girl my Cleo loves. Best I can tell, she's always been sweet to her. And how can I stand in the way of my child?"

"I think you can speak your mind! You saw when that shrimp got thrown at me! You know those girls dabble in the dark arts."

"So do your friends—Connie and her hoodoo work."

"White folks even stole our magic."

"Now, Sharon." The floor creaked again, weight redistributed. Ray was hugging his wife.

Another creak—she guessed Sharon had pulled away. "Don't 'now, Sharon' me! I keep white people at arm's length. I know that's not what you do, but it's what I do, because it works! When I don't—I literally have scars."

Never had Joanie felt so bad for a moment of Puabi-Ekur's magic. At least Puabi-Ekur had helped heal her.

"The doctor says they'll disappear over time."

"I'll be polite to that white girl, but no more than that. Ever."

Joanie, holding onto the bathroom door handle, subsided onto the now-closed toilet seat.

One moment of damage had confirmed Sharon in her hatred.

Sharon had a right. On her mother's side, Joanie's great-grandparents had enslaved people work their land. Her mom still had the unconscious racism she'd been raised with. Sometimes even now in herself Joanie caught the odd thought—doubts about Black men, a turning toward white people that felt instinctive but was just fear. You had to be actively anti-racist. She was working on it.

She'd do her best to treat Sharon like a queen. Without letting Sharon walk on her, which Cleo would never stand for even if Joanie did.

Cleo and her parents, talking with animation, barely noticed when Joanie alighted on the couch next to Cleo. She put on her shiny whore smile, designed to cover everything.

"We could host the wedding in our backyard—" Ray got a look from Sharon over that and paused.

Catching sight of Joanie, Sharon said, "Why don't we sit down at the table?"

In the dining room, an antique cherry dining set stood on a thick-piled Persian rug. The paintings were contemporary—big blocks of color, red-orange and black. The table's scarlet-banded chinaware matched the room.

Sharon moved toward the kitchen. "Can I give you a hand?" Joanie asked.

"No, thank you." She turned her back, not smiling.

Ray pulled out Joanie's chair, then sat himself, beaming, ignoring any tension.

"It smells divine," Joanie said.

"Sharon made her pork griot. A Haitian dish, got it from one of her friends."

Sharon came out with the steaming tureen, then went back and returned with roasted vegetables. For a while, there was no talking.

"This really is amazing," Joanie volunteered, to Sharon. "I wanted to ask, how is your leg healing? I'm so sorry about all that. It was so weird."

Cleo cut her eyes at Joanie. Sharon leveled a stare at Joanie and said nothing.

Ray said, "Luckily, the doctors say she'll heal up fine. In the end, there may not even be scars."

Sharon looked from Ray to Joanie and back again. "Oh, there'll be scars."

Silence fell again.

Cleo broke it. "How serious are you about our doing the wedding in the backyard? We need to settle on a venue and get the invitations out."

Sharon gave Ray the side-eye.

Cleo turned to Sharon. "Sharon, if you don't want that, just say so."

Her big dark eyes batted. She didn't want it, but she also didn't want to be the person who said no.

Ray stepped in. "When do you need to know, Cleo?"

"Within a week."

Cleo drove back. She liked driving, though it was Joanie's car. Joanie was still tired from her vision work.

Thoughts clamored in her head, but she needed peace. She let herself fall half-asleep. They made their way through the forest toward Witch Farm, turning and turning again, as black silhouettes of firs passed. Wet air seeped through a partway-open window, carrying a scent of conifer.

Close to home, Joanie roused herself. "How do you think that went?"

"Better than expected. Though not good."

"I overheard them talking in the hallway, when I was in the bathroom. Sharon says I'm a white devil."

"You know that's based on a quote from Malcolm X."

"She's got a point about white people. I get that."

Cleo looked across at her, the whites of her eyes blue in half-darkness. "She may never give in. But she's fair. She won't do anything to hurt our relationship."

"I suppose that's something."

"Sharon's had her share of hardship." They came to a dark corner, shaded by a cedar, drooping limbs holding darkness. Cleo turned.

"Her parents were both schoolteachers. Her dad wanted to become a principal. He got passed over dozens of times—white men got the job. They were some of the first to integrate a white neighborhood, and Sharon and her brothers routinely got beaten up, till her mom got their older cousin to walk them to the bus. White people have always made Sharon's life worse. White bullies, at every turn."

Sharon at eight, proud and skinny, facing down her oppressors—it was easy to see. "I'll do my best."

"I know you will. Sometimes your best does nothing, though. And it's not your fault."

In the end, Sharon and Ray agreed to have the wedding in their backyard. It meant Cleo and Joanie saved money on a rental, and it meant there was no pressure on Witch Farm's fragile plumbing.

A few mornings after they heard, Joanie sat on the floor in a drift of invitations. Rays of sun illuminated the steam from her coffee. She had a pile finished but needed to do several handfuls more. At the same time, she needed to be in to work early—one of her co-workers had caught the new bird flu. And her contract had a deadline today.

Another fourteen-hour day loomed. Would she ever see the end of them?

She needed to do all the witchcraft she could to make sure Sharon healed. She needed to unearth all her memories of the black-winged spirit. There could be more around that block she didn't know about—a lot more, if it was big enough to affect Nergal. He was a god.

But she had to put it all in a box and get stuff done.

Chapter 17

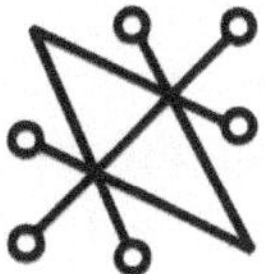

The eternal present

Puabi-Ekur and Samyaza were alone in his garden—the rest of the war band had gone to reconnoiter and locate their dead. Over time, those fallen in battle would return, though not always the same as they'd been. As Puabi, she wore a loose scarlet-red robe, color warm against the warm tone of her skin.

Heavy atmosphere hovered, dense summer. Bees buzzed under the press of sunlight, amid the scent of flowers. Lying on her chaise, she let her eyes drift closed. Even as a spirit, she needed rest sometimes.

She felt him staring at her, but she left her eyes shut.

His gaze, like the sun, warmed the body under her clothes, small breasts on a slender, wide-hipped frame, full rounded ass. Now she was spirit, but the memory of the body compelled.

She let her eyes open to slits.

"Are you thinking of me, Samyaza?"

Almost, but not quite, his hand moved to himself.

"It is only thought."

"It is energy."

How long would Azazel be imprisoned? Samyaza would not seduce her till he was free. Such was Samyaza's honor. Doubly the reason, then, to free Azazel.

Maybe she shouldn't think like that, but she did.

"What now?" she asked.

He smiled, drawing a line under their interaction, then let the smile drop away. "We find him and try again."

"I suppose that's on me."

"Who else?"

"Then tell me—presumably the heavenly angels are warned now. You've been at war with them for millennia—what blocks and magics will they have against me?"

He leaned back on his chaise, scratching his chin. "Well, Suriyel will certainly be paying attention now. They will have deduced we came for Azazel. So, subtly, not to draw attention, because his abduction of Azazel was highly questionable, Suriyel will have him guarded better. Angel guards are being shifted, so that means more magic instead. Magic of Suriyel's type, moon magic—shifting, confusing, trapping."

"That makes sense."

"To guard against moon magic, we use sunlight."

Puabi screwed up her face. By nature, she was a creature of the night.

"This is not a situation where you can slink by in shadow."

"How do you propose to protect me with sunlight?"

"We change your form and make you a sun sprite."

"A solar flare?"

"A type of fey. Most fey folk I work with are from the world of plants, but plants have an intimate relationship with sunlight."

"They eat it!"

"Just so. So we call in sun sprites and get them to dress you and surround you. Those can go unnoticed into the upper reaches and the Demiurge's realm. Even the lowest dungeons have the occasional sunbeam."

"I see."

She could do sunlight. Millennia ago, she'd been human. But since then she'd been a night dweller. Sunlight meant exposure.

"Is that such anathema to you?"

She made a face. "I have never been a creature of sunlight."

"Not even to rescue your lover?"

"For that, and only that."

She stood from her chaise, came to stand in front of his, looking down. "And then, after that, plant boy, you owe me."

He reached for her hips and stood, using them for leverage. On his feet, he was nearly a head taller then she. With a finger-breadth of space between them, she felt his heat. "I will pay then, in any coin you desire. Are you ready to do this work?"

"I am."

"Very well."

A wave of his hand, and there descended a glittering cloud, a raft of sun sprites.

A scattering of shine, and she was as they were, though larger. Samyaza waved to them again, and she rose, leading a cloud of shining sprites on the airless currents of space, following the golden cord of energy that linked her to her lover.

Then she was there—wherever there was. Flat light shut her in, a white nothingness. The sun sprites glittered around her, encouraging. She changed form, to a simulacrum of Puabi, and stepped forward into the nothingness. Under her feet, sand crunched.

It seemed she walked mile on mile. It was all perception; no harm came to her body. She didn't have a body. No fatigue, no sunburn, just the boredom of trudging forward in invisible sand —the outlook never changed. She saw nothing, a dull shine, no shadow, not even the sand below her; she only felt it.

A speck appeared in the distance.

When she got to it, though it was the only feature for miles, it was next to nothing—a tiny hole, a depression in the sand. She fell into a squat, onto fine, nearly translucent off-white sand.

She stuck one hand into the hole, all that would fit, and dug.

Presently she shoved in both hands, then got her arms into it. Then the sand gave way and she was falling. With a soft thump, she landed in a cave.

The sand spilled down, filling in around her. She was stuck. If she'd been in a body, she would have suffocated; as spirit, she did not.

Above her, she sensed, the sun sprites still glittered, but they could be no help. Sand was not a place for them.

She began to shift, ever so slightly, after an eternity wriggled herself up and out, lay flat upon the sandy ground.

Still there was near complete nothingness, the gleam and dance of sun sprites, wordlessly encouraging. The sand shifted easily, loose, like dunes.

She began to dig again, at random. The tiny depression was gone.

In front of her, a sandal-clad foot appeared, the sandal clasped with golden buckles. Her gaze traveled upward along a long leg, tanned, fuzzed with blond hair, to the edge of a Greek chiton. The owner of the leg cleared his throat, and she met his eyes, azure blue. A man in golden armor stood there, breastplate emblazoned with a lion.

She scrambled to her feet.

Mitzrael had not unfurled his wings, but he looked ready to, for intimidation's sake. He glowered.

"What are you doing here?" he asked.

She stood silent. The sun sprites surrounded her, close to her skin, tiny flares, prickling and supportive.

"I can guess. It is the same errand as before."

She said nothing, letting her form do the speaking.

She wore only the appearance of Puabi's naked body, a

woman at the height of her beauty: smooth brown skin, brown eyes lit amber by the glare, small high breasts, hips and ass a man might die for. The Demiurge's archangels did not dally with humans, but they were not immune to their attractions. But as spirit, he could see into her as spirit.

"You truly love him."

She did, and if she let herself fall into it—ah, she couldn't go there.

A tear rolled down her cheek.

"I did not know succubi could love. Perhaps you are on an arc of redemption."

She rallied herself. "As are we all."

"That is not in scripture."

"I don't believe in your scripture, and neither do you. We both predate those books."

He still frowned. Maybe he'd thought about the accusations Samyaza had made when they last spoke. Mitzrael hadn't debated that Suriyel had captured and preyed on Azazel for his own desires, whatever Suriyel's claims.

"If I am challenged, I will need to report your visit."

"Of course."

A burst of light, and he disappeared.

A channel opened below her in the sand, a tube like glass curving downward into darkness, the only darkness in the dully shining landscape.

"Follow me," she told the sun sprites—a ray of sun could fall into any darkness. Back in the form of pure spirit, she went.

Down, down—deep sand turned to rock, the basalt of hells' dungeons. Adamantine reinforced it, angel-stone not of the earth, and iron bars as she came into a dungeon. Vast, labyrinthine, cold, and nearly empty—some cells had sluggard life in corners.

She followed the golden cord, and there he was.

As with the old dungeon, in the new one the walls and ceiling of black adamant shone, sharp-edged crystals in the rock. Iron rods barred an opening; heavy chains lay to the side. All was enclosed in walls of ultraviolet fire, anathema to many creatures of darkness.

In sun sprite form, she was not that.

He seemed smaller than before, hunched into himself, skin grey in the unearthly light. His long hair hung dull, his face long —she'd never seen him so dispirited.

"Azazel," she whispered. "Azazel."

He did not turn.

He could not hear her.

He was ensorcelled with Suriyel's spellcraft, stuff of the moon —misdirection, glamourie, shadows; blindness, deafness. But the sun routed the moon.

"Come," she whispered to the sun sprites. "We must glow on him."

They surrounded him, an orb of sunlight, out of place in the dark, dank space. He warmed under their touch. He sat up, stretched, shook his head back and forth as if shaking off flies.

She drew away from the swarm of sun sprites and stood before him, a simulacrum of herself in dancer's gear, glinting gold with sunlight.

"Azazel," she said.

His eyes blinked open, and he saw her.

"Beloved," he said.

What if they were seen? They'd already been seen. This time it was defiance.

"Still we shall rescue you," she said. "I will try and try until we succeed. Your brother and his people are helping me, and other armies."

Their eyes met, and held. His were that topaz-blue, grey-blue, twilight. It seemed like centuries since he'd been free.

"I am sorry," he said. "I should never have banished you."

"Let us free you, and then you can apologize properly."

Chapter 18

The eternal present

$\mathcal{P}$uabi-Ekur returned to Samyaza exhausted. Even with the glass passageway, even with the support of the sun sprites, who radiated energy like their father the sun, returning from the depths to the heights through the realm of sand wore them out.

In the timeless garden, Samyaza received her as Puabi. She stood before him trembling. He sat on the edge of a fountain, letting his hand dip into the falling water, and nodded that she sit. She settled on a garden bench, green-tinged wrought bronze with an array of velvet pillows. Furniture in Samyaza's space was mysterious, moving and changing at whim.

"While you were gone, I was not idle," he said. "I have enlisted armies of the fey, who have never been friends with the Demiurge."

He gestured toward the edge of the garden, where there stood a line of new trees, hollies, behind them oak and ash: spiky, stalwart, martial.

"Tree warriors," she said. A blackberry vine rolled toward her, wicked thorns as long as her thumbnail. "Vines as well. But how can they fight in heaven?"

"They can travel on the spirit plane. Dryads, hamadryads, plant spirits." With Nergal, the angels, and the Rabisi, they might tip the balance.

"How do we fight this battle? I had the hardest time getting to him. I had to go through an endless realm of sand and glare, and the only way I found him was because Mitzrael showed me the way."

"Interesting. We may turn him yet."

"He did it because he saw I loved Azazel. He's hardly going to let our army pass."

"But you have way markers."

"I do. But I'm far less sure than I was last time. The whole thing is designed to confuse folk of darkness." Samyaza smiled. "You were right to send me with the sun sprites! If that's what you need to hear."

"My point is, many of our folk are not of the darkness. All my new recruits are from the daylight, eager to fight the heavenly host for reasons of their own. And of the underworld folk—the Rabisi are ancient spirits of the wind, who can fight in many places. Nergal himself, though a ruler of the Great Below, is a god of sudden death. Battle and plague deaths often occur in sunlight."

On her garden bench, she rolled onto her stomach, propped her chin on her elbows to look out across the garden. At the edge, by the wall, the trees massed, looking back at her.

"We need a phalanx to hold off the heavenly army," Samyaza said. She felt him approach behind her, and held her breath a moment. Her whole back listened to him. But nothing sexual would happen now. "Then we need scouts armed with sun energy to penetrate the dungeon and retrieve Azazel, with you."

"When we last fought heaven," she said, "Joanie cut us

through with her knife. But her past with Azazel is invisible to her. How do we escape to a stronghold now?"

"Azazel still has his ancient hell, and that place retains affinity for him. We just need a direct door from his current dungeon to his old one. And since it's like to like, we may be able to persuade the new dungeon that the old is an annex of sorts. For that, we need folk who talk to rocks. Luckily the tree-spirits know such folk."

"Who is that?"

"Huldufólk. The hidden folk."

She nodded, but she didn't understand. Such communication seemed far-distant to her. She had been human, long ago, and for a while she'd travelled on the wind, like the djinn. She'd never been a creature of rock, or earth, or even for millennia a farmer. She admired Samyaza's poison path, but it wasn't hers.

Yet this was her task.

"I need to meet these huldufólk and see who they are."

"Go to their home. They are earth spirits, so on Earth. Iceland is the easiest place to reach them."

On a green hill overlooking the sparkling ocean, she touched down. She'd traveled with a companion of Samyaza's, the dryad spirit of a birch tree, one of the few trees native to Iceland.

Preparing to converse, the dryad presented in near-human form—tall, pale-skinned, slender, with long, spiral-curled strawberry-blonde hair the color of birch leaves in autumn, her shift matching in color. "Best we talk to the big rocks in the north, here," the dryad said, as they climbed the hill, moving away from the ocean.

"The rocks?"

The dryad thought a moment, translating to human speech.

"Rocks dropped from the glaciers of the last Ice Age. Some of them still have huldufólk in them. Though the ones by the road-ways will not talk at all, they have been so bothered by humans."

"That makes sense."

"No talking now. This rock person will hear us and hide."

They crossed the hill in silence.

Coming from the water along turf studded with tiny daisies, they approached a rock formation. Like all of Iceland, this was volcanic, black with reddish streaks, basalt with iron in it. As they closed on it, she saw the clump of rocks formed a natural circle around an enclosed space—perhaps a giant lava bubble, burst long ago.

"Shhh," said the dryad, but that was unnecessary. The place itself enjoined silence.

A wall of jagged red-black rocks shaped like teeth circled a round of emerald grass. In the middle hulked a huge brown-black rock, like an animal from the age of megafauna—a small mammoth here in the far north. A dangerous animal that kept to itself, now asleep.

The dryad approached, step by step, Puabi behind her. Putting her hands to her mouth, the dryad breathed out a breeze, and the cool insinuating current circled within the rock forma-tion. It lifted Puabi-Ekur's hair. She'd gone as Puabi dressed for formal ritual planning, in a tiered Sumerian robe.

The wind circled the humped brown rock, stirred it awake—its outline rippled.

"Greetings, honorable one," the dryad said. "I am Berkana of the birch, of this land."

With a rumble, the land twitched, like the beginning of an earthquake. Puabi glanced around in fear, but it was the rock talking.

"Greetings," was all it said, but slowly, through the earth itself: "Grrrrrrrreeeeeeeeeeetings."

"Beloved elder, I would like to introduce to you a spirit from elsewhere. This is Puabi-Ekur."

A pause fell. The wind that had circled the rock returned and circled Puabi.

"What are you?" asked the rock.

"I am a succubus, of the land between two rivers. A desert land, now." It hadn't always been one. "Far away south."

"Why do you come here now?"

"Honorable one," said the dryad, "can you please make yourself present to talk?"

A pause, then very slowly: "Very well."

With a gentle shake in the earth, the being stepped from the rock.

Tall, slender, in that way like the dryad, this being was the brown-black color of the rock, his skin the rough texture of stone, inhuman. Male, but Puabi sensed this was almost happenstance, and if this elder chose to present otherwise, female would be natural too. He wore a simple tunic, also brown-black, lighter in color than his skin. He stood beside his rock, palm on it as if drawing strength from it.

"Forgive me if I seek words," he said. "I do not speak often. You may call me Alfstein."

It meant elf-stone. No one would give a true name in such a situation.

"What do you ask?"

Puabi stepped forward. "I am friends with fallen angels—angels that came to earth, now captured and jailed by the Demiurge. The Demiurge's folk have taken one of their number to torture, one I love. I seek his return to his usual place, and for that we need one who can talk rock to rock."

"And what will you give me for this, or what will that bring to me?"

"Beloved elder, none of us is on the Demiurge's side," the dryad said. "Do you not wish to strike a blow against the Usurper?"

"Striking has its consequences. We learned that long ago. We have worked out a peace, and I would keep that."

"This will not be a fight against the Demiurge's main force," Puabi said. "A rogue angel has captured my friend."

"Then this is a personal vendetta? If so, how does it strike a blow against the Usurper?"

"Some of his number will know that he is weak if we succeed. That we can take things his followers desire."

"But does not such a move warn that the Demiurge must protect himself?" Puabi had no ready answer for that. "Everything you say persuades me it is best I stay in my rock."

The dryad said, "I hear what you say, beloved elder, and were it two hundred years ago, my people would agree. But now the earth is changing, and the Demiurge makes ready for a mass dying." How did the dryad know that? Perhaps Samyaza had told her. "In the meantime, the forces of earth have strengthened. I do not know this for certain, but I would not be surprised if the fallen angels hope to lead a war. A war that we of the earth might now win."

"You are bloodthirsty for a tree-girl," Alfstein said.

"My people are dying. We need to make change."

"The rocks endure. This land endures." Puabi felt then how truly he was of the land—the bones of the land, the volcanic rock below, still liquid near the surface, not far from spilling free. That was a part of his strength, the living magma that could flow as lava.

"But what of that which grows on it? The people are changing the earth. The Demiurge's followers lay waste to the land, the trees, all living beings—humans themselves. The rocks might endure, but you also love the rest of us. Are part of the rest of us."

"Hmm." The sound went low, into the earth—Puabi felt the rocks grumble. The rock circle, stuck up through the greensward like teeth through gums, shifted slightly. It was true, though the huldufólk lived in the rocks, they were land-spirits, people that watched after grass, trees, the landscape.

"Our glaciers are receding," the dryad said. "Our sea goes to acid. Our summers grow warmer—too warm for many delicate things."

Alfstein gave her a dark glance. "And freeing this angel will help how?"

"If we succeed," Puabi said, "it will show the Demiurge's folk can be challenged. Things have changed since the last great war." Which she knew little about, except that it was millennia past.

"Hmm," Alfstein said. "I will think on it."

The dryad stole up to him, wound him around with the breeze she could call. Her long hair shook, like leaves in wind. She was still a foot away from him, but it was as if she embraced him.

"Please," she said. "For all the old love we have, your folk and mine." In her voice, it was clear this love was not just between their peoples, but personal.

Alfstein said, "For you, Berkana, I will do this. But look you, I expect your folk to support this outing."

"Oh, we will," she said. "I will."

Alfstein declined the general war council, but agreed to meet Samyaza with Puabi and Berkana.

He did not look out of place in Samyaza's garden. He had dressed as an elf-prince—some Icelanders called the huldufólk elves, though some said otherwise. His dark skin harmonized with a dark-green tunic, on it silver embroidery, ancient runic patterns, not runes Puabi knew. Berkana had likewise dressed up, in a green like spring leaves, gold spirals in her ears and on her long tunic. The two of them looked like they belonged together, which perhaps they did.

The fey folk who served Samyaza led them to a circle of chaise longues, gave them each a glass of something sparkling. Puabi sipped hers—for her it was like pink champagne, and its color was pale pink. The others were colored slightly differently. Puabi guessed each suited the person who held them. Alfstein's was clear sparkling water.

Samyaza appeared moments later, in an extravagant robe of green-and-gold paisley silk, open to show his muscular chest. He wore golden hoop earrings and a sparking green-stone pendant. He nodded to each and took his seat, reclining on one elbow. A fey maiden danced up with a glass for him, his sparkling beverage pale gold.

"Well met. I am Samyaza, one of the Watcher angels."

"Alfstein, of the huldufólk." Berkana and Samyaza knew one another; she nodded to him.

"I trust Puabi has told you of our mission."

"Somewhat. But I would hear it from your lips. In particular, why should the huldufólk help here, now?"

Samyaza sipped from his glass.

Puabi leaned forward. "Berkana spoke to that. It is a personal quest, yes, but perhaps we can show or explore a chink in the Usurper's armor."

"And why should I want to do that?" Alfstein said. "I prefer the Demiurge ignoring my folk."

"To persuade others," Samyaza said. "To show that perhaps we have the strength to fight a new battle against those who style themselves heavenly."

"The Demiurge and the archons."

"Exactly."

"If we never have won a war with them, why should we try again?"

Alfstein made it sound as if there had been multiple wars, of which Puabi knew nothing. Clearly she'd have to shake some information out of Samyaza.

"Because the forces of earth have grown strong, and the forces of heaven have weakened," Berkana put in. She sat up, curling golden-red hair falling over her shoulders like a cape. "Because the earth needs us as never before."

"My people have a fragile truce and wish to keep it."

"Is not our island particularly susceptible to these changes the humans have wrought?" Berkana asked.

"I do not see how helping this errand would change that."

"It is, perhaps, the beginning of a process," Samyaza put in smoothly. "And if we can break or even bend the Demiurge's rule, to a more equitable peace, it is time to do that. Or so I believe. Also you would have my undying gratitude, which I would make sure to display, even in the short term."

A side glance told Puabi Samyaza had no idea how.

The leaves of the new army at the edge of the garden rustled. "We must act," Berkana said in a low voice. "It may not work. But I will not let the earth I know pass away without a fight."

Alfstein's gaze drank her in like water.

"For you, Berkana, I will do this thing."

"I will do my best to make sure you do not regret it."

"As will I," Samyaza said.

Alfstein turned back to the angel. "What do you want me to do?"

"The imprisoned one is Azazel, another of the Watchers and my brother. He was entrapped by Suriyel, who has ever wished his companionship. Suriyel perhaps hoped to persuade him thus." Alfstein raised his eyebrows. "Yes, it was a poor idea."

"I have the way to his prison cell," Puabi said.

"We can get through locks and bars," Samyaza said, "but we need to put Azazel somewhere the ranks of heaven cannot assail him. Which, by logic, is the hell that the Demiurge long ago assigned him."

"Yes," Alfstein said. "It will be magicked to belong to him."

"Because it is his prison," Samyaza said, "it has a likeness to where he is. We just need to persuade the two prisons they are one. They are mostly made of rock, so we need a being who can persuade rocks."

"A member of the huldufólk."

"Just so."

"I cannot guarantee I can make this connection. Ideally I would have time to speak to both sides. I cannot see how I can have this."

"I cannot sneak you into Suriyel's prison," Samyaza said. "But I can take you to my brother's hell."

Palms stood silhouetted against the cobalt sky. A light wind shuffled the sand, hummocked at the foot of a wooden bench sand-blasted for millennia, renewed again and again by the nature of the place.

So many times, Puabi-Ekur had spent an evening, a few days, in this space of Azazel's, in his arms, making love to him, talking to him, helping him research—or giving him water as he hung upside down chained to a cliff face, in the torture that the Demiurge called penance.

They missed him, his touch, his kiss, his low voice in their ear, everything. The scent of dark frankincense that was his. But he was gone.

Berkana hung back, standing among the palms. No birch trees grew in this desert.

Alfstein knelt to touch the paving stones of the path, and then the sand, his tunic trailing in the dust.

"This is an ancient place," he said. "Older in its way than the living earth, which changes. This was meant to always be the same."

"Can you speak to these rocks?" Samyaza asked.

"I believe so. They are like enough to earth."

He put his palm flat against the sand. Puabi sensed he was reaching deeper, to the living rock. He began to whisper.

A long time passed. Puabi could almost see the change he wrought, the conversation. Rock on rock, old, slow, dark, yet sometimes sudden: lava bursting through a skin that only seemed solid.

Then Alfstein stood, shaking the sand out of his clothes.

"The rocks desire Azazel's return, and will do as we wish."

Alfstein joined Puabi to travel to Azazel. Both would go as spirit, following the few way markers Puabi had been able to set. Following them would be a small group of sun sprites, signalers forward and backward, to the prisoner and to the waiting army.

Again Puabi travelled disembodied, like a thought or wish, to the plane of flat white nothingness. Changing to a simulacrum of her body, she landed, sand crunching below her feet. The rules of this landscape implied form. The sun sprites sparkled.

Behind a veil, the many legions poised in the form of spirit. Once she found the way, they could translate to wherever they were needed. The energy connection was the important piece.

In the shining sand, a tiny depression appeared, a divot of darkness.

This time, the way seemed created for her. Perhaps Mitzrael was helping. It wasn't the glass-walled tube but a passage made of dark rock, red-black basalt. Maybe the huldufólk worked to bring earth to this barely material place.

She wriggled downward, now almost entirely spirit, through basalt and adamant, following her sense of Azazel, a golden cord. She reached the dungeon—black crystalline walls and ceiling, mouth barred by iron rods, heavy chains to the side, encircled in ultraviolet fire. Azazel lay supine on a flat rock, staring sightlessly at the ceiling.

He looked worse than before. Had Suriyel done something new?

She called the sun sprites, who surrounded him with gilded light, warming him. He glanced at her, then away.

He knew what she was doing and didn't want to betray her.

It was time.

In her mind, she called Alfstein.

A heat like magma poured through the rock, and then he was there, as spirit—red-black as the basalt that underpinned the magical adamant. The basalt began to move, subtly.

A wisp of pure energy, she circled Azazel, mind to mind asked, "Are we being watched?"

His glance pointed out an orb half-hidden among rocks—some spy eye.

Thinking of Alfstein, she directed this to him, and the basalt moved even more subtly, silently, letting the barely upraised rock-bed that Azazel lay on form a sight-barrier.

A space, hidden by darkness, cleaved open. The sun sprites dimmed their light, letting there be vague shadow. The hot breath of the desert touched her cheek, carrying the susurrus of palms.

The connection was made.

Azazel sat up, head in hands as if fatigued. He grunted and let himself slide to the floor. Stretching out, he rolled back and forth, groaning as if tortured.

He rolled to the side of the bed, hidden from the spy eye.

He met her gaze.

They fell onto the sand, by the ancient wooden bench.

"Now we see if it succeeds," Azazel said.

Chapter 19

For a moment, as they sprawled there, all was still. The sky lay cobalt blue, tinged crimson in the west, palms silhouetted against it. The scent of hot dust hovered.

Then white wings burst through the blue as if a knife had slashed it open.

Thunderclouds boiled through the tear in the sky, belching phalanx after phalanx of white-winged angels. Black-winged angels rose to meet them, wings beating the air to wind, swords slashing. Around them flew invisible air-spirits, the Rabisi, armed with darts. The God of Sudden Death shattered angels with his mace. Winged elves in the hundreds, Berkana's friends, shot arrows and light spears. On the ground, huldufólk crushed fallen enemies.

Suriyel's forces were outnumbered, but Samyaza had a harder time getting his varied combatants into the fray. Suriyel's white-winged angels cut through the black-wings, Rabisi, and fey.

Puabi-Ekur, as General Ekur, leapt into the air behind Azazel. That angel led his own legions and Samyaza's. The winged elves followed Reynir, a rowan tree dryad, glossy hair berry-red, shooting arrows tipped in aconite. Angels did not die in full—they were immortal—but a death blow cast them out of battle.

Samyaza's forces rallied, knocking white-wings to the huldufólk. The elfin folk clubbed the fallen and rolled the bodies to the rock-folk, who crushed the remains.

Slash, cut, slam, spin. Many who fought them were nearly their equals. But Azazel and Ekur knew each other's minds perfectly. Slowly they hewed through the white-wings.

Suriyel sat aside, directing the fray from a high-blown cumulus. Occasionally their eyes turned to Azazel. Azazel returned a glare molten with wrath. But Azazel was busy.

At some hidden signal, Suriyel saw the battle was lost. They gave a piercing shriek of rage, and the white wings disappeared through the rift in the sky.

The winged folk settled to the ground, in the empty fields past the tents of Azazel's angel legions. The huldufólk collected beside them. Alfstein and Berkana, spokespeople for the allies, came forward, with Reynir and a few other captains.

Samyaza's green-and-purple wings flickered with excitement. "We turned them back!"

"How did Suriyel get so many to fight with them?" Ekur asked. It had been a brutal fight, and though angels didn't die, fey and huldufólk did. A very few had fallen, but not zero.

That was Alfstein's first concern. "I need to get my folk back to their lands, so that our dead may receive proper burial and return to their earth."

"Understood," Samyaza said. "How can we best repay you?"

Alfstein's grin was grim, showing a lot of teeth. "You spoke of this as a test, to see whether and how we might challenge the Great Above. Keep us apprised of further tests."

"We will remain in communication."

Alfstein led the fey and huldufólk to the edge of the pocket hell, and they disappeared. Samyaza turned to his brother.

"You are returned to your own hell, at least," he said. "Berkana mentioned she might persuade Alfstein to make a permanent connection between this place and their own, in Iceland, so you may come and go as you please."

"Lovely," said Azazel. "But now I desire to cleanse myself from battle. And rest, and consider. Many thanks for mounting this rescue."

Samyaza eyed him. "You are more than welcome. We shall debrief later. I thought I might host a small victory party. I hope you can attend."

"Give me a little time, Sam."

"Of course." Like the huldufólk and elves had, Samyaza and his forces walked off the edge of the world and away.

Chapter 20

The mortal present

The night after sending the last wedding invitation, Joanie slept fitfully, a shaft of moonlight poking through the curtains to cross her pillow. Toward morning, she fell into deep sleep.

Angel fighters floated tangling, battling above the oasis she'd seen in her earlier dream. Black-winged angels fought white-winged ones, among them fey like mayflies armed with bows, arrows, and thrown spears. Winds tossed and knocked about the white-wings. Among them, suspended in air by some magic, strode her lover Nergal, swinging his huge lion-faced mace, taking several with each blow.

The angel that haunted her dreams fought at the center, whirling and striking, dark hair flying, face always in shadow.

She woke in the pale grey of dawn beside her sleeping fiancée, full of longing for her angel. Grabbing her journal, she wrote down the dream.

Vital parts were missing. She'd tried all she could think of to unearth them. Somehow it was all enormously important, though she didn't know how.

What more could she do?

Chapter 21

*I*n the fallen angel's pocket hell, only Ekur and Azazel remained. A whisper of wind shook the palm leaves and made the dust spin.

"Let's get you cleaned up," Ekur said.

They followed the torchlit path to the grand pavilion and pushed through the curtain-door. Gilt candelabra lit the space, centered on the gilt-framed bed dressed in black silk. Azazel conjured a bath, a huge wooden tub big enough for three, with steaming water and herbs. The candles blazed up in the candelabra—Suriyel's dungeons had been dark.

They unbuckled their armor, dropped their clothing, and sank into the aromatic water. On the surface swam rose petals with bits of lavender and chamomile, breathing out sweet scent. Groaning, Azazel let his eyelids fall shut.

Ekur released himself to the hot water. They'd both avoided significant wounds, but Ekur had a slash along one leg, and

Azazel had black-bruised ribs where one of Suriyel's minions had barreled into him.

It was probably too early to have this conversation.

"So," Ekur said, swirling the water with his brown hand. "You apologized to me for banishing me, if in passing."

"I did. And I meant it. I am deeply sorry to have sent you away. I was foolish to do so."

"There's the question of how to make it up to me."

Azazel dipped his head into the water, rinsing out his hair. Emerging, he said, "I am listening."

"You must reconnect with Joanie."

The bathwater lapped the sides of the tub.

"I must, you say." Azazel's tone was studiedly even.

Clearly Ekur had piqued Azazel's pride. But he had to go on.

"It is she who first brought you your ally Nergal."

"You also helped secure him."

"She can bring the support of witches and humans, which may be essential."

"Many of her alliances are yours as well."

"Does she not deserve honor for freeing your soldiers? That's a boon she can promise others, a powerful enticement." Ereshkigal had given Joanie a knife that cut through to the next step on the path of life for each being. Azazel's warriors had been locked in his pocket hell with him for millennia, and by her actions many were freed.

"I trust those with me now will stay for the coming fight."

Perhaps they were in the wrong form to succeed in this argument, though they'd never been certain Azazel had a preference. They shifted into Puabi.

"I realize you're just back from this long torture. We can put off this conversation if you like."

Azazel shook his head, flipping drops of water from his hair. "We can have it now."

"Okay, then! Not only did she help you, she's still in as much danger from Suriyel if you still care about her. And you clearly do."

"Do I?"

"You haven't forgotten her."

"You seem hell-bent on reminding me."

"Your plan failed, or at least two-thirds of it did. You and I kept our memories. But now Joanie's longing for you, and she doesn't even know who she's longing for. Since it helps no one, surely you owe her this!" Puabi was starting to feel desperate, and also angry.

The blue topaz gaze fixed on her, clear as water and cold as ice. "I owe no one."

In frustration, Puabi smacked the water with her palm. "That's not how it works! We all owe each other. It's the web of existence!"

Azazel stood, water dripping from his magnificent form. Angels could appear however they wished; Azazel appeared like something out of a woman's dreams. He had a warrior's muscles, sculpted like a statue. Puabi tilted her head back, avoiding being face to face with his cock.

"I am done with this conversation."

"But I've barely started!"

"Take it up another time, if you so desire. I am going to rest, in my own bed, of which I have been deprived these many weeks."

It was time to be meek and demure. "Of course. May I join you?"

"Of course. But no talking."

The mortal present

Working the cash register while her cashier took a break, Joanie served half a dozen Seattleites their coffee. The calls rang out. "Two pumps of white chocolate mocha, 2% milk, extra whipped cream and extra hot to go." "Twelve-ounce three-shot cappuccino, extra wet." "Sixteen-ounce quadruple latte, half oat milk, half hemp milk." These were her people.

Then the impeccably blonde woman in the pastel blue hoodie asked, "What is this?" She held up her paper cup.

"An Americano, triple shot, like you asked."

"No, it's not!"

Maybe data would help. "Ma'am, an Americano is simply hot water with espresso. We make our twelve-ounce standard Americano with two shots of espresso. You asked for an Americano with three shots, so you got a twelve-ounce one with three shots."

"This is drip coffee! And bad drip coffee at that!"

The time and resources spent pleasing this woman might be

worth it, if she'd only shut up. "Ma'am, I'd be happy to remake your coffee in whatever fashion you'd like."

"Just give me a refund!"

It was a small pleasure to see half the room glare at the blonde woman.

By the time Joanie finished the refund, the cashier had returned. Joanie went in back to the tiny manager's office, desk lamp creating a halo of light.

Damn that woman to the depths of hell—Ereshkigal's hell. Demons could torture her forever.

All right, belay that.

Well... maybe a little torture.

She called the cash register company about their software. "Do you mind holding a moment?"

Yes, she did. "Not at all."

Bland jazz played. She sat still a moment, resting her hands on a stack of accounts waiting for her attention. They'd never shifted to a fully online system, despite her urging.

Images nagged at her from her dream of battling angels.

This angel, who was he? She'd done a lot to find out. What did she need to do—make some kind of sacrifice?

It was a big deal. She didn't even know how much information she was still missing.

How was she supposed to do everything at the same time?

The music paused, and the phone line clicked. When she moved to pick up the phone, the jazz restarted.

"Ow!" Her quick movement had given her a paper cut. She blotted her finger with a tissue.

Maybe a sacrifice was needed. Or something more she hadn't thought of yet. Who had she not talked to, who might conceivably help?

Dea, the spirit of the woods at Witch Farm.

And Pete.

The first foxgloves unfurled at the edges of the grass at Witch Farm. A few had sprung to bloom, one or two flowers open on the stems.

Along the path to the cabin, bright green leaves fluttered. The scent of flowers hung in the air, the first ox-eye daisies open in patches of sun. Reaching the cabin, Joanie opened the door and breathed in the aroma of cedar, cut here and milled to make the cabin.

It had been more than two years since Pete had fallen from the balcony fighting Mark. Her Horned God, he'd gone into the land, but he was still present. Given the passage of time, maybe his energy had settled, and she could call him.

The air in the cabin was chill and stale. She opened the windows and took a chair before the Lady's small statue, which squatted, wild-haired and angry-faced. The statue maker had made her in birth throes, though no child was shown.

"Dea, goddess of this land, elder goddess—" but she didn't have to go further; the goddess was there in all her power. For a goddess of the land, the height of spring was a time of energy.

"I don't know if you can help me." Neutral energy, a dark smile. Dea was a goddess of strength and not without ego. She believed she could help with anything. "I've been having dreams of an angel meeting me and battling other angels. I know this angel. But something is hiding him from me."

Dea appeared in her mind's eye as a bear-goddess. She growled. "He is hiding himself. He accepts no master—not me, not anyone."

In other words, Dea couldn't command him. "But why is he hiding? How does he do it?"

The bear gave a shrug of a huge black-furred shoulder. It was not Dea's affair.

"Okay, thank you."

She pulled a tiny pot of honey out of her hoodie pocket, left it on the altar in offering.

The only one left to try was Pete. The place to find him was the woods itself. She backtracked up the cabin path and dove into the forest. Here, years ago, Pete had heard his calling as an avatar of the Horned God.

Cedar fronds stroked her face as she clambered up the steep hill. New green showed on the Doug firs' branch-tips. She nudged past blackberries to where it was easier going, ferns bright with new growth.

By instinct she found it again, the grove where she'd found Pete when he first became the god. He'd taken her roughly then, throwing her to the ground, ripping her clothes. She'd given way —she'd understood.

She'd met Pete originally through Gus, at a protest—a red-haired punk anarchist boy, a little too forward. Something had ignited, then suddenly went up in flame, the hottest of any of her love affairs. He'd come to a ritual out of curiosity, and the god had taken him. She and Hannah had helped him deal with that. Later, the god inspired him to protect her. Then suddenly he was dead.

When she let herself think about it, she missed him like fire. To think of him was like sticking a knife into her side, so mostly she didn't.

Now she sank down on the wet moss and grounded, deep into the spring earth.

"Pete, beloved. Horned God, beloved. Come to me."

Nothing happened for a moment. Then the wind rose, circling the tiny grove, taking her in an embrace. She felt him beside her, felt the warmth of him. A rush of longing and love rose in her.

"Oh, Pete."

He was there, a shadowy form, a twelve-point rack of antlers raised above his head. Reddish-brown fur covered his back, the back of his hands, but his face was fully human, blue eyes green with reflected light. His arms, his hands roved over her. For a while, she communed with him wordlessly. Then she had to ask.

"My dreams have been showing me this angel." She gave him the image, mind to mind. "And yet there's a fog over him. I can't discover who he is, or why he's in my dreams. Dea said he was hiding himself. What do you know?"

"From what I see, you are almost there."

"Perhaps."

"What have you dropped, what are you missing? There is a way in here. Call him yourself. I see you must have been lovers. I see you miss him. He must also miss you."

The first two she could see. The last, she wasn't sure of. "You think so?"

"He has to."

Then there was no more talking. He laid her down among the ferns.

At the small shrine in her room, every morning, she added the angel to her daily devotions. Some things were a clean cut—some things you got to with a steady grind. Puabi-Ekur had told her they were doing similar work on the other side.

Each morning, after saluting her goddess Inanna and her spirits, in meditation she paced down a long spiral staircase that opened to her angel's oasis, to the whisper of wind in the palms, the scent of hot dust. Sometimes she caught a whiff of dark frankincense, but never yet his face or voice.

Sometimes she saw him among the battling angels. In a moment's pause, he stood above the fray—the body of a warrior, long dark hair, black wings, face in shadow. Sometimes a shaft of light fell across him, teasing her, but it never reached his face.

Pulled by that longing, she would start her day.

For the wedding, they had the venue; they'd sent the invitations. The coffee shop was going to cater. They were renting chairs and tables.

Her mother had her over for brunch again, with the requisite mimosas. Out the windows lay a sunny spring day starting to get hot. The roses were starting, the very first pink buds. If only Joanie were out among them.

"There's a lot yet to do, but I'm pretty happy with where we stand," Joanie said.

"I'd like to help you shop for the wedding dress."

Uh-oh. She was going to try to bully her into something she didn't want. "Mom, I can just do vintage. It's more my style anyway."

"No way!" Her mother set her glass down with a thump. "I only have one daughter, and I want to make sure you have a proper wedding dress! We'll go right after this."

This trip would blow away the time Joanie had that weekend for household chores—she'd planned a chill afternoon of laundry and cleaning, then dinner with Cleo—but to keep her mom mollified, it was worth it. They could return to the usual state of cold war after the wedding. As long as the resulting dress wasn't too bad.

If she had to say no to her mother—well, she'd done it before, she could do it again.

Her mother got the dishwasher running, and they were ready to go. She pursed her lips at Joanie as they stood in the shadowy foyer, pale mint green, a mirror reflecting them back and back forever. "You hardly look dressed to go wedding dress shopping."

"Mom, I'm not going home to change." They got into her mom's blue Pontiac. She texted Cleo to let her know she'd be home late, and why.

<Don't let her talk you into something awful.>
<I won't.>
They drove to the outskirts of town. A light cloud cover

obscured the sun, which flashed in and out as they drove. An outlet mall, of course, she hadn't expected a high-end store—her mother lived on a tiny pension.

"Mom, are you sure you can afford this?"

"For my only daughter, for her wedding, yes."

They parked and got out. A lot of cars sat out front, sedate sedans and nondescript four-wheel-drives. She would be a June bride—keeping the date was something Sharon insisted on, though it gave her more work. Sharon wanted things done right, even if she didn't want a white daughter-in-law.

Windows fronted the salon, each holding a mannequin, one dressed in froth, one in slinky satin. Through the door, they confronted a faux wall, palest pink, with a couch in front of it, a bored and angry teenager sitting there chewing black-painted fingernails, hiding from someone's wedding-dress shopping.

It was like a younger Joanie. She drew a long breath for strength.

They walked around the wall to the cavernous main room. Racks and racks of white stood on one side, on the other side the bright jewel colors of bridesmaids' dresses.

Joanie gravitated there—by her own desire, she never wore white. Her mother bustled up and took her arm. "We don't have all day."

Their taste was 180 degrees different. Joanie wanted something quietly diaphanous, pretty on her, not too much volume, not too much tulle. She was navigating a narrow path here, and needed not too much. She didn't care so much about "her wedding"; she didn't need a big wedding. But she did want the clans that came together to get along, maybe even enjoy one another. That was her focus, not being a bride. Her mother wanted the image—something a reality show star would wear, or as close as they could get with their budget.

"Honey, you've got such a great figure. You should show it

off!" Her mother held out on a hanger a satin sheath, cut nearly to the navel.

"Mom, we're going to be in Sharon and Ray's house. I don't want to wear anything that will offend Sharon."

"Offend her! It's just a little skin. You can't tell me that Ray married a prude." Under her breath, she said, "That woman looks like she came straight from Africa."

It was the kind of thing her mom's friends would say.

"How can you be so racist?! You've dated Black men yourself."

Her mother rolled her eyes. "I'm not *racist*. I just find Sharon objectionable."

"You just insulted her because of her color! How is that not racist?!" Joanie was having a hard time keeping her voice down.

"I've heard plenty of Black women say the same kind of thing!" Her mom clearly was having the same problem.

"But you can't say it, Mom! You're white!"

"Don't tell me what I can and can't say! I'm your mother!"

Joanie wanted to drop the dress she held, stalk off, and find a Lyft home. She didn't have to do this.

But she wanted her mother at her wedding. It would leave a permanent wound if she wasn't.

"Just listen to yourself, Mom." She glanced around. There was no one of color close, but plenty of people—hard to say if anyone had heard them.

She met her mother's eyes. Her mother had caught the drift.

"Think what you care to inside your own head, but I'd rather you didn't take this point of view into the wedding. Please don't ruin this for me." That was fair—more than fair.

Her mother shoved the sheath dress back onto the rack.

"You're telling me you want to dress like a Victorian to make Sharon happy? Fine."

Chapter 23

ᚾ

The mortal present

In the end, they purchased a slender gown with a side-slit skirt, satin with a lace overlay, pearlescent off-white—one look in the mirror told Joanie it was perfect, and even her mother didn't disagree. And it fit the budget.

Folded neatly in a pale blue box, enfolded in white tissue paper, it came home with Joanie from her mom's. She let herself into the house with her key, let the door fall shut behind her.

A voice she didn't expect was coming from the kitchen. Kirk.

She was instantly repelled, but why?

He wasn't so bad, was he? So many actively awful men studded her past—even ones she'd slept with—what was so bad about Kirk?

A vibe, she didn't know what. Trickster energy. That could mean a scam.

Setting the thought aside, she went up the stairs.

Cleo had left a note on the carefully made bed. A nod of apology, that was, the bed. "Had to go in. Emergency meeting at work. Back as soon as I can."

Cleo knew Joanie turned off her phone when she was with her mom, from a desire not to be distracted—anything could distract her, because she so wanted to be somewhere else.

She'd hoped for a quiet, chill afternoon doing chores, but the afternoon was minus Cleo and plus Kirk, an irritant she didn't need. Still she had laundry and cleanup and had better get on with it.

Cleo had left a few dark odds and ends to mix with Joanie's. Cleo dressed in brilliant colors, bold as a dahlia, Joanie more subdued, in greys and blacks, the occasional jewel-toned green or purple. She piled the basket and went downstairs toward the laundry room.

Halfway down the stairs, she met Kirk coming up.

"Hello!" he said, smiling.

Dressed down from last she'd seen him, he wore a brown-and-orange flannel shirt over a tan t-shirt, brown-washed blue jeans, grey hair up in a ponytail, as before that handlebar mustache. Ruggedly handsome, was the phrase he called to mind. It wasn't his looks, one way or the other—she just didn't like him.

Or she didn't trust him.

Hannah had called him a trickster spirit, but not in a bad way. But she'd been biased toward him. They'd been lovers, long ago.

Kirk had held space well enough in the first fairy dust ritual, and that was something. But one time out proved very little. He made her hackles rise. Maybe it was just that so many men like him had slimed on her, but still it was something to look out for.

"Hi," she replied. She wanted to move past him. He wasn't quite blocking her, not quite trapping her. He had plausible deni-ability.

"I wanted to let you know, I'll be here for a few days. I'm

looking for a place, and in the meantime, Nora's graciously letting me stay."

"That's fine. Thanks for telling me."

How long was a few days?

He raised a bushy pepper-and-salt eyebrow at her tone. "I can stay out of your way if you like."

To be polite, she said, "No need."

He stepped aside and let her pass.

The household had an informal habit of sharing wine or cocktails, or tea if preferred, in the early evening. Out on the back porch, if it was warm enough, and in late May it was.

A month from summer solstice, the evening's golden twilight stretched late. The last sunlight glanced off the greenhouse's top and burnished the far fir trees red-gold. Lower, on the porch, fell lavender light, the air sweet with marijuana smoke. Jonathan offered a hit on a joint to Joanie, but she shook her head. It was too likely to make her paranoid.

They kicked back on the ancient deck chairs, weathered to a grey tan. She'd collected a well-deserved glass of wine, some local red mix. She needed something to chill her out, let her not think about the things preoccupying her. Cleo was still working.

"So what do you think of him?" she asked Jonathan.

"Kirk?" She nodded. "I've seen his type before. I know you have too."

"For sure."

"I don't know him in person well enough to say, yet. I'm inclined to watch a while longer."

"Has Nora said how long he's staying?"

"She has not."

"If it's more than a month, we should say something."

"I have to agree."

"But it's early times yet."

"You don't like him much." This was a question from Jonathan, despite the phrasing.

"I'm not sure yet. These old hippie guys—some are fine, a lot are pretty entitled."

"Didn't he have something going on with Hannah at one point?"

"He did."

"And?"

"She still likes him, but I think it's because she knows she could still get him in bed."

Jonathan grinned.

For whatever reason, though he was a hugely attractive man, there had never been anything but ease and friendship between her and Jonathan. No spark. Not so with him and Cleo. She'd wondered for a while when the flicker between them would leap into flame. Maybe he thought it was inappropriate to bed her girlfriend so close to their wedding. Or vice versa. This last bit, getting ready for the wedding, neither she nor Cleo had the time or emotional space to take on someone new.

"That'd be bad, though," Joanie said. "Apparently when Hannah and Kirk stepped out, it almost caused a witch war."

"We don't want that."

"No."

"I guess it's wait and see then."

A movement through the glass of the French doors made Joanie look up. "Speak of the devil."

Nora and Kirk stepped onto the porch. Nora was dressed in hippie finery: a tiered maxi-dress, patterned with tiny maroon flowers on pale pink, with a satin paisley shawl that dripped long tassels. Dressing up for Kirk, Joanie assumed, and no diss there. Nora had a glass of the same red Joanie did.

Kirk still wore his brown-orange checked shirt and jeans. He slipped by her to find his own chair. He smelled of tobacco. He carried a highball glass with two fingers of, she guessed, Nora's scotch.

"Hello, all," said Nora, standing in the open French door. "I think you both know that Kirk will be staying for a bit?"

"Yes," said Joanie and Jonathan, in unison. Like good children at school. Though the household shared decisions, Nora was the eldest, the high priestess, and the original owner. There was always a hint of her running things.

"Not long," Kirk put in. He had a pleasant baritone, roughened by years of smoking and drinking. "I am hoping to find something in the city pretty quick."

Jonathan and Joanie traded a look. No apartment in Seattle could be found quickly these days, even with good references, a perfect credit score, and a lot of cash in hand. Joanie guessed that Kirk had one of these at most.

Joanie's phone buzzed for a text: <Will be here till late. Don't wait up. Stupid budget stuff.>

She sighed, but Cleo disappearing like this was rare these days. Northwest Farms of Color was on more stable footing than it had been—but there were hitches and issues, and Cleo was called in for her level head.

Nora and Kirk sat at the far end of the row of deck chairs. The sun had fully set now, leaving a band of pale orange along the horizon, narrow slate-blue clouds floating on it. Flower-scent hung dense in the warm air. Low voices and laughter came from the far end of the porch.

Jonathan and Joanie traded another glance.

The whole point of this back-porch gathering was that the roommates talked to each other. Sure, occasionally, the couples dipped into couples-only conversation. But not at first.

"Nora, how is the fairy dust process going? You doing another ritual soon?" Jonathan asked.

Nora glanced at Kirk, which was telling. Usually Nora drove

rituals on her own, or supported a co-covener or student. She was a sovereign high priestess. "We're talking about that," she said.

Something about the implied secretiveness, as if it were just theirs to decide, hit a nerve. "I'd be very interested in that conversation," Joanie said.

Jonathan eyed her. He hadn't partaken in the earlier ritual— maybe because of his feeling that Kirk was a trickster. Yet that ritual had gone well.

"Come sit with us, then," Kirk said.

He was telling Joanie where to sit, on her own back porch.

"I'd like to take part as well," Jonathan said, voice smooth. "It's a general conversation."

Again Nora and Kirk exchanged a glance.

"Sure!" Nora said. She drew her seat closer to theirs, and Kirk followed. "The first ritual went well enough. But I'd like to create an arc. Ideally we could set up some kind of training to teach folks to administer and hold space for the fairy dust. Over time, I think this could be attractive to people more generally, even for paid visits. If we fixed up the house, we could easily hold five or six people for a weekend."

"It's possible," Jonathan said. As the house's main handyman, he knew the state of the building. "It would take some work."

"What do you think would need to be done?"

"We've been putting off having a conversation about the plumbing for a while. If we're going to have people here regularly, we need to step up that conversation and several others."

"It's not as if people are going to be spending all their time in the bathrooms."

"No, but some days I feel one flush will take out the whole system."

As Nora spoke, Joanie watched Kirk, covertly. Kirk caught her glance, and she looked away.

What was his deal? Was he after her? She wasn't remotely interested.

Even besides that, he was pulling on her energy in a way she didn't understand. He reminded her a bit of Max, Gus's white-supremacist boyfriend, now years in the past but hard to forget. Maybe it was just white cis boy entitlement. Maybe something more—Max had been an antagonist on many planes, and it had taken supernatural help to banish him.

"I do think there's potential here," Kirk said, in his resonant voice. "I'd just as soon do all this for free, but we do live in a capitalist society, more's the pity."

He was clearly playing to them. It was a house of leftists.

"Are you still considering patenting your chemical compound?" Nora asked, drawing this point out.

"I am."

"I don't think we're quite ready to plan anything out," Nora went on. "Kirk is spending a lot of time apartment hunting. But soon."

"Maybe we table the discussion till then," Jonathan said.

They sipped and smoked in near silence for a while. Darkness fell, dark blue, flooding the space, turning the long grassy sward into a lake. Robins called, liquid sounds in the night.

"I guess I'll be going up," Jonathan said. He worked as a contractor, carrying piles of lumber all day—he had to be worn out.

Nora had spent the day working in the herb gardens. "Me too," she said, and stood. To Kirk, she said, "Don't be too long, or I'll be asleep."

He grinned and patted her ass. "Don't worry, honey."

Now Joanie was alone on the porch with him. But she didn't want to go up yet. The breeze drove off the mosquitoes, bringing the scent of flowers—she'd seen the first roses in bloom today, hardy climbing pink ones by the front door. She wanted to stay, sip her wine, think her thoughts.

Kirk moved to take the chair next to her.

Her eyelids fluttered, involuntarily. She almost stood up to leave. But since he was going to be around a lot, since by her guess Nora would want him to move in, it was best to keep him sweet. Or as sweet as she could.

Because she was never planning to sleep with him. She didn't like him.

"Do you mind if I smoke?" he asked.

"No, that's fine." The breeze was going the other direction.

He struck a match, lit his cigarette. The scent of burning paper wafted over, sweet, then tobacco.

"I feel as if we got off on the wrong foot," he said.

"Probably." She took a mouthful of wine. "I need to say this up front, though. I am poly—Cleo and I have a poly relationship. But Nora isn't. Not only is she my housemate, I care about her feelings. Even if Nora wasn't in the picture, I don't think I'd get with you. You're an attractive man, but I've never gone for trickster energy."

Not entirely true, but Kirk was not her type. He didn't seem like a dom, which might have tipped the balance, more just a sleaze.

"Whoa, whoa, I never said a thing."

"Just in case you planned to," Joanie said blandly.

"Nora said you were in the life, though."

An old-school term. He said it neutrally. Still, it made her hackles rise.

"I have done sex work, but that doesn't change the situation with Nora, so it's not on the table." Besides, if he was getting sex from Nora, and apparently if he wanted to other women, why would he want to pay?

She was hot, and she was good, but she didn't see it.

"I understand. I hardly have the money now anyway. But things change. You struck me as a woman open to negotiation."

It was no time or place to get angry. "Let's reopen the conversation when that's the case."

"Sure. I hope you take it as a compliment. That's how I mean it."

No, he meant something far more complicated. "Of course."

Chapter 24

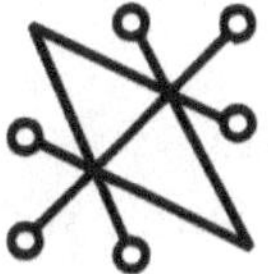

*P*uabi-Ekur woke before Azazel did, sat up pulling the black silk sheets over their knees. Azazel lay, profile in silhouette against the pillow.

He was back, the gorgeous one, that cut-crystal profile, that luxurious dense brunet waving hair, those shoulders. He smelled of dark frankincense.

But Azazel had cast Puabi-Ekur out, and Joanie too. That was a betrayal. They'd gotten an apology in passing—Joanie hadn't even gotten that.

Let the angel wake up alone, then. It would take him a while to rest and recuperate, and his people could address any immediate needs. Puabi-Ekur would eventually return.

They appeared in Samyaza's garden as Puabi, dressing in Samyaza colors, green and lavender, gold necklaces burnished by warm light on her warm brown skin. She wore the scent of cinnamon. She'd never shown up unannounced before, but there was no reason she'd get a bad reception.

She appeared in the arch all twined with moonflowers that served as the garden's doorway. A fey servitor led her to a couch beside a fountain, falling water shimmering in pale light, an arbor nearby dripping pink grapes. Another servitor brought a glass of green wine.

When Samyaza strolled up, she stood, politely.

"Puabi-Ekur, greetings."

"Greetings, Lord Samyaza."

He raised an eyebrow. "Surely we are on a first-name basis?" Taking her by the elbows, he leaned in and kissed her on the cheek. Today his scent was lavender—peace and familial love. Just when she was warming to his embrace, he stepped away.

"Come, sit." She did. "What brings you here? I did not expect to see you so soon after Azazel returned."

"We had our homecoming," she said. "He has business to attend to, and his legions to celebrate with. I would be welcome, but I'm not necessary."

"And you come to me why?"

"We have succeeded in freeing Azazel. I know that was important to you as well as me."

She paused. The sound of water falling behind her was distracting.

"Without both our work, it would not have happened," he said politely, waiting to see what she said next.

"We have forged a new alliance with the fey and huldufólk. You want to move forward toward taking on the Usurper. But for me, next—we have to break this geas on Joanie."

"By geas, you mean the stricture that made her forget Azazel? Perhaps it's unfair. But it might save her much trouble, even her life. We must break this binding?"

"I think so."

"My brother would not take kindly to hearing you say he must do something. He is one of the most stubborn of a stubborn race."

"What do you think would persuade him? Or force his hand?"

"We cannot force his hand in this."

This was annoying. Samyaza was just trying to stymie her. "What would work?"

"He was not swayed by the argument she could bring him extra allies, although I still believe that is true." Samyaza tapped a finger on his beautifully carven lips. "The only reason he would break this binding would be if it were somehow essential to help her. But I do not see how that would be. If she were in danger, he would save her. I doubt his love for her has died. They have been together for millennia, since the beginning of the world."

"I agree."

"But he could save her from danger without her knowing it was him."

"There must be something. It's just wrong for them to be apart."

"You see his point, though. If they are lovers, she will always be a pawn in these angel games."

"She will always be a pawn if he cares. And he has not stopped caring. It would be easier and better for all to know, and him to protect her properly! Now she misses him, and she doesn't know—she's lost all their history." Puabi bit her lip. "It just seems so unkind and unfair. And useless."

Samyaza shook his head. "I do not know how to help you, my dear. I will say, be careful trying to force his hand. Azazel does not like being forced. Especially now."

An empty throne, black adamant engraved with silver, floated in the depths of star-dazzled space. To either side, a torch stood, flame flickering in an airless wind.

Puabi-Ekur prostrated themself on the rug before the throne, woven black and silver. They would stay for an eon if they had to.

But when they glanced up, sandal-shod feet posed on the throne's step, lapped in spectral red flames.

For a moment, the fire's whispering was the only sound.

"Puabi-Ekur, beloved servant. I know your quest, but I would have you ask in words," Hekate said.

Puabi-Ekur sat up on their knees, watching the goddess's face, shining like the moon, features painted on silver light. "Joanie is under a geas that prevents her remembering her time with Azazel. Azazel has broken their tie to protect her. But she had memories and dreams and longs for him, and is seeking to know more. I wish to break this geas."

The Lady inclined her head. "If Azazel desires to break with a lover, is that not his call?"

A meteor shot by, scattering fire.

"There are some solutions you cannot force, o incubus-succubus. Gentle persuasion or events unfolding must do the work."

"But it's so unfair!"

"You are thousands of years old." In other words, don't act like a child. "Karma works itself out, I am certain you have seen. But it does not do so suddenly. Supernatural beings rarely learn quickly."

Did Hekate mean Azazel, or themself?

"Go and look after your loved ones. I have given you Azazel to care for, not manipulate."

"I didn't manipulate him!"

"The path I describe is the one most true to your nature and most likely to gain you what you want."

It was true it wasn't their approach to force their will, but rather to persuade, to seduce.

"You are still my agent, unless you wish to end that agreement."

"No."

"Then perform the task I ask of you, and be at peace."

Puabi-Ekur retreated to their spangled wisp of cloud, their tiny home in the depths of space. A pink nebula behind them glowed, rose sparkles. Usually they liked that, but not now.

The goddess had spanked them. It hadn't been fun.

They could see it wasn't theirs to force Azazel's hand. They'd been told so by his brother also. Inanna, their tutelary goddess, had washed her hands of this errand long ago, as had Ereshkigal and Nergal.

But Joanie was her lover too, tormented by memories that couldn't be reconciled. It hurt to watch her hurt.

But it was time to pause, wait, and see what the universe brought.

It wasn't what they wanted. But that didn't mean it was a bad idea.

Chapter 25

The mortal present

*S*omething Kirk had said stirred Joanie's mind.

She had been paused on her calling as a sacred whore quite a while.

She climbed the stairs to her and Cleo's room, to the small black-velvet-covered altar she'd made on a bookcase shelf.

She pulled up a straight chair before the altar, lit a coral-colored candle, and focused on the small poured-stone statue of Inanna, which Cleo had bought her. She'd dressed the Lady in necklaces and set her among colored scarves—the sunrise colors she thought of as Inanna's, pink and gold and coral.

She led herself down into trance, and the goddess was there.

"I will wait for you a lifetime, if need be," the goddess said.

"But now is a good time to start." Even with her wedding coming up.

"It is always a good time."

"If I do this work, I need you to make the way clear for me, in a good way." She had so many demands on her time. She needed to support herself, and have a way forward to a career in the daylight world, for cover if nothing else.

"This I will do—I will always do."

"What about Kirk—who is he to me?"

A long pause, a silence. "Not Kirk."

"Do you mean, he's not for me, or... what exactly?"

The goddess didn't answer, but what she got from the silence was, avoid him.

"Okay. I take your point. As soon as I'm married, I'll go back to my calling as a sacred whore."

She communed with her goddess in warm silence a few minutes, Inanna's presence like an embrace. Then she shucked her clothes and climbed in bed, window half-open to the warm night, scent of flowers hovering, breeze making the curtain wave.

She'd expected Cleo would wake her coming in, but she slept through till dawn.

In the morning, they got ready together. She knew what Cleo would say, but she had to speak.

Fear circled, trying to take over. Cleo had to want what she wanted. What if she didn't?

Now was time to check.

"I got some information from Inanna last night. I think I need to go back to sacred whore work." She sat on the edge of the bed, about to pull on her boots. She was going in to manage the coffee shop, and the boots always helped with authority. "You're cool with that, right? I mean, maybe it's a weird thing to do, especially as soon as we get married."

Cleo shrugged. "The timing hardly matters. The goddess has been wanting this for a while. It's your true work."

"I know that's the right answer, but do you mean it?" She let herself fall backward onto the bed. She had a minute or two to waste.

They'd decorated as Cleo always did, colorful saris pinned and draped above the bed. Now, spring merging into summer, she'd changed these to greens, vibrant chartreuse shading to dark sage. They hadn't painted the white walls yet—they'd both been so busy—but sunlight bounced off the thin silk tinting the room in spring greens.

Cleo came to sit by her, stroking her hair. "We're dedicated to the same goddess, girl."

"But suppose someone at your work found out your partner was a whore?"

"I don't care. If my co-workers don't like it, they don't belong working there." Northwest Farms of Color was fully staffed with leftists and progressives.

"Oh, Cleo." She sat up and hugged her girlfriend, hard, burying her face in her shoulder, the scent of sandalwood. It was tempting to bite that beautiful neck, but they needed to get on with the morning. "Why am I so lucky?"

"Because you deserve it."

On her way to work, Joanie stopped by the small produce co-op for which she'd had the accounting contract, figuring out a tangle of back bookkeeping. She had a few last paper files to deliver.

Stopping her little Volkswagen Bug in the gravel parking lot, she got out and walked along the long fence, wood weathered grey, a couple of rowan trees leaning toward each other over the open gate. She'd wondered a long time whether witches had planted these. Yet mountain ash was native to the area, especially in the mountains.

Letting herself through, she walked up and knocked, a red door in a white doorframe.

The owner answered. When it opened, the scent of oatmeal floated out. The owner was a woman in her fifties, in jeans and a hoodie, grey hair in a messy bun. "Oh, it's you! That's good! We're expecting a delivery of bark for the gardens, and we're not ready!"

Joanie handed over the papers in a manila folder. "These are just a last few files, from last year, which I wanted to double-check. I've done that, no changes needed. I think this is the last of everything."

"Thanks!" The owner flipped through the file briefly. "It's been such a pleasure working with you. I have to say, book-keeping is not my strength. You did such a good job, we'd love it if you kept doing our books."

This was such good news, for a moment Joanie didn't know what to say.

It was what she'd hoped for.

It felt like a good omen—Inanna had promised to pave the way so her world worked, and here was an example.

"That works for me!"

"Can you start this month?"

"Sure! I'm just going to be a little frazzled, juggling things, for the next bit. I'm getting married to my girlfriend next month." She made sure to put it that way, so that no one said, "Who's the lucky fella?"—which could be awkward, even in some situations dangerous, though not with these co-op farmers.

"Oh how nice! We can start in July if you want—I don't really think we'll get beyond you in two months."

Joanie grinned. "I appreciate that. Let's wait, if you don't mind." She leaned in and gave the woman a hug. "Thank you!"

It was like a ray of sun breaking on a grey day, and it sent her off to work happy.

She and Inanna had established a space together on the astral where they met. This was Joanie's best imagination of a

Sumerian temple, not a large public one but a neighborhood one —a one-story mudbrick building in the ether, holding a crude statue of the same mudbrick, Inanna with inset lapis-and-gypsum eyes. Before that astral statue on its plinth sat an altar, with a copper bowl to burn incense in.

In front of her tiny real-life shrine, Joanie lit cypress incense, dropped into trance, and entered the astral temple, making a deep obeisance before the statue.

"Lady," she said. "I need your help again."

She and Inanna had been trying various paths and tricks to getting the angel to reveal himself—stopping a moment in time, turning him around in imagination, combing the memories she had to see if he'd ever dropped a name. They asked attendant spirits—clearly Puabi-Ekur couldn't help or would have already.

She'd gone also to Samyaza, to his hazy, humid garden dense with flower scent. The fey servitors greeted her, gave her a seat, poured her a glass of pink rosé.

But when she asked, Samyaza cut her off, though he was polite about it.

"No, fair one, no, I cannot. Even if I could, and you have seen how the binding prevents me, I would not. I assume that any angel that put such a spell on you had a reason to. I believe likely it is needful."

"Do you think so?" She searched his face. All it showed was a rueful smile.

"I do."

Each time, she returned from trance empty-handed and slightly more depressed.

"My dear one, you have spoken to so many spirits," Inanna said. "We are running out of beings to ask, and you are running yourself ragged. Truly, now it is time to stop."

She'd been afraid the Lady would say this at some point.

She burst into tears.

Inanna comforted her, drawing her astrally into a warm

embrace, scented slightly with roses. She communed with her lady a while.

When Inanna drew away, Joanie stayed in the coral-lit space a little longer.

She had so many demands on her now. It was lucky the co-op owner had okayed July to start work, because she had no idea where she'd have fit it in. The coffee shop wasn't any less demanding—in fact, since Jeremy was planning to cater the wedding, he asked even more of Joanie. Now she had to do an inventory of cups and lids and shop for new types. A good idea, but it was definitely extra, at a time when she had no extra.

On the wedding, Cleo was giving her less help than planned. Northwest Farms of Color had leaned on her to do multiple site visits, often a day or longer with an overnight stay. Sometimes Joanie would go with her, but she didn't have time now. With help from Alyssa, Joanie got the wedding tasks done, and she understood Cleo's constraints. But it made her weary.

It took all her strength to pull herself out of trance.

Chapter 26

The mortal present

The day of the wedding dawned bright and warm, stray cottony clouds scudding across a deep blue sky. A light breeze stirred the trees' limbs, all in full leaf. The roses were in bloom—Sharon's yard had a full bank of roses along one edge, red and white alternating heraldically.

The front yard went up steeply, and anyone elderly or infirm had to be helped up the brick steps. The main event was in the backyard, surprisingly deep—Ray and Sharon had nearly an acre of land, backed up against a greenbelt.

White-clothed tables, one with a champagne fountain, stood against a line of close-trimmed juniper bushes, behind them a dark mass of firs. Once they'd lent their yard, Sharon and Ray had gotten into the swing of things. Much of the setup was Sharon's taste, but her taste was exquisite and classic, so Joanie didn't complain.

She just wanted to get through the wedding without things falling apart.

Now she was ensconced in a tiny upstairs guest bedroom to get ready, with floral wallpaper and a single bed. Behind filmy white nylon curtains, the window stood half-open, breeze lifting and dropping the fabric. Cleo was separated from her by old custom. She'd sent her mother to pick up the cake. The coffee shop girls helping her get ready had drifted away to find champagne, except for Alyssa and Kelsey, a dark-haired white girl, Irish-looking, nose all freckles, one of the bridesmaids. Gus was going to show up later, closer to the ceremony time; he had a final paper due.

Hannah was officiating. Her voice floated up from the yard, through the half-open window. "Pagans been jumpin' the broom for a long time. I've been doin' this ceremony for years."

"I thought it was just Black folks." Sharon's voice was friendly, but a glance into the yard showed her face was not.

"The first time I did this ceremony was in the 1980s, and at the time there weren't any people of color in my circle. Since then..." but they moved away, and Joanie couldn't hear them anymore.

"Joanie," Alyssa said, drawing her attention. "Which earrings did you want? There are these you brought, then these diamond ones from your mother." She held up the box, diamonds pinned to a fold of cardboard-backed pale-blue velvet.

"I'd better wear the diamonds."

"Do you want to?" Kelsey asked.

"The diamonds are fine. I don't mind them."

"Something borrowed, for good luck," Alyssa said.

"I can use all the luck I can get."

Despite the sun, there was a feeling of thunder in the air. Alyssa exchanged a look with her. She was the coven's main medium—whatever it was, she felt it too.

Joanie's mind trailed after Hannah, talking to Sharon. Did Sharon imagine they were going to take apart the whole ceremony now? Maybe she could insert a speech about what jumping the broom meant to Black people. Sharon had a right to her anger. But couldn't they avoid a fight?

The voices rose again, in the distance, though she couldn't distinguish words.

"Hannah can talk Sharon down," Alyssa said. "She'll work it out."

"Hope so."

"You ready for the dress?" Kelsey asked.

"Sure."

After Kelsey zipped her into it, Alyssa did her hair, high in a messy bun, a half-veil falling from a small white hat Alyssa had done over for her, balanced on top of the bun. Kelsey went downstairs to refill Joanie's glass of champagne and returned. When Alyssa was finished, she drew Joanie over to the standing mirror.

Slender in the pillar gown with a side-slit skirt, pearlescent off-white satin overlaid with lace, the play of pale colors brought out the olive of her skin, the shape of her neat figure. She met her own eyes, black in the mirror.

They showed fear. But Puabi-Ekur had promised to be on best behavior. Cleo's mom would show up right before the ceremony, then leave straight after—Cleo's stepdad, sick with the bird flu, might be developing pneumonia. She'd promised Cleo to leave her truce with Sharon in place and merely nod and smile at Ray.

From behind Joanie, Alyssa caught her eyes in the mirror. Hers too were full of fear.

They just needed to keep a lid on things and get through the ceremony.

A knock sounded on the door. "Who is it?"

"Celia." Another of the coffee shop girls. "Setup outdoors is just about done, so you know."

A couple thuds below came from a drum. They had a small jazz ensemble to play everyone in, and to give them a few standards after the rite. They'd finish with a DJ for the evening. The ensemble was friends of Ray's, and as Joanie peeked out, she saw him standing with them. Their instruments were on the stands, sound check done.

She had to go out and mingle, but she wasn't ready.

Commotion sounded at the door. "You can't go in there!" Celia's voice said.

"Just try and stop me!" It was Cleo. She came in and closed the door behind her. Alyssa slipped out, Kelsey in her wake.

Cleo had chosen an island-inflected dress, spaghetti straps and narrow bodice holding up a tiered white skirt, edged in crochet lace and tiny silver bells, which also adorned the long, filmy scarf she wore around her neck. White ostrich feathers on a band circled her close-trimmed head, very 1920s.

"You ready?"

"Just about."

"Hannah wants to start at one sharp."

"What time is it?"

"12:15."

"We're just waiting on my mother and the cake. I expect her any time now." Her mother would be on her own, without Dustin, traveling for business—too bad, because Dustin made her more reliable.

Cleo stepped forward and took her in her arms. She smelled like sandalwood, overlaid with jasmine. "Are you ready for this?"

"Ready as I'll ever be."

Cleo leaned back, arms still firmly around Joanie's waist. Big dark-brown doe's eyes met Joanie's. "What does that mean?"

"I want to be with you. But this event, all the possible fights below the surface, I want it over and done with."

"We don't have to stay a minute longer than you want. It's why we got the B&B." Taking the bridal suite of a nearby bed and breakfast that weekend was all the honeymoon they planned, at least for now.

"I expect I'll be fine once the ceremony's over." At least the main event would be over and they could take off if they chose. "What happened with Hannah and Sharon?"

"Ray talked Sharon down a bit, and she's going to say a few words about jumping the broom being a tradition for Black folks."

"As long as Sharon's okay with that." Hannah would be gracious, she knew.

"She is."

A loud voice below, her mother's, announced the last important straggler had arrived.

"Are you ready to come down?"

"Give me another minute or two."

She and Cleo stood in front of Hannah, hands clasped, staring into each other's eyes.

Around them, the yard lay decked in white, bright against the green grass—white tablecloths, white and red roses in bowls on the tables, white plastic chairs. Close in, the assembled people stood on a circle of white and red rose petals—a witch handfasting, in a witch circle. Joanie and Cleo wore crowns of white and red roses, the crown delicately set around the brim of Joanie's perched hat.

Hannah looked around the circle, catching the gaze of one person then another.

"As Cleo and Joanie's friends, one day you may be called upon to witness and support these vows. Are you ready to do that?"

The crowd murmured their assent.

On the far side of the brick house, in the street, a car squealed around the corner, loud against the quiet of a warm June Saturday afternoon.

"Louder! I need to know you'll be there for them! Are you ready to do that?"

The car, or maybe a truck, with a low growling transmission, drove up near the house and parked.

"Yes!" cried the crowd.

Commotion sounded in the front yard. The ushers' voices: "What are you doing?" "I wouldn't go up there. It's a wedding service."

"Let me hear you louder still!"

"Yes!"

Hannah turned back to Cleo and Joanie, satisfied.

"For you, do you come to this union free of encumbrances, threats or coercion, and of your own free will? Cleo, what do you say?"

"I do!"

"And you, Joanie?"

"I do!"

Three men burst into the backyard, all white men wearing black. The lead one held a pistol. He stopped at the edge of the yard and trained the gun on Joanie.

Time hollowed out, a black tunnel. The only people there were herself and the gunman.

Cleo's voice came from far away: "Down, Joanie! Down on the grass!"

A tiny bubble of time—did she want to stain her dress?

Cleo grabbed her and threw them both down together.

The wind rose. The whine of a bullet passed. It grazed through the grass beyond her. Screaming, crying, shouting surrounded her. She lay in the grass, too scared to get up.

Chapter 27

The mortal present

Gus arrived at the wedding with only a half-hour to spare. The other ushers grabbed him and shut him in a room to change. He clambered into his tux—a simple rented one, black and white. He'd eschewed the tailcoat, though Alyssa had turned big blue eyes on him and threatened to beg. She and the bridesmaids wore a motley of pinks.

He found her in the backyard, kissed her cheek. She wore a perfume like cherry candy. It made him want to lick her. He nuzzled her pale neck.

"Go! It's about to start!" she whispered.

He found his place in the side yard, between the brick house-wall and a rank of juniper bushes. He stood beside a stool with a handful of programs. Most of the ushers and the bridal party had joined the circle, but he was one of two who'd agreed to hang back and greet latecomers.

In the backyard, Hannah cut the first circle. "Before all else, I honor earth and sky, without which we would not be." He'd heard the words dozens of times in coven rituals. He was still technically in the coven's outer court, but he came to nearly everything.

"I cut this circle from sacred fire, to contain the magic of our desire." Hannah had tapped Jonathan as high priest for the rite —he'd been to Nora's rituals and knew his way around a witch circle. His deep, sonorous voice grounded the second circle, and Gus saw the fire he called.

Hannah cut the third circle. Quieter invocations came next, as coveners and friends summoned elements. Nora was audible calling water—Gus cheated backward to watch. Kirk stood behind her with a big grin.

A friend of Cleo's, an actor and priest, called Aphrodite in a poem based on an Orphic hymn. White, a hipster in presentation, he wore an fluorescent orange tuxedo with a hot pink ruffled shirt. Somehow it worked.

"Great goddess, queen of Cyprus, praised by all peoples, seaborn lady mother of all that lives, I call you. Beautiful and comely goddess, come to us." The strike of a match, a hollow sound in the glass, and the candle was lit on an altar heaped with roses.

A pretty gay man called in Pan. Medium height, mixed-race with hair in loose black curls, he'd dressed as a satyr—tux coat and frilly shirt but goat's horns blended into his curly hair. From the waist down, he was all fur; boots made his feet into cloven hooves.

"I call Pan, the shepherd god, who lives among the snowy crests and mountain peaks. Come to us, goat god, father god, we hail you, lord!"

He lit a great brown candle, as close to a phallus as they'd thought Sharon would allow.

Hannah stepped up, grinning ear to ear.

"We've gathered y'all here to witness a witch handfasting, a wedding, a celebration of the commitment of these two women

—Joan MacEwan and Cleo Gleeson—who will be bound in holy matrimony here before you. In just a moment, these fine young women will give vows to each other to form the basis of their marriage.

"As Cleo and Joanie's friends, one day you may be called upon to witness and support these vows. Are you ready to do that?"

The crowd murmured agreement, rustling as they shifted to watch the center of the circle.

At the front of the house, a car squealed around the corner, and he moved toward it. The car revved down the street, almost spinning in its haste. A dark, low-toned growl rose from the engine—a souped-up engine. It was a late-model American car, medium blue.

From the back, Hannah's voice came: "Louder! I need to know you'll be there for them! Are you ready to do that?"

The car pulled up in front of the house and double-parked.

He caught the eye of the usher across the yard, a friend of Cleo's from Farms of Color, a burly Black guy, Leon. They were both seeing the same thing.

Each of them stepped forward.

Three men threw open car doors, leaped out, and ran up the front yard's steep hill. Not unusual with the bird flu outbreak, they wore medical masks. These obscured their faces.

"What are you doing?" Gus yelled at them.

Leon stepped forward to intercept them. "I wouldn't go up there. It's a wedding service."

"Outta my way, Black boy," said the lead man, big-framed, wearing a black t-shirt, black jeans, and a black leather vest covered with Odin's Hunt patches. The other two dressed the same. The first man shouldered past Leon and kept running.

One ran toward Gus. Gus shoved him into the juniper bushes and ran around back.

The lead man untucked a Glock from his belt, at the small of his back. He took a three-point stance, aiming toward the women in the center of the circle. "This is for Mark! This is for Max! This is for Bruni!"

Wedding guests screamed. People ran. A mother flung herself down on the grass, folding herself around her toddler son. Two women hunkered below a serving table.

A shot rang out.

At the same time, a burst of wind punched across the bullet's path.

Leon threw himself at the shooter, tackling him at the knees. Running up, Gus stepped on the hand that held the pistol. He squatted and pried the man's fingers off the gun.

He loosed the pistol and kicked it away. Another usher grabbed it. A fourth usher and a guest Gus didn't know threw themselves down and grabbed the shooter's legs to stop his escape.

The other Hunt man pulled out his own pistol. Ray ran up with a baseball bat and smacked him across the arm. He dropped the gun and Ray picked it up.

Another man grabbed the Hunt guy from behind. They struggled. A wedding guest in a blue tux picked up the fallen gun and pointed it at the struggling men.

"Calling 9-1-1," said Sharon, calmly. Putting a hand over the ear not on her phone, she retreated toward the rosebushes.

"Get the car's license plate number!" Gus called. Kelsey, one of the bridesmaids, ran to the front yard.

The man Gus had shoved into the bushes pitched himself forward and grabbed her. Taking his own pistol from his belt, he shoved it under her chin.

"Don't say a word, don't do a thing, or I'll kill her!" He gestured with his jaw toward the shooter. "Let him up!"

The shooter dragged himself out from under Gus, knocking him over.

"Go!" the man holding Kelsey yelled at the shooter. "Run!

Both of you!" At the man struggling to hold the last Hunt man, he yelled, "Let him go!" He waved his gun, and the blue-tuxedoed man stood down.

The two freed men ran past the house and away. The third man dropped the girl he'd held. She fell, sprawling. Eyes full of malevolence, he turned and shot at her from point-blank range, but she was rolling away.

He shot again. The shot went wide. A woman's cry—it had hit someone. The man ran. Doors slammed. The car started and squealed away.

A pause fell, as if the event that had just happened hung in the air.

"Joanie, help me!"

<hr>

Chapter 28

<hr>

The mortal present

*J*oanie pushed herself up from the grass.

It was her mother's voice.

A faraway part of her mind noticed stains on her dress. Cleo steadied her where she stood, kissed her cheek, and stepped away. Joanie's mother wouldn't want Cleo there.

Joanie crossed the yard and knelt down. Mom was panting, blood seeping from her powder-blue polyester dress at the hip.

Joanie waved at the nearest guest. "Call 9-1-1."

Gus ran over and threw himself down beside them.

"Do you mind if I take over?" he asked Joanie.

"Not at all."

To her mother, he said, "May I pull up your dress to take a look?"

"He knows what he's doing, Mom." Gus didn't have EMT training yet, but he'd taken advanced first aid classes.

After a pause, her mother said, "Okay."

He pulled the fabric off the wound gingerly. The bullet had

grazed her thigh but only had hit flesh. A flap of skin hung loose and would need to be stitched. The blood didn't pump out like arterial blood, but might be coming from a vein.

Sharon hurried over. "Do you have a first aid kit?" he asked her.

"Yes." She went to find it and returned quickly. Opening it, Gus unwrapped sterile gauze and pressed it to the wound, slowing the bleeding. Joanie lifted her mother's leg gently, and Gus wrapped a bandage around it.

"I'd expect the ambulance to be here within fifteen minutes," Gus told them. "In the meantime, maybe just sit here." Sharon grabbed pillows from a garden bench to prop Mom's leg and let her sit up.

"I'll sit with her," Joanie said.

The backyard was a shambles. Crying and shaking people were everywhere, standing alone or in huddles, sitting at tables or on the grass. There'd been nearly a hundred guests. A knot of people clustered around two Native American elders from the Yakama Tribe whom Cleo had invited. The bullet shot aimed for Joanie herself had gone wild, embedding itself in the lawn, but the damage was done.

"Ow," said her mother. "This really hurts. I'm sorry."

"It's not like you got shot on purpose."

"I mean, it's such a shame for your wedding." She closed her eyes against the pain. "Before all this—it was good. I talked a bit with Ray. I think you belong with Cleo."

Ray had probably flirted with her. Whatever worked.

"I'm glad," Joanie said. "Thanks for picking up the cake. I really appreciate it."

"You think this shooting stuff was that same group harassing you?" Joanie had sketched in the tale of Odin's Hunt some time ago.

"They were all patched up, wearing Odin's Hunt regalia."

"Too bad we couldn't see their faces because of the masks."

This was baiting Joanie—her mom was in the anti-mask camp with the new bird-flu outbreak. "It is too bad, isn't it? But Jenna got a picture of the car's license plate. So there is hope."

"Why would they even do this?"

It was a question she'd asked herself.

"To scare us, to keep us nervous. Who knows, maybe they're even trying to run us out of town. I think they underestimated the chance that they'd get caught and charged, though. They're not the sharpest knives in the drawer."

Joanie and her friends had—however inadvertently—been picking off the most intelligent ones.

Her mother rested a few moments, then opened her eyes again.

"After the ambulance comes, I want you to keep going with the wedding. I want you to get married to your girl."

"Mom, don't say it unless you mean it." Sometimes her mother said what she thought was the right thing when sober, then took it back drunk. That hurt worse than if she'd never spoken.

"I do mean it. This has been nice. If this is what you want, I want you to have it."

Maybe she really meant that.

"Okay, Mom. I will."

Chapter 29

The mortal present

Gus went to Kelsey, sitting in the grass next to Celia. "Are you hurt?"

"Oh, not badly, but—" She gestured toward her legs, a flail. "I tried standing up, but I fell. I think I sprained my ankle."

"Let me check it out."

He gently stretched out Kelsey's leg. The ankle was swollen and red. "Ow."

"Do you mind if I touch it? It may hurt."

"If you think it will help, sure."

He pressed on the swollen area, puffy enough that his touch left an indent.

"Ow."

"Can I try moving it?" Gus picked up her foot and moved her ankle to check range of motion.

"Ow, ow, ow."

"What exactly hurts? There?"

"No." Gus kept moving her ankle. "There!"

The joint felt loose, as if a ligament was torn. "Can you stand up?"

"Not really."

"You should get this checked out by a doctor. We can send you in the ambulance with Joanie's mom."

"Do you think so?"

"If you can't stand up, yes."

Hannah had floated over to check. "Are you going to be able to cover the cost of the ambulance?" she asked Kelsey.

"I think I can," she said. "I'm on the shop's insurance."

"I'll go with her to the hospital," Celia put in.

"If you don't mind riding with Kelsey and Joanie's mom, it would be a kindness," Hannah said. "You've got Joanie's number, right? You can keep us posted."

"Sure, I can do that."

Hannah nodded her thanks. To Kelsey, she said, "Are you okay with us sending you healing energy?"

"I am." She grimaced and stroked her leg. Celia handed her a glass of champagne.

Getting up, Gus found Alyssa, who'd been standing on the circle. She was sniffling, her eyes red. "I can't believe this! I can't believe they'd ruin this!" He put his arms around her.

Hannah came up and hugged them both. "It's not going to stay ruined. Once the ambulance is gone, we'll have the ceremony. It's what Cleo and Joanie want. We just need to regroup."

"I think a few people left," Gus said.

"Let them!" Hannah said. "It doesn't matter."

"What did they want, do you think?" He meant the Hunt invaders.

"To do what they've done. To disturb the wedding. Shoot Joanie, if they could. They blame Joanie for things she didn't do."

Hannah stalked to the center of the circle.

Raising her voice, she said, "An ambulance is coming for

Crystal and Kelsey. The two brides want the wedding to go on. When the time is right, I'm going to ask everyone to rejoin the circle. I'll do a cleansing exercise to let go negative energy, raise energy for Crystal and Kelsey's healing, and we'll go on with the ceremony. When the police arrive to investigate, we'll do what's needed there."

Chapter 30

When Joanie stood the second time in the circle's center, a half-hour later, grass stains on her pillar dress, she was shaking. Cleo held her hand tight.

The ambulance had taken her mother and Kelsey away. For Kelsey, Gus had guessed she'd need a cast. For her mother, he hoped she'd mainly need stitches and time to heal. It was hard to say.

Now they were going to finish the wedding.

The vows were the central part of the ceremony. They'd each written theirs separately, then brought them together and compared them, smoothed out discrepancies, and memorized them.

Joanie gazed deep into Cleo's brown eyes.

"I vow that, for as long as we are together, you come first for me. I put my love and friendship for you before all others. You are my true love. I vow always to listen to you, even when I'm angry, and I vow to try always to communicate fairly. I vow to respect your voice and concerns."

Cleo's voice came lower-pitched than usual—she was fighting off tears. "I vow to help and support you in all your work and dreams, even the ones I don't understand. I vow to support you through thick and thin."

The wind kicked up, tossing petals off the rose hedge, shuffling the petals on the circle. It circled the pair of them, stroked Joanie's cheek.

It made her think of something—some spirit that had come to her as wind. No time to consider that now.

They had connected each vow to an element—earth, air, fire, water, spirit. With each vow, the element callers tied a ribbon around their wrists, binding them together.

The last element caller, a young woman from the coffee shop, all in pink, tied her strand of purple organza. "You are wed in spirit, and may the boundless nature of the infinite support you and protect you as you go into married life."

Would married life be different? She'd felt married to Cleo for years. They'd been sharing finances for a while.

Hannah stepped forward, beaming.

"Your hands are now tied fast! You may kiss to seal your commitment!"

Cleo smelled of sandalwood and jasmine. The warmth of her presence enveloped Joanie. The tension and shock of the day dropped away. Her thoughtful lips touched Joanie's, reassuring; their mouths connected, love pouring through them.

"It's time to jump the broom!"

Sharon had given her broom-jumping speech earlier, so now they were free to take the leap.

Gus and Leon sauntered up, holding the broom wound with ribbons and ivy, roses braided among these. They held it in front of Cleo and Joanie, raising it shoulder-high.

"Think you can clear that?" Leon asked.

"Maybe a bit high," Cleo said, and they lowered it to knee-height.

"Try going under!" someone said in the crowd. "How low can you go?"

Joanie and Cleo ignored them, dropping back to give themselves a run-up.

"Ready?" Cleo whispered.

Joanie nodded.

They took a running jump and cleared it.

They hugged each other.

Again a breeze curled around Joanie's shoulders, intimate, another layer to the hug.

Now the handfasting was fully sealed. They'd sign the marriage certificate later.

"Now it's time for champagne and wedding cake!" Hannah cried. "We have a few preplanned toasts, but after that anyone can give one."

One of the coffee shop managers had taken possession of the cake table, cutting cake like a professional. They had no plan to smash cake into each other's faces, but Joanie decorously took a bite of Cleo's. Chocolate—why would anyone want any other kind of cake? Now the ushers and bridesmaids snaked through the crowd, dispensing glasses and plates. The jazz ensemble started their second set, and people milled. A few had left after the attack, but there were still seventy-odd people left, and cake and champagne distribution took time.

Then came the sirens.

The cop cars turned the corner and parked in front of the house, like Odin's Hunt before them. They'd have showed up sooner, but Sharon had called to say the active shooter was gone.

Ray and Sharon traded a look. Though they spoke low, Joanie stood close enough to hear them.

"I'll do it," Sharon said.

"You can let me."

"We can all have this conversation," Cleo said, drawing Joanie forward. They planned to be tied together at least till after the toasts.

Gus came up. "I can help."

Together, all five went to the front yard. The cops were mounting the steps. Ray stepped forward. Joanie did as well, but Cleo put a hand on her arm.

"Let him have the first part of the conversation," she said quietly. "He takes being the man in the situation pretty seriously."

"Okay."

There were two cops, the first one up the steps a well-set-up Black man, behind him a thin, nervous-looking white woman.

The two introduced themselves. "I'm Officer Colman Carpenter, and this is my partner, Officer Nancy Sneed. We got your original phone call about 1 PM this afternoon, and then you called back fifteen minutes later."

Ray glanced at the two of them and turned toward the Black man. "Yes, Officer, my wife here called this in." He nodded to Sharon.

"We were just starting the wedding. My daughter, Cleo, and her girlfriend, now wife, Joanie, got married." She gestured to the two of them. "Then these three men arrived in a late-model American car, skidded up, came up the yard and into the backyard, where we had the ceremony, and the one started shooting."

"May we see the backyard?"

"Of course."

"One of the wedding party got a picture of the car's license plate." She showed him on her phone.

"This may have something to do with Thomas Mueller, who goes by the name of Bruni," Gus said. "He's part of an white supremacist group called Odin's Hunt. I helped put Bruni behind bars earlier in the year. The shooter yelled at us, 'This is for Mark! This is for Max! This is for Bruni!'" All three are people Joanie had some connection with—she's one of the brides." Joanie gave the officers a small wave.

"So you think it may be a revenge attack," the Black officer said.

"I do," Gus said.

Ray cleared his throat. "We'll be doing the toasts now."

"I can help show them where the bullet went and so on," Gus offered.

"That would be great," Joanie said.

Returning to the backyard, Ray stepped up to the microphone on its stand in front of the jazz ensemble, who'd gamely started a third set. The musicians tailed off the song, and Ray adjusted the microphone.

"Now we're going to start the toasts. It's going to be a little broken up, as these officers"—he inclined his head toward the two police—"are going to come around and ask some questions. I'd like to ask everyone to answer to the best of your ability." Whatever differences this gathering of youth, activists, and people of color might have with the cops, Ray asked them to cooperate. "Gus here will be helping them out. He's close friends of both Cleo and Joanie."

More of Joanie's—Cleo had always held him at arm's length. She didn't forget his time with the white supremacists.

In Cleo's case, Ray took on the initial toast. Fearing what her mom might do in front of the microphone, Joanie had asked an old friend, Danielle. "Danielle really wanted to do it," she'd told her mom. "You can do yours a bit later."

She couldn't have predicted her mother's change of heart. Her mother was on her way to the hospital anyway.

A pang crossed her chest—would her mother be okay?

She'd deal with that later.

The two cops split the crowd between them. A couple other

cops had appeared but seeing the situation under control left on another call. Now the white policewoman appeared at Joanie's side, hovering like a curious wasp.

Joanie looked to Cleo. "I guess we need to untie ourselves for this?"

Cleo gestured Hannah over. Closing her eyes, Hannah put her hands over their bound wrists. "In the name of our gods and spirits, you continue to be connected as partners, though these physical bonds are loosened."

She gathered the ribbons. "I'll braid them."

"Let's get out of the crowd." The policewoman drew Joanie to the side, to a table away from the microphone. Ray had finished, to light applause, and Danielle's toast had been short. Now came the random, unplanned ones, generally also short.

Joanie'd had her share of run-ins with police; she'd spent time in lock-up. Her prostitution charge had been wiped off her record, but it wasn't the kind of thing you forgot. Now she needed to act like the cops were on her side.

They sat below the hedge of roses. A breeze picked up a few petals, threw them across the white table. Two white, two red, soft, a fleshy curve like the interior of a delicate ear.

If you read them as divination—half and half. Even chances. Enter at your own risk.

"Do you mind if I record this?"

"No problem."

"Your name is?"

"Joan MacEwen."

"You were one of the brides."

And still am. "Yes."

"You've been together how long?"

She wasn't sure how it was material, but she answered. "About four years."

A long and sometimes bumpy ride it had been. She'd first met Cleo when she was doing Inanna shrines with Sasha, who they later found out trafficked teenagers. Alyssa had been one of those teenagers. Then they navigated the journey of Alyssa's boyfriend, Gus, through white supremacist heathenry. Then Joanie got together with Pete, the red-haired punk anarchist who'd died for her.

But the woman was talking.

"What was your first run-in with Odin's Hunt?"

"I knew Gus through Alyssa, who's one of the bridesmaids and who works at the coffee shop where I'm a manager. Not long after I met him, he started dating Max Dwyer, who was one of the leaders of Odin's Hunt. In fact, one of the men came in shouting, 'This is for Max.'"

"So you and Cleo have a history of friction with Odin's Hunt?"

Friction was an awfully neutral way of putting it. But it wouldn't help anyone if she argued with a cop.

"You could say that, yes. Gus has even more details on that."

The woman pursed her lips. It seemed to be one of her tells, of what it wasn't clear. "My partner's talking to him."

"Probably the biggest thing is that they blamed me for Mark Walker's death, though in reality that was just an unfortunate accident."

"Tell me more about that."

She'd rather not. She'd rather if this woman showed a little more empathy. It was, after all, her wedding day, and she'd been shot at.

But she plowed forward.

"Mark Walker was a client of a company I worked for, the Gunnar Group. He invited me up for a nightcap in a hotel at one point and got a little handsy. I called my boyfriend for help. The two of them fought, it got out of hand, and they ended up falling from a balcony. They both died."

Shrewd brown eyes narrowed on her. "It sounds like you came out the loser there as much as anyone."

"Well, yes." This cop wasn't a friend, but she was listening, not dismissing Joanie out of hand. It was the benefit of her being a woman, whatever her unfortunate job choice. "But somehow they thought I wanted Mark dead." She was hard-pressed not to roll her eyes at that point. "Mark wasn't my very favorite person, but I didn't want him dead. Why would I? He hadn't done anything that merited that. Pete Martin, that was my boyfriend—he took it way over the top, way too far." She sighed. "But they're both dead now, as I said."

"How long ago was this?"

"About two and a half years ago. In December. Holiday time."

"Not much of a holiday for you that year?"

The cop was trying to be nice, for whatever reason. "No."

"Anything since then?"

"Not for me. Gus has been pursuing putting Bruni, that is Thomas Mueller, in jail for a while, and finally got a break earlier in the year. But I'm sure your partner has asked him about that."

The cop nodded.

"Anything else in particular I should know about?"

"There's been a couple attempted break-ins, at Gus's house and at a friend of his. But again, he's the best source for that. I wasn't there."

"Anything else you were there for?"

It came out as sarcastic. She couldn't tell if the woman had meant it that way or not. "No."

Cleo and Joanie extricated themselves not long after the police left. Theirs was an older bed and breakfast, a Craftsman cottage on Capitol Hill lovingly restored to the time of its greatest splendor, its exterior the blue of a twilight sea, with cut-glass inserts in the windows, furnished with well-polished antiques. Their suite had a four-poster bed with a canopy, and the owners had filled the suite with vases of pale pink and yellow roses. Celia had texted—at the hospital emergency room, Kelsey had gotten a cast and gone home. Joanie's mother had been sewn up, given pain medication, and kept overnight. She'd gone to sleep.

There was nothing to do now. Joanie could go to the hospital tomorrow.

She let her dress fall in a puddle on the floor and jumped in the shower—it had been such a long day, hot in the sun. The mirror showed a touch of sunburn on her nose and cheeks. Wrinkling her nose, she felt the burn. It hadn't been the kind of day when she remembered to reapply sunblock.

The pale grey bathroom, with its clawfoot tub and hexagonal period tile, also had an excellent showerhead. Hot, sharp, pulsing water got rid of her surface dirt and some of her tension. She let go as much as she could to the water.

It was over now.

Angry, she was angry. And sad. Those men had broken up her wedding and shot her mother. But the wedding was done. Her mother was out of pain and asleep.

Hot water poured over her, washing it all away.

Toweling down, she came into their room, painted a dusty rose and scented with roses.

Cleo had thrown herself across the bed with no shower, all sandalwood and jasmine. "Come here, you," she said.

Joanie dropped the towel and crawled into her arms.

"What a day," she said. "I mean, it was always going to be. But I had no idea."

"How could you? I'm pretty resentful too. But let's not talk about that now. I need a nap, and I think you do too."

They woke midevening. The bridal suite rental included a bottle of champagne, and Joanie let Cleo do the honors of opening it.

"Aim that cork away from me!"

"You think I'm going to take my wife out on our wedding day?"

"Fuck, wife. What a word."

Cleo filled two champagne flutes and handed her one, sitting down by her on the bed, white chenille spread mussed after their nap.

"We don't have to use it."

"I don't care. It's just so… heavy."

Setting her champagne on the bedside table, Cleo leaned and kissed her. She kissed back, sinking into it: warmth, love, and a hovering bit of lust, still, again, forever. Cleo's orchid lips were still faintly plum-colored from her wedding lipstick.

They settled back onto the bed, Cleo curled around Joanie, enveloping her.

"Are you happy you married me?" she asked.

"Yes."

"Despite all the bullshit that went down, despite everything about the institution of marriage?"

"Despite everything. It was the right thing to do." It had settled into her, a reassuring weight.

Besides their strong emotional connection and the ongoing journey of their sex, Cleo had her back—forever, without question. Now, somehow, the bond felt stronger. Perhaps it was the legality behind it. She had no conscious belief that this made the connection sturdier.

She was no fan of the state. The Odin's Hunt boys almost certainly had supporters within the police precinct. At least maybe the Black cop would take the whole thing seriously. But if it had been three Black men shooting up a white wedding, the response would have been more significant—more than two cops taking statements!

But for some deep part of her, beyond her critique of the state, that signed legal document made a difference.

"Are you ready for dinner?" Cleo asked. They'd made a reservation at the restaurant next to the hotel.

"Is it that late?"

"There's a little time yet."

She rolled over, took Cleo in her arms, and kissed her deeply. "How'd you feel about a quickie?"

As she dove for another kiss, Cleo's lips smiled against hers.

Chapter 31

The eternal present

The cobalt sky lay underlined with sunset coral, dunes silhouetted black against it. A light wind shook the palm leaves.

Azazel had kept Suriyel's toy, which let him look at his favorites on earth. Now, idling on a bench in his pocket hell, he watched Joanie at dinner with her new wife.

Alfstein had created a pathway, so now he could go to Earth anytime he liked—to Iceland, but it was the work of a moment to go anywhere from there. He could go as wind, rattle the Venetian blinds at the restaurant, stroke Joanie's cheek.

That path had saved Joanie's life.

She didn't know to call him now. She didn't know he existed. She didn't realize the wind that punched across the backyard and shoved aside the bullet had been him, watching out for her as he always did.

It had worked, but it had worked by chance, underlining the flaw in this silence between them.

Only his obsessive watching of her let him protect her, and he had other things to do. Samyaza was hot to move against the Demiurge and wanted him to consult. He still had his weekly punishment from the Demiurge, hanging on a basalt cliff face, upside down, tortured, a thing baked into his hell. If he were there and didn't undergo it, worse would happen. Puabi-Ekur often brought water to slake his thirst, but they were elsewhere now, avoiding him, angry over this very topic.

They were right. For him to protect Joanie properly, she needed to be able to call him.

It had taken her nearly dying for him to realize that.

Puabi-Ekur had stung his pride, but he should be above that kind of petty consideration.

There was the argument too that Joanie was a diplomat. Puabi-Ekur had many of the same existing contacts. But perhaps Joanie was a nexus point, an important point of connection, or at least a witch who'd poked her head above the line from the mundane plane into true reality. Someone who would be noticed and would always be in danger.

A witch naturally on his side, in the line of the Watchers.

It was his job to protect her the best way he could, which meant reconnecting.

The ban would need to be let up carefully. Restoring memories was best done bit by bit. Perhaps he would send her a dream first.

He'd have to seduce Joanie all over again.

He smiled to himself. That was no hardship.

But Azazel wasn't ready for any conversation, even to agree and make up the argument, with Puabi-Ekur or with Joanie.

He needed a period of peace and restoration. The worst part of his imprisonment in Suriyel's dungeon hadn't been the time alone, but the time that Suriyel came to him, nagged at him, forced him into sex—bound his mind, even, sometimes, forcing him to enjoy the attack against his will. Forced togetherness with his enemy had abraded some part of his soul.

With the new passageway, he was more free than he'd been in millennia. It came from this coalition that Samyaza was building. But he wasn't ready to help.

He needed to spend the beginning of his freedom healing himself.

Angel time was not as human time. His pocket universe could have its own pockets of time. There were ways he'd have to pay for creating one, and his energy wasn't infinite. But this time, it might be worth it. He could create a space of time to heal and still move forward at pace in the mundane world.

And reconnect with Joanie.

Chapter 32

A few nights after her wedding, Joanie had a dream.

A white truck sped down a Seattle highway, passing car after car. Rain pummeled the roadway. As the truck crossed a bridge, a gust of wind slammed it against a barrier. It spun away, and another gust threw it on its side. A third picked it up and dropped it, crushing it. Max's blood poured out the window onto the street.

She woke, to a warm night, overcast, moon hidden behind clouds. She sat up, found her glass of water, and sipped. Some residual horror of death surfaced, but far away.

The dream was a memory.

Max had threatened to kidnap and kill her; he'd been planning to try again. Her angel friend turned into wind and killed him first.

Who was it, this being who had killed for her? The familiar longing rose.

She drifted off again. Cumulus clouds rose against blue sky;

among them stood a platform of white stone. A star of light burned at the edge of the platform, too bright to look at.

To one side, wrapped in golden chains, stood Puabi-Ekur as Puabi. Beside her, chains lying in pieces on the marble below him, was a dark-winged angel.

He had dark-olive skin, a warrior's muscles, long, black, curling hair, full well-curved lips, and high cheekbones. Kohl lined his shockingly bright grey-blue eyes. He was so beautiful it hurt.

Also, he had a strong resemblance to Samyaza. A family resemblance, maybe.

It was him. This was her angel.

Her excitement woke her up.

Cleo was already gone to work. She scrambled out of bed to meditate, chair facing the black-velvet shelf where her altar lay.

Barely in trance, she called out, "Puabi-Ekur, Puabi-Ekur! Come talk to me!"

Gus caught up with Joanie during her break at the coffee shop.

June in Seattle—in between bouts of rain, summer poked its head out. Today bright sun bounced off the puddles, filling the coffee shop with light.

"How's your mom doing?" Gus asked.

"Still in the hospital for observation. I go see her every day or so." When she wasn't there, Dustin texted her updates. "They found deep-vein thrombosis and they're afraid the injury might trigger blood clots."

"That's a bit concerning."

"It is. But they have her on blood thinners and they're monitoring her. I think they're doing all they can."

A wave of fear threatened, but she held it back. "You had news?"

"They're interviewing Odin's Hunt, bit by bit, closing on an arraignment," he told her, hands wrapped around a cup on the blonde wood table. "There are three persons of interest, though they're not releasing names yet."

"At least things are moving." Joanie followed the story in the newspaper and the Capitol Hill crime blog, but Gus had inside information. "What do you think will happen?"

"My guess is that they'll take it to court. Since your mom's doing okay, it'll be attempted murder. The guys might get suspended sentences, or some time in prison, depending on their past records."

"I'm curious to see what the police do about the group as a whole. It's clearly a pernicious and destructive group, if multiple members do these attacks. They could release a statement or form a hate-crime task force. But do they really care about white supremacist groups?"

Gus grimaced.

"A lot of them sympathize. You know that," he said. "I'm no fan of policing. On the other hand, they did put Bruni behind bars. So all of us are safer."

"They did." She took a long sip of her iced coffee. "What I want to know is how Odin's Hunt found out the details about the wedding."

Gus scratched his head. "That I don't know, but I have a theory."

"Which is?"

"Too early to share. I might be completely wrong." He took a mouthful of coffee. "I need to talk to Julia."

"I thought she wasn't going to spy for you any more?"

"I think I can talk her into doing it one last time."

～

"But Mom, when are you getting out of the hospital?" Joanie asked, switching the cell phone to the other ear. Ready for bed, she was checking in.

The hospital had kept her mother more than a week now. A blood clot could cause a pulmonary embolism and so a heart attack, the nurse had told her, so they were monitoring her.

Dustin kept Joanie posted by text—he was able to stop by the hospital more often. That he was noticeably Christian bothered her, but he seemed to love her mother. Crystal had always been at least nominally Christian, and Dustin's flavor seemed better than most. He was helpful, which got him points.

"It could be as early as tomorrow," her mother said. "But it's one thing after the other, and it's always better that I stay. Thank God I've got decent insurance."

"Now you're taking the Lord's name in vain." It was something Dustin would say. Her mother laughed.

Witch Farm stood on the edge of a forested area, some of that forest owned by individuals, much owned by the state. That area shared a boundary with national forest. The woods were full of game—deer, bobcat, coyotes, the occasional black bear, no grizzlies till the north Cascades.

Sometimes a domestic cat got ambitious and went out to the woods to catch chipmunks, wood mice, squirrels, and birds. Very few cats survived, but they sometimes made good, especially if they could find a hiding space. If they did, they bred.

Joanie's sleep was uneven those days. She had plenty of stress. The mom thing ate at her on a low level, and though she loved the effect of the filmy curtains in their bedroom, they didn't shut out light. She'd put off changing them—it would take finding and hanging blackout curtains, and she and Cleo both worked too much.

Joanie was up before anyone that dawn, even before Nora.

She sat with her coffee on the back porch. The view faced north, past the garden beds and the greenhouse to the woods. Rays of yellow light outlined the eastern tree branches—the joy of the summer sunrise, before the day began.

A broad swath of grass, close-trimmed, grew into the salal at the woods' edge. They meant to return the bits that weren't garden to natural vegetation.

Now a wiggle shook the grass, with the tiniest mew.

Two kittens emerged—one a tiny black one, one tuxedo.

They looked at her uncertainly.

What did she have for cats? There was a tiny bit of smoked salmon on a plate in the refrigerator. She sneaked in, grabbed it, and went down the porch steps to the bottom one.

"Pss, pss, pss," she said. "Here, kitties."

Chapter 33

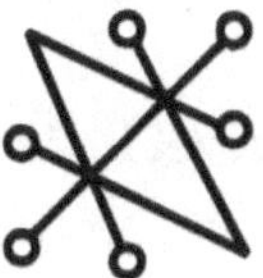

*A*zazel hung on the cliff-face.

Upside down, chained to the basalt with massive, rusted iron bands, he sagged, black wings gashed, torn, and bleeding.

As pure spirit, Puabi-Ekur floated down into the chasm of Dudael toward him.

They knew he made little of his pain, they knew he would heal himself as soon as he drew away, but here and now, this was utter agony.

As they had many times before, they manifested a cup, held it to his cracked lips.

"Only a psychopath would require anyone do this for millennia," they said.

Azazel sighed, a breath that shook him. His bound wings struggled to unfurl. "Yes."

"I understand you contacted Joanie."

"Wait for me in the pavilion, will you, please?"

The pavilion lay almost dark, a few candles lit in the golden candelabra. The huge ebony bed was made. A coverlet of black fur lay on it, unusually. Maybe Azazel felt the cold more, after his imprisonment.

They'd need to handle him with care this next bit. Physical damage for an angel took a moment to heal. The spiritual damage Suriyel had inflicted would take longer, especially on top of the centuries of injury Azazel had sustained.

The crunch of feet along gravel gave warning the angel approached—on purpose; he could have appeared with no sound. Puabi-Ekur took the form of the dancer of Uruk, slender yet well-curved, with long, crimped brown hair. She curled up catlike on the fur coverlet, in a simple black robe with gold trim.

Azazel pushed through the curtain-door to the pavilion. He wore a loose black robe, wings hidden. He sat on the bed on the far side with no comment, putting a few pillows between himself and the bedstead. He patted the space beside him, and she crawled to sit there.

She leaned and kissed his cheek. "I'm glad you talked to her, beloved," she said.

A side glance toward her—those blue topaz eyes. His physical beauty almost made her wince, so close up.

"Am I forgiven?" he asked. His tone was joking, yet she knew he was serious.

"Of course. I know you had your reasons... just..." Don't say it, Puabi-Ekur. Don't say, "But your reasons were wrong."

They knew each other well enough by now; she knew he heard the words in the silence. But she got points for not saying them.

"What changed your mind?" she asked.

He smoothed his hand upon the coverlet. On his thumb he wore a silver ring inlaid with ancient Arabic script in gold, a protective charm. Old scars crossed his hands and arms, their pale tracery heavier as they went up his arms, from battle but also from his punishment in the chasm.

He'd had so much pain in his life. She didn't want to add to it. Yet they had to talk through things.

"I have been watching her through Suriyel's orb, and I was lucky enough to see those djinn-followers attack, Odin's Hunt they call themselves. I was able to shift that bullet so it didn't hit. But that was only luck. She's a prominent being now, perhaps a nexus point; she will always be in danger, whether allied with me or not. She needs to be able to call me for protection."

"Well, bravo."

He rolled his eyes. "You are not helping, Puabi-Ekur."

As an answer, she pulled her robe over her head.

"How can I help?"

He smiled.

Chapter 34

ᚾ

The mortal present

In the humid late twilight, citronella candles drove the worst of the mosquitos away. Lined up against the back wall of the house, the housemates sat on the porch. Nora sipped red wine; Joanie had a glass as well. Cleo had made lemonade. Jonathan preferred a joint. Kirk was elsewhere—he drifted in and out of the house, ostensibly apartment-hunting, though no one thought he'd move soon.

"I'm thinking another fairy dust ritual at the new moon," Nora said. "Same format. I'll need a down payment from everyone, to pay back Kirk for his materials and time."

"That's fair," Jonathan said. "Could you give us an itemized bill?"

Nora raised her eyebrows. "Sure, I can do that. But the materials aren't cheap, and it's his only livelihood right now."

"Sure." Jonathan offered Nora the joint. She shook her head.

"I should ask her if she's charging Kirk rent," Cleo said to Joanie in an undertone.

"I'd like to do at least one more fairy dust ritual before we run him out of the house."

"If that's what you want."

"We can talk later."

Joanie felt called to the enlightenment space, and this was one way to reach it. Though Kirk's part of it was an issue.

The roommate conversation broke up. Upstairs in their room, windows thrown open and fan on, she set herself in the breeze. She'd grabbed another glassful of wine.

"He's sliming on me," she told Cleo. Nothing recent had been as obvious as the night he'd offered to be her sugar daddy, but a look here, a hint there. "He needs to learn that no means no."

"You could just bop him one. You're the one who knows martial arts."

"I don't want to have an argument with him when he's clearly going to be staying here indefinitely."

"We can change that."

Cleo was probably right—among the current four official roommates, only Nora wanted Kirk there.

"Like I say, let's not stir things up yet. I want to try the fairy dust one more time. Who knows how that will go, if we kick Kirk out?"

"When we kick Kirk out."

Kirk presented a bill in person a few nights later, again on the back porch, flames of citronella candles winking against near-dark.

"I don't blame you all wanting details," he said, in his warm deep voice. "I would myself."

He passed around a slip of paper. Most of the raw materials weren't expensive, except for a couple that were hard to source. "I could make do with some substitutions, but I haven't been happy with the results."

His labor came to almost nothing.

Joanie was the first to speak up. "This seems extremely reasonable."

"I'm glad you think so."

"I agree," Jonathan said, and Cleo murmured something. She'd stood down the active belligerence for now, for Joanie's sake.

"Are we on, then?" Nora asked. "For the new moon? I'll ask Sandy and Mike too, but I have a feeling they won't be up for it. They both found it pretty intense last time."

"I'm down," Joanie said. The roommates nodded their agreement.

No one stayed on the porch long after that. Despite the candles, the mosquitos drove them inside. Joanie wandered into the kitchen.

The light over the sink as the twilight deepened made the room dramatic. Kicking off her shoes, she padded to the refrigerator.

She'd come home late and missed dinner. She poked through the fridge—there was some leftover curry Cleo had made a few days before. At the counter, she dished it into a bowl.

Kirk came up behind her, too close to her, as if he'd materialized out of thin air. She moved away, putting space between them.

"I want to thank you for being willing to go forward with the ritual," he said. "I know you've had some compunctions about me."

"It's not so much that I like or dislike you. I'm interested in the work," she said. True enough, but it skated around the main subject. That was her intent.

The lighting brought out the flecks of amber in his brown eyes. He'd be an attractive man if he wasn't a sleaze.

"I understand," he said. He meant more than that he understood her words.

She didn't care to parse it. She didn't care about him.

"I'm glad," she said, at random. She'd been meaning to eat at the table, but she took her bowl upstairs.

He needed to move out of the house. He made her feel unsafe. But she'd wait till after the next fairy dust ritual to start the process.

A hot, dark night, nearing the new moon—a sliver of moon would rise late. Cleo was away, visiting a farm in the center of the state, near Centralia.

Joanie had traded a bottle of wine for some of Jonathan's stash of weed. Smoking weed was something she did rarely, but she had problems sleeping in the heat, and getting stoned made her sleepy.

She lounged with the window open, the smoke driving away mosquitos. The sky was hazy, only a few summer stars poking through—the Northern Cross, beside it blue-white Vega.

The two new kittens made a small pile, asleep at the end of the bed. With a neighbor, she'd traced the cat family to an abandoned shed on property owned by absentee landlords. The neighbor committed to bringing the other kittens and mama cat to a no-kill shelter. Joanie felt no compunction adopting the kittens who'd presented themselves—two boys, Jareth and Jinx.

What she'd forgotten was how horny weed made her. But she felt listless, not willing to find her vibrator and get herself off.

And you a sacred whore! she thought. But sex was about consent. You could say no out of laziness.

After a bowl, she went to bed. It was too hot to wear a nightgown—even the sheet felt oppressive. She set the fan as high as it would go and fell into a half-sleep, drifting downward.

Chapter 35

The eternal present

Knife-edged dunes cut an outline against a dark-blue sky, past the trees of an oasis where tents stood. Closer in stood buildings with lamp-lit windows.

Joanie sat on an ancient wooden bench, sand inlaid in its whorls, alongside a sandy path. A lantern at the end of the bench gave light. She wore the short nightgown she hadn't worn to bed, black cotton.

As she glanced along the path, black against the blue twilight, an outline came into view. A thrill of anticipation poured through her, but she held herself still. Ambient light painted in details as the figure approached.

He wore a long dark-red kilt but was naked from the waist up, broad-shouldered and brown-skinned, a gold sigil necklace against his muscled chest. Curling black hair framed a face with kohl-lined eyes that shone pale grey-blue.

In no hurry, he strolled toward her, sandals rasping on sand.

Arriving at the bench, he looked down at her. Behind him flickered the outline of wings.

She leaped to her feet. He was nearly a head taller. She caught his scent, dark frankincense.

"Greetings, most fair," he said. "Sun of my heart, glory of my existence."

"You are my angel," she said.

"Always and forever."

She took a deep breath.

She could flirt, go to bed with him. It would be lovely.

But she'd been hurt, and she had to speak.

"It was you who made the break between us, wasn't it?" Everything pointed to that. "Why? Why did you build a wall between us?"

Taking her hand, he sat them both on the bench. "I shall tell you. But will you drink wine with me, beloved?"

She nodded, her heart too full to speak.

Beside them appeared a silver tray, wine pitcher, and cups. He poured for both. She took her cup between both hands and sipped, looking at him through her eyelashes.

"I have an enemy among the angels of the Demiurge," he said. "Suriyel, the Angel of the Dark Moon. More than once, he attacked me through you, capturing or threatening you. I thought to protect you by separating us."

"Mmm-hmm." She had opinions. But he wasn't done.

"Separation did not work as I hoped. I never forgot you. I never stopped loving you. Neither did you drop the connection. It only made you blind to me. It was torture for you."

"Go on."

"I believe you have been noticed by the powers that be, particularly the djinn, even if Suriyel ignores you. I believe this group Odin's Hunt is riddled with djinn, and there may be others around you. The djinn are a variable people, by no means always opposed to the Watcher angels, but those you have encountered work against us. I believe both Max and Mark Walker were djinn."

"Maybe so. Max, for sure." Even after his death, Max had harassed her. They'd trapped him and taken him to hell in a lead box for Ereshkigal to guard.

"If you cannot call me, you are in greater danger than if you can. It was only by luck I could deflect that bullet meant for you."

"You did that?!" A gust of wind had risen. Perhaps it had shoved the bullet aside.

"I did not tell you to earn your gratitude."

"But you have my gratitude."

"You have saved me as well. Century after century, we trade. We are bound up in each other's fates. We can be together using sight, or we can be blind. It is better to see. This is why I removed the wall."

She took a mouthful of wine.

Emotion poured through her—she wanted to forgive him and fall into his arms. But she owed herself more than that.

"I'm glad you did. But I'm still angry about all that. It was painful. It was humiliating. Other people knew things that I did not." She shook back her long brunette hair. "You say I've been noticed by the powers that be. I feel that. And that's partly because I have my own power too."

"Of course."

"Treating me like a pawn denies me my power."

"I never meant that. But I acknowledge I misstepped."

Setting aside his wine-cup, he knelt before her.

"Beautiful Joanie, love of my many lives, I am sorry I ever caused you pain, or ever seemed to think less of you than you deserve. One may be human and still wield great power. As you do."

It was frightening to hear him say it to her and mean it.

"I made a mistake. Can you forgive me?" he asked.

"Yes. But not yet. This is a lot, and I'm still processing it." He nodded, blue-topaz gaze still burning into hers.

Setting aside her wine-cup, she threw her arms around his neck.

"You're happy to have me back, then?" she asked. He opened his mouth to speak, but she shut it with a kiss. She drew back again. "Show me."

He picked her up in his arms.

Gravel crunched under his feet as he took her beyond the palm trees. She hid her head against his chest. She'd had sex with him many times, and all she recalled had been amazing, but what if it no longer worked like that? A betrayal could break things.

The scent of dark frankincense enveloped her. Full night had fallen; the stars were out. She didn't recognize any. Fear-thoughts ran around her head like trapped mice.

He leaned and kissed her hair. She breathed in, let it out, let go.

The pavilion was near full dark, only a few candles lit in the standing golden candelabra. The bed—it was huge, four people could sleep in it—lay under a black fur coverlet.

He set her on the bed, and she curled up there.

"Wine?" he asked.

"Sure."

Fear clutched her stomach. She breathed.

She was a skilled professional and a priestess of Inanna, a sacred whore. The task before her was not only in her skill set, but also part of her calling.

On the bedside table, ebony she thought, a silver pitcher and cups appeared, embossed with scenes of battling angels. He poured. Her breath sounded loud in the cup. She drank.

He sat beside her, and she put the cup on the bedside table and wound herself around him in a hug.

His face, released a moment, fell in planes of sorrow.

"Oh, beloved, are you sad?"

"Always."

"Don't be sad about me. I'm here with you."

He set aside his cup and took her in his arms.

She leaned back a little, ran her hands through his hair, drew him in for a long kiss. Her mouth dipped, explored; she sucked his tongue. Had the separation changed things?

The rhythm caught; the kiss went deeper. He took her by the shoulders, pushed her back on the bed. Kissing her face, her shoulders, he reached under her, swept off her nightgown. She pushed herself back up to sitting, kissing his face and lips.

"I missed you," she said. "I didn't even know it was you, but I missed you."

"I missed you too." He pushed her back, kissing and gently biting his way down her torso, burying his head between her legs.

At the top of the pavilion, currents of candlelight flowed along curving, billowing black silk. Sensation built, threatening to overwhelm her, but she didn't want to be so separate, even if he pleased her.

She grabbed his hair, and he lifted his face gleaming with her juices. She tugged upward. He snaked out of his kilt and slid up, planted himself inside her, and started to move.

She held her eyes open, fixed his grey-blue gaze, and the rhythm built. Her eyelids fluttered, the flicker of candlelight, the sensation pouring, pouring, cresting. She cried out.

A moment later, he released into her, the circuit linking them, binding them.

Afterward, she lay curled up in the curve of his arm, letting the wash of emotion pour over her. She fell asleep.

When she woke, his eyelids were closed. The whuffle of his breathing sounded, not quite a snore.

What now? They'd reconnected. He'd apologized; she'd accepted the apology. Or begun to.

He'd said she was a powerful witch. She didn't know what to do with that. It implied responsibility.

With the even cadence of his breathing, he seemed to sleep.

Listening, breathing in his frankincense sweat, she went back to sleep herself.

He woke again, kissing her, stroking her, her parts still juicy and engorged. Moving his hand, watching her face, he gave her another orgasm. The waves passed through her and rolled away.

She reached under the covers, stroked his cock with her fingertip, met his eyes with a question. But he sat up against the gilt headboard, shaking his head. She pushed herself up next to him and nudged herself under his arm.

"What now, my love? What do you desire?" she asked.

"I would rest and enjoy the moment. It is a prize of my life, to have you back with me. I was wrong to bar you away."

"You were." She picked up his hand and kissed his palm, which smelled of her. A scar lay at its heel below his thumb, a divot that was a stab wound. His thumb and one of his fingers wore rings, one silver and one gold, each with an ancient script. Another ring was inset with a broad black stone, perhaps chalcedony. All over his wrists and arms lay scars.

"So many battles," she said. "Over millennia."

"We are all that old. You and I have been together in many lives."

"You say I am a powerful witch. What does that mean?"

"You know how to connect to the spirit world; you have allies and personal power. Most magical work on the mundane plane is done by alliance with spirits."

"Is this true among spirits as well?"

"That is one way. There are gods too who grow up out of devotion—devotion is like food to them."

"Like Inanna. Or the Demiurge."

He frowned. "Yes."

"Puabi-Ekur said Samyaza believes it's once more time to face off against him." She continued to stroke his palm. "You call him Yaldabaoth. But he is not like in gnostic texts, at least not the ones I know of. Who is he?"

"There are many types of gnostic, and all gods have many faces. Some say Yaldabaoth created the world of manifestation to trap us, the angels. Some of us bowed to him. Some did not."

"Some made a feint at it but didn't really."

He smiled. "You are thinking of Samyaza. We Watchers do not abjure the physical world as gnostics may do, but we do believe that Yaldabaoth endeavors to keep humans from the truth. To keep them in bondage."

"So what is the truth?"

"It is not hidden. You are gods, we are all gods, all sentient beings. You can play the game on earth, the game we began together millennia ago, as long as you like. You can return to the embrace of the Star Goddess, the All That Is. Or you can return and turn back again, seeking to free others."

"Be a bodhisattva."

"Yes. Yet there is no time, and we shall all be free at the end of days."

"Then what is hell?"

He gestured out the doorway, to the pocket hell. "A trap. Either one made by yourself, or one that is made for you."

"Is Yaldabaoth the king of the material plane, then? Is it him who makes it so bad now?"

"What the All That Is does, we all do together. Even myself, trapped as I am. And Yaldabaoth is merely a principal player, not the king of the world. For all his pretense."

"What does Samyaza hope to gain by fighting him?"

"You would have to ask that angel himself."

"But will you ally with him?"

"Of course. He is my brother. Besides, if I understand him, I agree with him. But we should hear his thinking from his lips."

Chapter 36

<I need to talk. There's things I'd feel more comfortable saying in person> Gus texted Julia.

He left it vague—she might think he was breaking his heart over her, and that might make it more likely she'd come. He wasn't proud of the subterfuge, but he needed to talk to her, and in person was safer.

Back at the same coffee shop, he sat outside—less chance of anyone overhearing. Though he wasn't so afraid of that. Like most Seattle spots, the coffee shop didn't have air conditioning, and outside they might catch a breeze. He grabbed a black-painted wrought iron table. The maples along the sidewalk were in full green leaf, and he sat in the shade.

Half-done with his iced coffee, he was scrolling idly through his phone when Julia walked up. Hearing a click of heels on the pavement, he looked up to see her, in jeans and a retro halter top, blue and yellow stripes. Her long brunette hair was up in a high ponytail. She wore lipstick, a good sign—meeting him still invoked her vanity.

"Okay, so what's up?" she asked, swinging her purse down beside a chair and flopping into it. She'd never been so late before. She didn't want to be there.

He let the rude greeting pass.

"Last time we talked, you dropped the hint Odin's Hunt had figured out a way to spy on us. You probably saw in the news about the attack on Joanie and Cleo's wedding?"

Her eyes widened. "No, I didn't. Tell me!"

"Three men with guns, all in Odin's Hunt regalia. One shot at Joanie, though the bullet went wide. Her mom got shot in the leg, though I think she's going to be okay. Me and the ushers and guests were able to stop the worst of it. The police are investigating."

"Those stupid fuckers! I can't believe them!"

This was a better start than he'd expected. "Buy you a coffee?"

"I'll get my own. Give me a minute."

She went inside to order and returned with an iced coffee. She took her seat, this time with more patience.

"Obviously Odin's Hunt knew where the wedding was," Gus said. "My question is, how?"

She twisted her mouth, staring at the table. "That I don't know. But I bet I know how to find out."

"Don't do anything dangerous."

"I don't think this will be dangerous." She picked up her plastic cup and drew on her straw. "Linda hasn't been comfortable with a lot of stuff lately. Like most of the women's auxiliary, she's mostly there for ritual and fellowship—she's not interested in the politics. Or even, she's uncomfortable about them. I think if I nudge her a bit, she'll spill everything."

"Just please stay safe."

"I will." She stirred her straw in the ice. "I can hand off the information somehow, I guess in code?"

"I don't think that's wise."

"Gary's the kind of guy who doesn't appreciate me seeing my exes."

"I get that. But you can't get a lot of nuance across in code, unless we set up something complicated."

She stirred some more. The ice rattled. "I guess we can meet up once. But Gary's a good guy, and I don't want to make a practice of hiding things from him."

"I understand."

Chapter 37

The mortal present

The new moon fell a week later. The fairy dust ritual was set for the Saturday just after, starting in the early evening. This time it was five of them: Nora, Kirk, Joanie, Cleo, and Jonathan. Jonathan was new to the work, but he'd taken psychedelics before and had no concerns.

The sun hung at the horizon, western sky pale gold, light pouring through the yurt windows. Nora had placed a couple of fans; a boombox released a loop of trickling waterfall sounds to blot out their oscillations. A purple sleeping mat spread in the center, around it throw pillows, paisley and solid purple and black. Joanie and Cleo arrived early, sharing chilled lemongrass green tea, sprawled on yoga mats off to the side.

"What do you think?" Cleo asked. "Are you going to do a heroic dose?"

"I paid enough that we both could, if we wanted to. But I'm not sure."

She'd returned from the angel's space fuzzy and drowsy. It

had taken a day or so to recover; being there didn't refuel her as sleep would.

A golden ray stretched across the faux parquet floor. "Part of me wants to reach... whatever," she said. "Universal love. Enlightenment. Get past this ego and go. Another part of me wants to sneak up on it, bit by bit."

Cleo took a mouthful of tea. "That seems like the long way around. You'd spend more money. And you'd see more of Kirk."

"True. But if Nora's there, I have protection."

"But he slimes on you every time she steps away."

"Also true. I'll decide in the moment, or as close to it as I can. What about you?"

"I'm going to go for it, though who knows what I'll hit. Enlightenment, universal love, what have you. Wherever Sandy went, when we did it this spring. As for doing a repeat later, I don't care. I'm not a fan of Kirk, but he's way too smart to hit on me."

"My tough girl."

"You're the martial artist."

"Hardly." Gus had shown her some moves, and occasionally she sparred with a pickup group he was part of. She practiced, sometimes. She stayed in shape. But she'd fold before anyone serious—she knew that.

"Enough to surprise people."

"Enough to run away."

"But that's enough, isn't it?"

"It helps."

She picked up their shared glass, took a swallow.

In the earlier ritual, she'd floated to rest with the Star Goddess and gotten an injunction to remember. Remembering had brought her to her angel. It was what her deeper self had wanted her to know, but it had been a side road, not a full breakthrough.

Movement showed beyond the yurt windows. "Here they come," Cleo said.

Jonathan entered first. He wore loose clothing, as instructed, a splash of yellow and green tie-dye in a pajama-like set, his dreads tied up. He nodded to them both. Nora pushed the door open next, in hippie finery, a loose tiered natural-fiber-colored dress trimmed with embroidery in reds and blues. Kirk followed her, in jeans and a loose linen henley. All three left their shoes at the door.

Sitting down, Nora gave an expansive smile. "Good to have you here! I'm excited! Are you all comfortable?"

Cross-legged across the mat from Cleo and Joanie, Jonathan grunted a yes.

"I'm fine," Joanie said, and Cleo nodded.

"I might turn the fans down," Kirk said. "Don't want to blow the fairy dust around." He turned both down a notch. "Does that work?"

The group murmured agreement. With windows to either side, the high-ceilinged space breathed, despite the summer weather. It would cool off toward evening.

"Let's get started," Nora said.

They stood up for the circle. She led them in a grounding, connecting them to the green summer earth and starry space. Joanie and Cleo helped put up a witch circle, a small wooden table draped with a silk scarf as an altar. They called in elements —Cleo fire, Joanie air and water, Nora earth—and lit a candle for each.

"As goddess I'd like to call in Dea, our goddess of the land," Nora said. On the altar stood a small goddess figure in terracotta, a wand of foxglove laid before her. Nora closed her eyes.

"Now in the green summer, foxglove in full bloom, I call you, Dea, in summer garb, flowers in your hair. Smile on us today, help us navigate blocks and burdens. Help us go to the right place."

She lit a candle in glass for the goddess, bright yellow-green.

"Blessed be," she said, and the circle echoed her.

"Joanie, would you call the god of the land?"

She hadn't expected to, but she could rise to the occasion.

On the altar stood a small Cernunnos statue, horns held high. In her heart, though, the horned god of this land was Pete.

"Horned god of these woods, beloved one, come to us. Bring us the best energy to do the work before us. Bring us, as always, your love. Blessed be."

She lit his candle, and the others said, "Blessed be."

Energies flooded the space, the goddess a stream of green with gold sparkles, the god a stratum lower, red-brown like the fur of a deer. His embrace slipped around her.

Nora called the fey, and everyone settled themselves. Nora sat with Kirk across the mat from Joanie and Cleo, Jonathan beside Kirk toward its foot. Kirk handed Nora a glass vial. She raised it, poised in her palm, so everyone could see.

"This is a different synthesis of the dust, and I'm going to pass it around so you can greet it. Like before, be careful not to lose any, though it's not the end of the world if we lose a tiny bit."

Tapping the vial, she released a bit into a grey marble bowl and passed it across the mat to Joanie. This dust was pinkish-grey, scent woody as before.

Did it have a spirit, as datura did? A presence hovered, but it was hard to distinguish from the other spirits.

The bowl returned to Nora. Using a small funnel, Kirk returned its contents to the vial. He turned to ready his green glass pipe.

"Before we start," Nora said, "I'd like to talk about any barriers or concerns anyone has, coming into this work. We'll go around the circle and speak. I'll go first."

She stared at her hands a moment, then looked up.

"I'm worried for the world. I think we all are. I'm worried about climate change and the global rise of fascism. I'm also worried about my place in the world, keeping the farm together. It's been so important to have more help than we did."

She glanced around at her farm roommates. Before they moved in, she'd only had one part-time helper, who left when Jonathan arrived. Since then, Witch Farm had started selling raspberries in a few local markets and planted blueberry bushes. On the internet, Nora sold soothing balm and witch flying ointment based on her datura.

"But we're still hanging on by our fingernails. I think we can survive, and thrive, but I worry."

"I hear you," Joanie said.

"Let's run some energy of stars and earth and let this go," Nora said.

The circle turned expectantly toward Kirk.

He shook his head. "I don't think I'll partake this time. I've been doing some trips just with me and Nora, and I'm feeling pretty grounded right now."

Interesting. It looked as if Kirk didn't want to make himself vulnerable.

Jonathan went next. "I don't have a lot of specific blocks I can think of, but I'm a grounded person, and it takes a lot to move me to a psychedelic space. We'll see what happens."

In turn, Cleo said, "Last time, I came up against a lot of sorrow, both mine and my ancestors'. I wouldn't be surprised if that happened again. But if that's where I need to go, that's where I need to go."

Last came Joanie.

The real thing getting in her way was Kirk. How could she address that in a way that was kind?

"Though I've worked as a prostitute, and I believe being a sacred prostitute is my life calling, I'm a very private person."

She looked up, at Kirk. Dilute sunlight brought out the amber flecks in his eyes. "I guess this is my way of saying that I'd particularly like Cleo and Nora, who I have history with, to hold space for me during the trip."

"Of course," rumbled Jonathan, from the bottom of the mat.

"Sure thing," Kirk said. His face was studiedly neutral.

At least she'd said it. Maybe he'd heard it.

"Other than that, a few things. My mom's in the hospital, and I'm worried about her, so that might come up. Also, last time, I got I was supposed to remember something, which had to do with my spiritual life. I think I've done that work, but who knows? My main fear probably is getting sidetracked, not reaching the All That Is. But I also know anything that comes up will be useful."

"Of course," said Nora. "Anyone have anything they want to add?" The circle shook their heads. "Then let's get going."

"Who wants to go first?" Kirk asked, picking up the pipe.

Joanie found herself saying, "Me."

"Small, medium, or large?"

The image of Pete, her Horned God, rose for her. He'd always gone big.

"Large." She took in a full lungful, held it, then a little more, and dropped back onto the mat.

Up and up and up she went, alongside Dea and the Horned God, also Hekate, Inanna, and Ereshkigal. Rising, she came to a place of hovering gold light, threaded with shimmers and sparkles of silver and brighter gold.

"Look," whispered a voice. As if she was on the shore of an ocean, below her rolled the web of interactions of all beings on earth, humans, animals, plants, a field dense in many dimensions. "Here," said the voice, and one spot winked like a star. A flood of information cascaded over her, too much to hold: how she connected in this field, what her purpose was. Some spots floated almost separate, but she had connection upon connection, a nexus spot.

"You will remember," the voice said, echoing her last assay. "When there is need."

Letting go, she floated, suffused with love.

A voice again said, "Look," and among the net shone one strand, which threaded down and down and down, toward another nexus point. Some great being shining gold and silver joined her, who she didn't know, and they dove to follow the thread.

"Where are we going?" she whispered.

"You will see," said the voice.

Carried by the unknown spirit, she moved through the starry universe, as before, but the scale was different—now stars were tiny. She could hold one in the palm of her hand. The sky arched dotted with puffs of lit dust, nebulae further on, in the distance galaxies, spirals glimmering.

Two thrones shone from far away, a web between them like a rope-bridge. One was black incised with silver, encircled with low blue flames, to either side torches. A shadowy being sat there, erect, a chain around her neck with a silver key—Hekate.

The other was gold set with lapis lazuli, carnelian, and crystal that gleamed in the diffuse light. In front of it stood a bejeweled gold incense burner, whose smoke wafted into the airless void. A shining being half-reclined there, in a tiered dress and Mesopotamian crown—Inanna.

For a time, she floated between the thrones, basking in the goddesses' presence. These were her two main deities—Ereshkigal was more a lover than a goddess she worshipped. Love and vision, the finding of paths, the seeking of futures.

"But what do you have to tell me?" she whispered.

Holding out a long-fingered hand, Hekate released a ray of silver.

Against the ground of the night sky, in a flash appeared the arc of her best future. She would forget, she had to, but she saw the path entire.

In Inanna shrines, warm bedrooms draped with gauze and silk, lovers entwined. Each orgasm, a meteor, burst across the sky, leaving a trail of stars. Her work linked spirit to spirit, helped beings find their paths—connected Puabi-Ekur to Azazel, Pete to his apotheosis. She herself was a shining pathway.

The thrones pulled nearer each other, dark silver and shining gold. She bowed in obeisance before her goddesses. A wave of energy broke over her.

After a while, she sat up. Cleo handed her a water bottle, and she took some sips.

"That was lovely," she said.

Nora scanned her face, making sure her needs were met, then said, "Let's all take a fifteen-minute break."

Jonathan beat Joanie out of the yurt. The green rise of grass lay ringed with purple and white foxgloves, early daisies. Crossing, she picked a daisy and put it behind her ear. She let Jonathan take the bathroom off the kitchen and went upstairs.

Bits and pieces of her passage drifted in her thoughts, a wash of gold energy, the arc of her future. Some pieces were clear; much had fallen away. Knowing all the dangers ahead would only muddy things and maybe shift her path.

But her arc was key. Sacred whoring was truly her calling, not just an excuse for rebellion. She needed to start the Inanna shrines—she'd dragged her feet too long.

Through the end of twilight, she returned to the yurt, the farm spread before her. Love for it all washed over her, for the green earth, its deep comforting sense pouring over her, tactile.

The yurt interior now lay in shadow, and Nora turned on a standing light. She sat, and the others collected.

"Did you want to talk about your passage before we go on?" Nora asked Joanie.

She shook her head. Not yet.

Jonathan took his place and inhaled the fairy dust smoke.

Falling back, he lay quietly, frowning slightly and then smiling. He drooled a bit, and Nora wiped his face. His body was quiet. He felt deeply grounded, as he'd predicted. His passage felt earthy—she caught a scent of earth.

After a break, it was Cleo's turn. "I've been thinking about it," she said, "and for my session, I want Joanie and Nora to hold space. I often get naked, with psychedelics. It's like a purely bodily place, for me, like an infant."

She turned to stare at Kirk. "Can I do that without you sexualizing me?"

"What do you think, Kirk?" Nora asked.

He gave them an opaque look. "If it's easier, I can go outside. Just come get me when you're done."

"That works," Cleo said.

The door shut behind him, and she tugged her sundress over her head. Nora fed her the smoke. Under the influence, she tossed and turned, moaning. Joanie stayed close, held her hand, then curled around her in an embrace.

After the peak passed, Cleo stared into space a while. But she was smiling.

After another fifteen minutes, Kirk returned, and Nora took the smoke. She cried as if her heart would break, and Kirk spooned behind her, holding her.

Nora's breathing quieted. After a time, she sat up, wiping her face. Kirk settled back.

"Let's take another fifteen minute break," Nora said. Heaving herself up, she left the yurt and retreated to the house. Kirk sidled out to smoke a joint around the side of the yurt, and Jonathan followed.

Returning, they sat once more around the mat. Kirk put away

in a tote the smoking equipment, a carven box holding the fairy dust in a set of small bottles.

"We've completed the process," Nora said. "Now is a time for each of us to talk about the experience, if that's what we want. Sometimes feedback can help."

Jonathan cleared his throat. "I saw the farm," he said, "but the farm of the future. We will survive the current chaos and political bullshit and keep going. I saw that."

Jonathan did all right for himself, but Joanie knew he was concerned for his extended family. His uncle, a retired barber, lived on almost nothing. In his voice, she heard he'd found reassurance.

"That's lovely," Nora said. "Let's send golden and green energy of sun and earth to Jonathan." Drawing from earth and sky, the group sent energy.

At Nora's nod, Joanie went next.

"It seemed to go on for hours and hours. I saw Hekate and Inanna on their thrones. And then I was just taken by a wave of golden energy. I saw the arc of my future too. I don't know if it was *the* breakthrough, but it was *a* breakthrough."

Kirk gave her a toothy grin. "Bravo!"

Nora's gaze glazed over, holding back some emotion. Was she jealous of Joanie's breakthrough, or unhappy about Kirk cheering her? Surely it wasn't a competition. But humans could be rivalrous over anything.

With a glance at Nora, Cleo went next. "For me, it was the ocean, which I got last time. The sorrow of my ancestors was there, but it was moving and changing. Mostly I got that I'm on the right path, which is what I needed."

Joanie squeezed her hand and let it go.

A pause fell. It was Nora's turn.

"If you don't want to talk, you don't need to, any more than any of us," Joanie said. Nora as a high priestess wanted to set a good example, but that thinking could get in the way.

After a moment, Nora said, "Old stuff came up. I've been here before, and clearly I need to revisit it. Old pain, my family, the pain of the world, you know?"

She met Joanie's eyes. "We all seek the gods in other people, and we call that love, even it's just infatuation. But you have to find love, deep love, within yourself. And yet, we all need human companionship, and to be held and comforted and loved. It's a balancing act."

She was talking about Kirk. She was trying to be honest and do the work.

"I know what you mean," Joanie said.

Chapter 38

ᚾ

The mortal present

By the time they closed the circle, it was midnight. They collected their things and trailed out of the yurt one by one. Nora went directly up to bed. Kirk stayed, the last in the yurt, puttering, putting things away.

In the kitchen, Joanie stood with Cleo. Light from the track light over the sink cast shadows in the corners. Terracotta tiles lay cool underfoot. Cleo was making chamomile tea in a pot, for them to split, one of the things they did to go to sleep.

She leaned against the white-enameled gas stove as the kettle heated. They kept their voices low, knowing Jonathan and Nora had gone to bed. From Jonathan's room sounded muffled snores, but he slept lightly. Joanie herself was only half awake.

"Looking at my path, I got very clearly the sacred whore thing," she said. "I guess I've been in retreat from that for a while."

"Honey!" Cleo set her arms around her neck, delicate long

forearms balanced on her collarbones. She drew her in and kissed her. "It's scary! It's not something the culture supports."

"I guess I expect myself to buck all that."

"It wasn't a bad idea at all to finish your degree and do accounting work." Having the wedding so close to finishing her degree work had been insane, but Joanie had completed it. She hadn't walked at graduation—her milestone had been the wedding. "And keep your manager job at the coffee shop. Having a foot in the regular capitalist world is not a bad thing."

"But I need to do it for real now. I need to cut back my hours at the coffee shop. It's too much. If I keep the contract with the co-op and get a couple others, we should be able to stay afloat."

"Will Jeremy let you cut hours?"

"At this point, yes. I'm doing his accounting for free."

"Plus you are the most reliable and well-respected manager he has."

"Sadly, that's true."

Cleo hugged her tighter. "If you ever need to just quit, we'll make it work."

Joanie released herself to kiss Cleo's cheek. "We need both incomes, and I'm not there yet with accounting. I'd have to get some kind of entry-level job in accounting or finance. You know how that went last time."

"Lots of people need accountants, though." The kettle squealed, and Cleo poured hot water into the teapot.

"I've worked for Jeremy for years now. He can be a pain, but he does honestly share my core values. It's a good jumping-off point for the real work."

Cleo handed her a full cup. "So you're going to do the Inanna shrines."

"I got that pretty strongly."

Cleo kissed her again, lightly. "I'm going to bed."

"I'll be up soon. I just want to sit with all this a bit more."

Despite her exhaustion, Joanie wanted a moment to sit on the back porch and gaze at the night garden, to chill, sip tea, and start re-entering regular life. It was almost too easy to go back to the golden space. Part of her yearned for it. But if you went too far that way, you found madness.

Going out, she pulled up a chair, on the table nearby lit a couple citronella candles. Past their glow, a clear sky arched, full of summer stars. She picked out the Big Dipper. The Great Bear —of course a bear would be high in the sky now. Summertime the bears were deep in the woods, foraging. The Lady Dea too was a bear. She imagined her carrying the foxglove wand from the altar in her mouth.

Following the goddesses, she could live a life in alignment with the world. She might dip her foot into accounting or finance, but her real heart was in this liminal space, bordering the forest. Witch Farm was full home to her now.

A flashlight's beam skittered on the path between the yurt and the house, then steadied, traveling toward her. Wooden stairs creaking, Kirk came up the back porch stairs. "Mind if I join you?"

It wasn't outside Witch Farm's courtesies to ask for time alone. But old habit told her to keep Kirk sweet. "Sure, go ahead."

He took the next chair over, falling into it heavily. It had been a long day for everyone. He had to be tired.

"All cleaned up?" she asked.

She'd give him a few minutes of conversation, then go. Her re-entry process was begun, at least, and wouldn't finish this evening.

"Yup." He patted the wooden box he'd set down beside his chair.

"What are you thinking, about how the drug is working? Are you happy with it?"

"I am," he said. "I'm considering patenting it, which is one of the new angles people seem to be taking."

"It's still technically legal?"

"Technically. Of course, that can change at any minute, depending on politics and so on."

"Is it hard to synthesize?"

"Not particularly, if you have the background. Most of the people who make this kind of thing, of course, have been extralegal for a while."

She wasn't sure where he was going with that. "Sure."

"I mean, most of my competitors are probably not considering a patent. But I have some friends in the world of science. I think I could make it work."

"As what?"

"Most psychedelics work as antidepressant therapy. See things in a new light, and so on. Reconnect with your purpose."

"It did that for me."

"Exactly. By the way, do you mind if I smoke?" He meant a cigarette—lighting up weed was common on the back porch.

"No problem."

He lit and drew, tip cherry red against darkness.

"So you identify as a sacred whore, huh?"

"I do."

He leaned in, face lit by the candles' glow. "I believe I'm in need of connection to the goddess."

It was always the question, who you ministered to and who you sent away. When she'd whored for money, in a way it was easier. She'd turn away anyone who seemed dangerous. She mapped the dangers. She was used to that, although her mapping hadn't been perfect. Giving a blow job to a cop had gotten her two years probation and trapped her with a sugar daddy who tried to kill her.

That had taught her ignoring her intuition got her into trouble. She was feeling floaty and at one with the world, but Kirk was a raft of red flags.

Puabi-Ekur. Help me.

Azazel.

Puabi-Ekur swept in, a wisp of sparkling purple on the astral plane, invisible on the mundane one. Behind Puabi-Ekur hung a presence, a shadow with wings.

Just watch. Don't move in yet.

To Kirk, she said, "I haven't really restarted my hierodule work yet."

He smirked. "Is that a fancy name for it?"

He leaned close enough she could smell his breath and body scent—laden with tobacco, sweet because he smoked all-natural, but something under that. A tang of sweat, she didn't mind that, the yurt had been hot, but also something else.

"You could start it with me," he said.

"I don't think I'm ready."

He put his hand on her wrist, taking it between his fingers as if testing its strength, or taking her pulse.

"I'm interested now."

She drew her hand back toward her. He held onto it.

"Isn't it your sacred work?"

Did he think he was going to persuade her?

Standing up, she jerked her hand away. "I think I'll go up now."

He stood and stepped into her space. This close, he smelled of whiskey. He grabbed the back of her head and smashed his mouth against hers, forcing his tongue between her teeth. His other hand grabbed her breast.

She squirmed, got her hands up and pushed him away with a grunt. They stared at each other.

"Leave me alone, Kirk. I'm going upstairs."

He closed on her again, trying to block her.

She elbowed him aside and escaped.

～

Someone had left the front porch light on. Its glow spilled into Cleo's and Joanie's room. As Joanie came in, Cleo lay propped on her elbows.

"Come to bed, honey."

Joanie let herself fall seated on the bed. "Give me a moment."

The past half-hour had left slimy energy all over her. She wanted to take a shower, though not as much as she wanted to sleep. She pulled down starry light to cleanse herself, again and again.

The Kirk thing was always going to come to a head eventually. That time was now.

Was he holding off finding a place in hopes of seducing her? If that's how he thought about it. Men like him had different ideas about seduction than her friends.

The whole thing was nauseating. She'd dealt with it so many times, with Kirk and other men.

Jinx, the black kitten, leapt onto the bed. She let him climb into her lap, scratching between his shoulders. Jareth joined them, lying beside her leg. Cleo scooted over to Joanie, putting her arms around her from behind.

She was surrounded by love, but it didn't make her happy.

"What's wrong?"

"I was sitting on the porch, drinking tea, starting re-entry, when Kirk came out of the yurt. He'd been putting stuff away."

"And?"

"He wants to be first in line when I do sacred whore work. He told me that, then he grabbed me and kissed me."

Cleo growled under her breath. "Did he hurt you?"

"No. But it was pretty gross."

"That is so fucking wrong. Especially in coming-down head-space. He absolutely knows better. He's a predator—we need to get him out of here."

It was time. Joanie'd had her breakthrough. Though who knew how he'd act when he found she wanted to get rid of him.

"Let's talk to Nora, scope things out," Joanie said.

"Is Nora on our side? She's sleeping with him."

"You think she'd turn a blind eye to him creeping on me?"

A silence fell, broken only by Jinx's purring.

"She might," Cleo said. "People do. She hasn't had a boyfriend in a long time."

"But he's also—aren't they exclusive?"

"Who knows? I think we should talk to Jonathan, find out where he's at. Then call a house meeting."

First thing, a few days later, they sat over coffee at the dining room table, sun falling all around them, windows open to the sweet air of summer.

Jinx perched beside Joanie—both kittens considered her mom, though Cleo or Nora would do in a pinch. Jonathan, who came in with his own coffee in a double-sized brown pottery mug, was clearly a big cat, but nervous-making. Jinx glanced at him sideways from golden eyes.

"We wanted to talk about Kirk," Cleo said.

"I'm not surprised," Jonathan said. "It's time we get him out of here. I've offered him many opportunities to help with farm work —mulching, watering, cutting brush back around the house. I have a bunch of corn starts; it's the work of a day or less to clear out the land and plant them. Over a week was fine. He was too busy."

"Busy doing what?" Cleo asked. "All he does is lie around getting stoned."

"To be fair, he is apartment hunting," Joanie said, sipping coffee from her mug, tan with a blue interior, a product of one of their potter friends.

"He goes out a lot, saying he's apartment hunting," Cleo said. She blew on her coffee to cool it.

"How long has it been? Two months?" Jonathan asked. "I wouldn't care if he helped in the house. Cooked dinner. Ran errands. Paid rent. Anything." He went to the coffeemaker, refilled his cup, and sat back down. "He could give us a break on his drugs. He could stop bumming weed and buy sometimes."

"The other night, after the fairy dust ritual, I was on the back porch," Joanie said. "He came up and said if I was restarting my sacred whore work, he wanted to be my first customer. Then he grabbed me and tried to kiss me."

"He tries anything, I will fuck him up," Jonathan said.

"If he was just a guest," Joanie said, "we could just have him not come back. This is harder. But I don't want him in my house."

"I want him out of here," Cleo said. "He said it was for a few days at first. Now he's being a leech."

"Yeah," said Jonathan. "I didn't want to push. Nora's done me a ton of favors. I figured I was doing her one. But yeah."

"I've wanted him gone for a while," Joanie said. "It's just—I've wanted to be courteous and compassionate. It's not easy to find a place in Seattle. And I don't want to mess things up for Nora. But I can't deal with him anymore."

"It's time to talk to Nora," Jonathan said.

The phone call woke her from deep sleep.

Sitting up, she scrabbled for her cell on the bedside table. Dustin's number showed on the screen. "Hello?"

"Joanie?"

"Yes?"

"Your mother has passed."

"What?"

"Your mother's dead, Joanie."

It fell like a rock into a pond.

Could it really be true?

The hospital had sent Mom home a week before with blood thinners, compression stockings, and a sheaf of things to read. Dustin had agreed to stay over for a bit; Joanie had planned to trade off with him.

"I woke up beside her, and she was gone." Dustin's voice caught. This was a lot for him to say—ordinarily he'd never have told Joanie he and Crystal slept together. "They're sending an ambulance."

"I hate to ask, but are you sure she's dead?"

"She's cold, Joanie."

"I see."

"I'm so terribly sorry."

"I'm sorry for you! That can't be easy! I'll come right away."

"Please do. I'll let you know if the ambulance gets here before you." He signed off.

Cleo was awake now. "Do you need me to come with you?"

"You're so tired. You stay here." Just back from a site visit, Cleo had hardly slept the night before.

"You sure?"

"I don't see how you could help, really. I mean, if she's dead, she's dead. You should sleep." Joanie climbed out of bed. "I might check in with Hekate, make sure Mom has an easy passage."

Dressed, she spoke to the Lady, then drove. The middle of the night, the moon had set, the humid darkness thick black felt. Few cars were out.

At her mother's house, Dustin let her in and hugged her, standing in the foyer. He seemed as numb as she was. A tan man, tan hair, tan polo shirt above blue jeans, he had circles engraved under bloodshot blue eyes. It came to her he'd been crying.

He led her to the living room. Her mom's ficus tree cast shadows, leaves crossing beams from the floor lamp. They sat, awkwardly, her legs cold against the brocade on the couch.

"They took her to Harborview. The county wants to do an autopsy."

"An autopsy?"

"They need to determine cause of death, particularly with the gunshot wound. We can go in tomorrow if we want."

"Will they let me see her?"

"Generally you'd do that at the funeral home. They'll need you to sign the release, then once they're finished with the body, the funeral home picks it up."

"Really?"

"I can help take care of that. A friend from my congregation runs a funeral parlor."

She frowned. "I don't want it to be too expensive. And I don't want them to be weird with me." To someone else, she'd have said, "I don't want it to be too Christian"—though her mother would have been fine with that. But she wanted to say good-bye without the funeral home getting in the way.

"I don't think you need to worry. Gerald's a kind man, and his team has seen a lot. But you don't have to decide now."

"What she wanted is in her will, I think." She vaguely remembered discussing it with her mother. "Cremation, ashes scattered by the ocean."

She should have taken her to the ocean. They'd talked about it.

"I believe so. Cremation's pretty much the same across the board. You just need to choose an urn."

They looked at each other—full stop, 3 AM. Earlier, she'd felt Hekate's blessing, but now she felt nothing. A little cold. The room was air-conditioned.

"Let's go with your friend's funeral home."

"They won't make any arrangements without talking to you."

"Will you go with me to the hospital tomorrow morning?" Dustin seemed like the right companion, bland as he was. She loved Cleo, but Cleo was brash and loud. She needed quiet.

"I will."

At the hospital, the receptionist directed them to the morgue. At the nearest desk, they found a nurse, a tall man who looked Native American, judging by his skin tone and long dark hair in a ponytail.

"I'm ready to sign the release for my mother, Crystal MacEwan," Joanie said. "Do I need to identify the body?"

He checked his computer. "No need. We know who she is. Here's a photograph so you can check." He showed her his screen.

She glanced at it. "Thanks, but I'd like to see her."

Part of her insisted this couldn't be real. She needed to see the body for herself.

The nurse raised his eyebrows. "You can arrange a viewing at the funeral home."

"I need to see her sooner rather than later."

"Okay. You have the legal right. It's not in a viewing room at this point."

"I don't mind."

"Follow me, then." Dustin stayed behind.

The nurse gave her a surgical mask and gloves. They walked through the medical examiner's office, a space of tan file cabinets and desks. The morgue door was an ordinary metal one with a window in it. They pushed through into a huge refrigerated room, sheeted bodies on gurneys lining the walls. A body with rigor mortis was in a seated position on one, its legs up in the air, tented under the sheet.

The nurse moved among the gurneys, looked at a few tags, and found the right one. He motioned to her, and she went over.

"Ready?" She nodded. He folded down the sheet.

The odor hit her, and she stepped back. Even with refrigeration, her mother's body smelled of rotting meat: dense, earthy, sickly sweet.

The face lay calm and pale, eyes closed.

It was her.

Knowledge fell into Joanie's body, a solid weight. Her mother was dead.

She touched her arm through the sheet. It was hard, not yielding like flesh. Rigor had set in.

A pang rose, the beginning of anguish. She hugged herself and nodded. The nurse drew the sheet over her mother's face.

Driving away, she held back waves of sorrow and anger.

Never mind the thrombosis, or the pulmonary embolism that followed.

Odin's Hunt had killed her mother.

Chapter 39

The mortal present

Saturday morning, Gus woke early. He was done with school for now, though he was starting a summer class soon—American literature. He needed one more humanities credit. Alyssa had work and slipped out with a kiss.

A few moments later, he got a text from Julia. <I think I have the answer to that question. Coffee?>

<11 AM, usual place?>

<It's a plan>

Seattle had shaken off its mantle of rain. It was hot, especially in the sun. Gus found a table in the shade of the huge maple tree, shadows moving and shaking in a light breeze.

Julia had made it clear they would no longer be lovers. She'd found a boyfriend, a steady guy, and he had to be happy for her. Still he was looking forward to seeing her in her summer clothing.

She did not disappoint.

A deep V-neck tank top, dark floral colors, hugged her torso above a sheer skirt, tight around her hips, flowing to just below her knees. She wore strappy sandals, her painted toenails purple glitter.

Seeing her approach, though she was fifteen years his senior and planned never to take him to bed again, he was proud to be the man she was meeting. A smirk crossed his lips as she arrived.

"You like what you see?"

"I do."

"I'll go in and get a coffee."

"The special looks good." Julia appreciated a frappuccino, and the special was that, with peach syrup and sprinkles.

"I might try that. Back in a few."

He himself had iced black coffee. He'd been studying a lot, spring into summer, which meant he'd been more sedentary than he liked—no whipped cream for him.

She returned, the peach-flecked monster in a parfait glass. "It looks amazing," he said.

"Amazing good? Or amazing bad?"

"Try it and tell me what you think."

She drew a deep sip. "It's kind of special." She set it on the wrought-iron table. "You should try."

There was only one straw, but she didn't seem to care. He took a mouthful. It was pure sugar, the tiniest of peach taste. Somewhere deep in the mix was coffee.

"It is amazing. Not for the purist."

"Nope."

He let her enjoy her drink a while. The humid day was dense with scent. A whiff of diesel poured in from the street. Above that, her perfume flickered in and out, a floral scent, maybe honeysuckle.

She looked at him, head slightly to one side, assessing—for what, he didn't know.

"I had dinner with Linda. She wanted to get out of the house. They have her niece staying with them, and it's hard to find time for herself." She took a long sip. The straw sucked noisily at the bottom of the glass.

"Her husband is pretty close to leaving the Hunt." Her husband, Jake, was the gothi of the Hunt, the spiritual leader. "It's all just white supremacism now. There's a new guy running it."

"Who's that?"

"I'm not recalling his name. It'll come to me. Anyway, I got who the spy might be. There's a couple options. One's a friend of someone at your friends' farmhouse."

She meant Witch Farm. "Tell me more."

"There's not much to tell. It's a guy, friends of some of the Hunt dudes, but that's all I know. The other potential spy is some chick from the coffee shop where your girlfriend works."

That clicked into place. The coffee shop had catered the wedding. It might be one of the servers at the event. Though it could be almost anyone—the whole shop knew it was happening.

"Did Linda know her name?"

"No. She came to a few meetings, then stopped. And you didn't find out any of this from me." Julia had been harassed enough.

"Of course not."

"Ah, the new guy's name is Chico. I think he comes from the Caribbean somewhere, which makes it super weird that he's interested in Odin's Hunt."

"Yeah, I don't think the Vikings got that far south." He took a mouthful of his own coffee—he would need to finish it quick, the ice was nearly gone. Now it was a dilute and rather acid cup of cool coffee. "So do you mean he's Black?"

"Mixed-race, I think?"

"He wants to throw in with the white supremacists?"

"Like I say, it doesn't make sense to me."

"People do this. It's like sucking up to a bully or something."

He'd done it himself, in a way, though that had been about sex. "People are weird."

"For sure." She laid her head down on her arms on the folded table, a move that seemed oddly flirtatious. Chin on her hands, she looked up at him. "It was fun, hanging around with you. When I did."

He grinned. "I thought you had a boyfriend. You're monogamous. All that."

"Yeah, but let's—I don't know. Let's try and stay friends. Life is long, and who knows what's going to happen?"

Chapter 40

ᚺ

The mortal present

*B*efore they could talk to Nora, they had to wait. Cleo had two back-to-back overnight trips, and Joanie pulled double shifts to cover a co-worker's vacation. The shop had offered her bereavement time, but they were short-staffed and work kept her mind off sorrow. The moon waxed through the hazy, humid summer nights.

At the funeral home, the next step was choosing an urn. Dustin offered to go with Joanie. They picked a powder-blue one, with a spray of cherry flowers.

On the way back, she sat silently in the passenger seat.

Halfway to her mom's place, where she'd left her car, Dustin asked, "Do you mind if we have the memorial at the church? Your mom had friends in the congregation."

She swam up from the depths. Her life had gone underwater —everything dragged, pulled by the undercurrent of death.

"Sure, that's okay." Her mother would have liked it. "We should make sure Carrie-Anne and my cousins can be there."

Carrie-Anne was her mother's half-sister, who lived in Hawaii. When Joanie called, she wanted to attend the memorial but had a hard time getting to the mainland quickly. "We can wait," Joanie told her.

She picked up the full urn on her own. At home, she put it on the house main altar, in the small ancestor section.

With Cleo, she went to her mother's lawyer for the reading of the will, to a corner office in an Eastside tower, windows ten feet tall. In the conference room, sitting at a walnut-stained table, she read it page by page. She knew it would be simple, and it was. She was her mother's only child, and her uncle was dead, luckily—she never again had to face the man who'd abused her through childhood. Joanie had inherited everything there was, except for a handful of jewelry and heirlooms for Carrie-Anne and Joanie's cousins.

She'd inherited a house, though not one she liked or had attachment to. Apparently she'd also inherited several hundred thousand dollars.

Cleo drove her home. Again she sat in silence.

It was so weird, getting money and that lifeless house in exchange for her mother.

If only they'd had a little longer. Mom had just decided to accept Cleo.

If only they'd gone to the ocean.

"Honey, it's okay to cry," Cleo said.

She grabbed the tissues out of the glove compartment.

After a double shift, Joanie got back late from work. They stayed open till ten on weekends now, and after a half-hour to close and her drive home, she got back after eleven.

After a shower to get off the food and coffee smell, she settled with a glass of wine on the back porch, guarded by a citronella candle.

Movement in the kitchen—a shadow traveled across the room, and the door to the porch opened: Kirk.

A weight fell into the pit of her stomach. Her body went into high alert.

"Mind if I join you?" He sat in the chair next to hers, between her and the door.

"I was just going in." She tossed off the last of her glass of wine and stood.

He stood up, as if to let her pass by him, but instead stood in her way. The only way she could get around him to go inside was to jump off the porch into a rosemary bush.

"So are you for real about this sacred whore stuff?" he asked.

Could he be more of a narcissist? Her mother had just died.

"I am," she said. "But I get to pick and choose. No priestess takes all comers. I'm choosing not to now."

He closed the space between them. His scent was as usual, weed and tobacco, but overlaid with a heavy hit of alcohol.

"For me, now is good."

"Not for me."

Again she called her allies. *Puabi-Ekur. Azazel.*

A whirring of feathers, a wisp of purple—her angel and incubus arrived.

Just watch for now.

Again Kirk took her wrist, drawing her toward him. "When will it be good? I just find you so attractive."

He'd been drinking again. Was it whiskey?

In her moment of distraction, he kissed her neck. He nibbled at it.

Anger shot through her. "Don't!"

She shoved her arms outward to push him off. But he stayed in place, leaned in close again, grabbing her wrist to anchor her.

"It's your sacred work, you said."

Gritting her teeth, she took a step back. She relaxed her wrist, turned it, and pulled it out of his hand. A move she'd learned long ago.

"Let me past." She tamped down her fury.

"But honey, you're a whore. I'll drop you some money. Don't worry about that." He lurched toward her again.

Rage rose like the lava spit of a volcano, flashing upward. She held it in, hard.

He put his arms around her. She struggled. His grip held. One hand landed on her ass and squeezed. His fingers inched between her buttocks.

She dropped, falling out of his hold, and nudged his knees with her shoulder, hard. He toppled off the porch into the bushes.

Scrambling up, she ran upstairs, taking the steps two at a time. She shut her door behind her and locked it.

Feathers brushed her cheek. An unseen hug enveloped her.

She let go the adrenaline, and rage swallowed her.

She should go downstairs and beat him up.

But violence was a last resort. It might not feel like it, but she'd won that encounter.

A wave of disgust broke over her.

The same feeling, over and over again, all her life—you'd been a person but you became a thing. This time, she'd lashed out. Old voices said she would pay.

Frozen into tension, she curled into a fetal ball. Resonances rose, discordant and clanging.

She could go very far away if she wanted.

But she was a grown-up now. She could stand up to him and make it stick.

She had allies, on the spiritual plane, on the mundane plane.

She could do this.

The next day, she sat in the bright June morning kitchen. She had a closing shift, and should be working on accounting tasks, but she was taking her time over coffee.

"Hi, Joanie," Nora said. "Can we talk a moment?"

Sticky emotion washed over her, like glue. She was being called on the carpet. "Sure."

Nora sat down across from her, blowing the steam off the coffee in her cup. She took a sip.

"Kirk says you two were talking last night, and for some reason you went ballistic. I'm not interested in people using violence to solve their problems."

Joanie had to swallow her first answer, which was a child's— he started it.

But he did start it.

"Let me tell you what happened. I was there, on the porch, minding my own business. He came and sat by me. He smelled like whiskey. He asked me about being a sacred whore, and I told him, not for the first time, that I haven't started again. I stood up, and he grabbed me and started kissing and groping me. I needed to get out of there, so I did." She met Nora's eyes. "I spent my childhood getting raped, with my mother ignoring it, okay? You knew that, right? Now I can protect myself, and I will. Maybe Kirk shouldn't do that shit."

Nora and Joanie stared at each other.

Maybe Nora would support Kirk.

Then her gaze changed subtly. In it, Joanie read this wasn't the first time this had happened.

"I should have known. He can be like that when he's drinking."

"Did he honestly complain I pushed him?"

"He had bruises on him, so I asked."

Joanie held onto her cup hard, with both hands—otherwise Nora would see they were shaking.

"Jonathan, Cleo, and I were going to talk to you. I think we should have a house meeting. Kirk really needs to step up apartment hunting. I know Seattle's a hard market, but he needs to get out. In the meantime, he needs to back off."

Nora had been alone a long time. Joanie hated to prevent her living with her partner. But Kirk had to go.

"I'll talk to him," Nora said.

"I think he should get out immediately," Cleo said. "Though he should apologize to you first."

They were in their bedroom that evening, fan on. Back from her trip, Cleo perched on the bed with her suitcase half-emptied next to her. A lime-green scarf, a typical Cleo color, hung half off the bed, pooling on the floor. Cleo had gotten the whole story.

Joanie had never considered getting an apology.

Probably that reaction was a childhood thing. She'd had her share of counseling. Her neutral position was she had to be perfect and no one was going to listen. And she had to disappear as soon as she could.

But her home was at stake, and now she was an adult and a witch.

Still, part of her was sure she'd never win this game.

"We should sort things, I guess."

"Honey, you're one of the least violent people I know. If you pushed him off the porch, congratulations! It's about time some of that rage came out. You're absolutely not the person to start a fight unless backed into a corner."

"That's true."

"I'm really proud of you! I know it's not always the easiest thing to stand up for yourself."

"People don't listen to me."

"But they do. Or they can. You can be really persuasive. And I'm on your side. You know that."

A week later, on the rare Sunday afternoon they were all there, they collected for the house meeting. Nora had asked Kirk expressly not to be in the house for it.

They met in the small, library-like living room, its dark-varnished shelves full of old leather-bound books. It was too hot to sit on the porch, and the living room had a small portable air conditioning unit to help preserve the books, some of which were valuable antiques. Jonathan took a striped upholstered chair, a balancing act—it was much smaller than he was and looked as if it would break under him.

"You could sit on the couch," Joanie said. She'd taken a corner of it, strictly for comfort, her arms wrapped around herself. Three against one, they'd succeed in pushing Kirk out. But the little kid in her was scared.

Jonathan shrugged. He hunched forward a little, focused on his hands a moment, then looked up.

"You know, Nora wanted Kirk at the meeting. She wanted him to be able to speak in his own defense. Cleo and I vetoed that. This is house business, and he's not part of the household. A lot of my problem with him is that he doesn't act like part of the household, though he seems to want to stay indefinitely."

"I assumed he was at least helping with the gardens." She herself didn't do much of that—until recently, she'd been working two jobs and going to school. Doing accounting for Nora's businesses was her contribution.

"Nope. Though I guess he knows about this meeting and he's not happy. He thinks I'm on his side. I'm not."

"In a perfect world, there wouldn't be sides." But it was too late for that.

Cleo sailed in on a wave of sandalwood and took her seat on the green velvet couch next to Joanie. She rubbed Joanie's shoulder, giving Jonathan a sunny smile.

Nora entered, face drawn and tired. She'd fought with Kirk earlier in the day—it would have been hard not to hear it. She settled into a wingback chair facing the couch. "All right, let's get this started."

Jonathan and Cleo traded a glance.

"I'll just speak my mind then," Cleo said. "I know Kirk has a different point of view, but I've never known Joanie to raise a hand in anger when I was there. Ever. If she pushed Kirk, she must have felt menaced."

"I think we're all on the same page about Kirk's and Joanie's altercation," Nora said. "Let's back up a little."

Generally their house meetings were loose affairs unburdened by rules of engagement. Nora had to be feeling ruffled, not to let the conversation go where it would.

"What do we want out of this meeting?" she asked.

Cleo checked the others' faces, then dove in again. "I want Kirk out of the house. I want a timeline for that. I want the timeline to be short."

Nora's gaze went to Joanie.

She shrugged one shoulder. "Same with me."

Jonathan was once again staring at his hands. "Jonathan?"

"I'd say the same," he said, looking up. "He's not pulling his weight. He's done no yard work since he got here. He didn't cut us any deal on his drugs, while he bums my weed all the time."

Nora looked shaken. Maybe Kirk had convinced her Jonathan was on his side.

"Is that so?"

"What, you think I'm lying?"

"No. I'm just surprised. Kirk never announced he was doing yard work, but he let me think he was."

"That's how he is, isn't he?" Cleo said.

Joanie watched Nora's face.

Nora had known Kirk a long time. Joanie had known guys like him too—beautiful lightweight boys who eroded the social contract but with charm. At some point, the charm eroded as well. Kirk had pulled every string to make them do what he wanted, till there were no strings left.

"All right, I hear everyone. How about a month? That takes us to the start of August."

"That long?" Jonathan asked. "Joanie, what do you think?"

"I just don't see how he can find anything sooner," Nora put in.

"He can sleep somewhere else, can't he?" Jonathan said.

"I can get him to stay somewhere else as often as possible. I can't see him moving out entirely till the end of the month." The Seattle rental market was far from flexible. Kirk had friends in town to stay with, but he'd been gone too long to have many.

"Joanie? Does that work?" Jonathan asked.

"I guess it will have to."

It had seemed fair while she was sitting on the green velvet couch. But before she got to the top of the stairs, a month seemed like too much time.

She let herself drop onto the bed. "How can I be around him for a whole month?"

Jinx leaped up on the bed and sniffed her face, then curled up next to her. His brother leaped up and settled next to him.

Cleo trudged up the stairs after her, stood in the doorway

watching her sprawled on the bed. "We could go back and ask for less time."

"That hardly seems fair." The constraints were real. "He'll mostly be elsewhere."

"He's already had two months." Cleo smirked. "Hannah would put him up."

"Let's not go there." Outdoors, a robin called from a nearby fir tree, warbling as if its throat would burst. Maybe there was a predator nearby.

"I guess we've got him for a month."

"Maybe Jonathan can talk him into going sooner."

Kelsey returned to the coffee shop one sunny afternoon to say hello—ligaments badly torn, she couldn't stand on her feet long enough to take a shift. Joanie hugged her carefully, fed her a vanilla latte and an apple danish, and put her in the back booth, the one the employees used if the shop wasn't crowded. Baristas stopped by to say hi, and on her break Joanie dropped into the seat across from her.

"How are you?" she asked. "I mean, I feel like I owe you one. You nearly took a bullet for me!"

Kelsey blushed, dark pink below her freckles. "I was in the wrong place at the wrong time, is all."

"I'm so glad it wasn't worse!" If only her mom had gotten off that lightly.

Kelsey sipped her latte, getting foam on her top lip. She licked it off. "After I got home from the ER, I had the weirdest dreams. I saw Aphrodite, like we called at the wedding, but also —do you work with Inanna? The Sumerian goddess?'

Hiding her surprise, Joanie said, "I do."

"She came to me and said I should worship her, with you."

"Hmm." They stared at each other. "I am starting a set of shrines to Inanna over the next bit."

She looked around the sunny shop, full of customers. This wasn't the time or place for details. "I'll text you, and we can talk."

Besides Kelsey, Hannah had signed up, and Cleo, though neither could make every shrine. Nora was a tentative yes, Sandy and Mike and Hannah's witch students each a maybe, waiting to see how the shrines played out. Gus declined—he didn't have the time. He was focused on starting EMT work. Alyssa also declined. To her, whoring was tainted by her early years on the street, under the thumb of a pimp.

Chapter 41

After they made love and Puabi-Ekur went to sleep, Azazel remained wakeful, restless, a couple of times wakening them. They weren't sure if he ever fully slept.

It was going to take a long time for him to heal.

The third or fourth time she opened her eyes, she let herself come fully to consciousness in her form as Puabi. A few candles glimmered in the gilt candelabra, burnt low but giving enough light to see across the pavilion. He stood in the doorway, a cup of wine in his hand. It was full night, stars glittering above the palm trees.

"You can escape now," Puabi said, lounging in the black sheets. "The huldufólk made you a bridge."

"I am aware." He turned to look at her, took a sip from his silver cup.

"You seem better. Did something happen?"

"Of a sort." Coming to the bed, he set aside the cup and lay down next to her. She took his head in her lap, stroking his long hair.

They stayed like that a while. He had beautiful hair, waving, a dark brunette but in the light with a reddish burnish.

"You were saying?"

He sat up, tucking his hair behind his ears, looking very human. "Mine is a pocket universe, created when I was thrown into exile. Yet it retains, or I retain, some of the original spark. I can create my own pockets outside time. I do it rarely, because it takes considerable energy."

He paused, gazing through the half-open tent door at the fiery stars. Picking up his wine-cup, he took a mouthful.

"Yes, and?"

"I sat a long time in such a one, in contemplation. An eon, considering my deeds and misdeeds, seeking how to change, how to let go my hubris."

"An eon?"

"A timeless time. I cannot say how long. I believe I have at least begun to release that which I need to."

She stroked his hair, his back, feeling his thoughts far away.

He did seem better. There was an ease, a grace, a letting go.

"Well, that's cool."

He laughed and kissed her.

In Sam's garden, she was again Puabi. Bees buzzed in a golden haze, and fey servitors brought fizzy concoctions and multicolored wines—bubbling apricot, astringent pale green, deep blood color. That one tasted of smoke. A pale girl dressed in luna moth colors proffered glossy blackberries and cherries piled on a plate. Tiny savory pies with perfect golden-brown crusts broke to pesto or bits of chicken.

"These are delicious," Puabi said, sitting up from her couch to take another.

"Quite." Azazel had one in each hand.

"So we're agreed," Sam said. "It's not time yet for a formal war council. It's a time for discreet conversations, testing the waters."

The peace of his long contemplation had softened Azazel's features. It made the brothers more similar in looks, despite the threads of green and purple in Sam's hair.

"Yes, and we cannot take too long at it," Azazel said. "Our conversations need be far-ranging, which opens us to espionage."

"But we must have our alliances and plan solid before we move," Samyaza said. The Demiurge was overpowered even compared to millennia-old gods; it would take a well-coordinated coalition to fight him.

"What's really our desire here?" Puabi asked. The brothers tended to speak in shorthand. "Do we want to conquer the Demiurge and imprison him as he did the fallen angels? Or what?"

"I believe we can take the Demiurge down," Samyaza said. "Or at least negotiate more favorable terms with him and the Council of Archons. I would take an equable truce. But I am tired of these tiny, pointless battles with the white wings, and of being subjugated by this bully. And yet we must act carefully."

"To be more clear, it is a war for freedom," Azazel said. "Ours, and that of all the so-called lesser spirits."

"Sure," Puabi said. "I didn't know." The brothers stared at her. "I haven't been a Watcher angel for millennia. I'm an incubus-succubus who used to be a human. I'm small fry."

"No one is small in this conflict, Puabi-Ekur," Azazel said. To his brother, he said, "These first conversations are needful. But we should be ready to move soon."

Iceland was the easiest place for Azazel to emerge, the huldufólk's home and a land where every volcano could be a gateway. Puabi-Ekur went with him as spirit.

It was interesting to see him enthusiastic. All the time they'd known him, he'd been trapped. He was freer now. Maybe soon he'd be entirely free.

They themselves had been free, a wanderer, going here and there on earth as an incubus-succubus, seducing and trading energies. They'd stayed an observer. Distancing themselves had been their self-protection for centuries.

But now there was Joanie. There was Azazel.

Iceland's active volcano lay on the southern coast. In a gap on the mountain's flank, red blood of the earth pooled. On it floated a black skin of new rock. The two of them set down there to meet Alfstein.

"Have there been earthquakes?" Azazel asked him.

"There have," Alfstein said.

"Nothing large. We will need more. And more eruptions."

Alfstein raised an eyebrow. "How do earthquakes and volcanoes affect Yaldabaoth?"

"He considers Earth his creation, although we all know better. Human prayer feeds him. If the people cry out, he will pay attention. Ideally we would frighten but not harm humans."

Alfstein shrugged. "We will not go out of our way to hurt them. But they should have a care."

"Are there others who might be open to this kind of conversation? Would you be willing to speak to them?"

"I can do that," Alfstein said.

Azazel and Puabi-Ekur flew away, along a rocky beach where lava boiled the ocean.

Ringing the globe, they spoke to pantheons of gods that had formerly ruled, many barely displaced. Shinto, Mayan, and Hawaiian deities still were worshipped in unbroken lines from the deep past. Greek, Roman, and Celtic divinities also had followers with sincere worship. Northern gods did as well, despite dallying with groups like Odin's Hunt, which put some in the imperialist Demiurge's camp. But the huldufólk had diplomatic relations with Northern deities who took interest in freedom.

Other spirits would not join or even converse. Anger had driven some to numbness. Some had gone so far to sleep that only the explosion of the planet would wake them.

On a mountainside north of Greece, Azazel called out a name Puabi-Ekur didn't recognize. "Ouros of this place! We met long ago, when the world was young."

In silence, in dense sun, the air hung unmoving, smelling of pine needles and dust.

Tiny pebbles skittered down the slope. Then bigger rocks tumbled, the size of a head, boulders as large as a wrecking ball, larger, bouncing a man's height, crushing size.

"I guess that's a no," Puabi-Ekur said.

Out the doorway of the angel's pavilion, above a line of scarlet sunset, the evening star hung. Palm leaves whispered, and a fall of dust went across the threshold. The realm had its own energy. Perhaps the dust was saying something.

Azazel paid no attention. He hunkered in a winged overstuffed chair, black with gold frame and embroidery, a cup of wine held in both hands. Puabi-Ekur, as Puabi, lay on the bed.

"Spirits and gods we have in abundance," he said. Besides these new allies of the earth—spirits of rock and land and plant and ocean—Samyaza and the other fallen angels had their own armies. "But never underestimate those who pander to the Demiurge."

"I don't. Should we approach the djinn, do you think?"

"I doubt it."

"I'd love to court the ones who might be on our side. But too many are already our enemies. They have a huge web of alliances—I don't claim to understand it. I'd be afraid to pull one string and get the whole tangle."

"Yes, we have enemies there. Joanie's enemies—Max, for example, and Mark. I have some thoughts about this Kirk who is bothering her, also."

He sipped his wine.

"I like seeing you enthusiastic," she said.

"Freedom seems closer than it has for millennia."

"You're very convincing when you talk about it, angel-boy. But I think there are some places I'd be a better diplomat."

"I would not debate that. You have made fast friends with Berkana."

"She has been talking to other tree and plant spirits."

"If you think we might work better now separately, you have my support."

In the Carpathian Mountains, spruce and silver fir went on for miles, untouched by humans since the forest began. Spirits here remembered the old agreements, before the Demiurge claimed a kingship that was not his.

Berkana and Puabi-Ekur landed in a dark circle of evergreen, beech trees guarding its edge. Night, a high half-moon in dense black that sparkled with stars, cold breeze whispering in the trees—up here nights were always chilly.

They collected, spirits of spruce, fir, beech, and larch—larch the pioneer, who went up to the ice. Rowan appeared, also lime, hornbeam, alder, and mighty oak with each leaf like a stubby hand. The meadow and the space above the meadow filled to bursting. Many of these visiting were emissaries—some woodland folks would never travel from their homes.

Berkana stood at the center of the circle. Tall, slender, hair the strawberry blonde of a birch leaf in autumn drifting down her back, she wore a shift of ombre fading yellow to summer green. Puabi-Ekur hovered, a dusting of shimmering purple like a scarf around her shoulders.

"You know our concern," Berkana said.

Murmurs grew like a wind in the endless forest. They rose, crescendoed, fell.

"Will you stand with us?"

A larger wind swelled, twigs and needles spinning away. Waves again and again lifted to a peak.

"Do you have connections south and east?"

A young larch-spirit stood forward, hair feathery and yellow like larch needles about to fall. "East and north I can go."

A beech spirit said, "I can go south to the lands bordering the sea."

"I can accompany you that far," Berkana said. Birch went south to the Mediterranean, into the Middle East. "We will need others to take the quest farther."

"We can make a connection at the edge of our range," the beech said.

"So be it." Berkana turned to the larch. "Larch-ones, can you go on your own? I can follow later." Birch ranged nearly as far as larch northward. Both had a foothold in the Americas.

Along the Mediterranean, above a margin of sand beach, stood hills full of pines. In high crags and fastnesses inhospitable to humans, dryads and earth-spirits gathered: pine and fir, poplars, plane trees, oaks, cypresses tall and rounded.

"We will work with you," a tall pine said. "We will talk to the rock-beings."

"Some ourea have turned emissaries away."

"Yet some await our word, and will aid you."

$$\backsim$$

"I would say easily two-thirds of the folk we talked to were willing to support a move against the Demiurge," Azazel said, as they reconnoitered in Samyaza's garden, in the familiar rosy haze.

"Even now, even still," Samyaza mused.

"It is time," Azazel said. "We have seen the changes to the earth. You have reunited nearly all the Watchers. We have made allies."

"What say you, Puabi?"

Something in Samyaza's tone made her want to be General Ekur. They needed to remember she'd led armies. Hanging back had been her way as a traveling spirit, but it was not right action now.

"We coordinate our efforts, and we move, I'd say. Coordination is the hard part. The time of spirits and angels, the time of spirits of earth, and the time of humans are all different."

"You would include humans?" Samyaza asked.

"At least witches and sorcerers, and leaders in Indigenous religions. Many spirit-workers still follow older ways."

"You're right," said Samyaza, sounding weary. "But how?"

Puabi tilted her head back and looked down her not-very-long nose at him.

"The same way."

"Although humans perceive time differently than we do, and it must be timed according to their senses, still I think we can do this," Azazel said. "What we need is a dream."

A minor goddess, Somnia spent much of her time sleeping. Her lair was a series of Roman loggia, crossed with a garden like a nymph's. When Puabi-Ekur and Azazel arrived, her attendants would not wake her—it would be bad luck.

In a room open to a courtyard, she lay all in lavender, under a dark-blue coverlet that might be wool and might be sky stuff, glittering with silver-gilt or stars. She looked Italian, olive-skinned, long waving brunette hair tousled on her pillow.

They waited in another loggia, at a table of grey marble, sitting on a bench set into the wall. Rows of whitewashed arches topped by terracotta tiles formed a courtyard, in a twilight wispy at the edges like cloud. The whole space felt dreamlike, as if you could walk through its skin and be in an entirely different place. A dream, embodied pale and ghostly, with face half a skull and eyes of roses, offered them pink fizzy drinks in martini glasses on a tray. Out of courtesy, they took them, and the dream drifted away.

"Should I drink this?" Puabi-Ekur asked, looking at theirs dubiously.

"If you like. If it is poisoned, it is unlikely to harm you, or at least not permanently. It might make you woozy. It would be a dream-poison."

"You're not very reassuring."

Azazel drank his off. "It is delicious. It is only mildly poisoned."

Puabi-Ekur sipped theirs, embodying a bit more to do so, as Puabi. The beverage tasted of faux strawberry, but good. "I thought somnia was a plural word meaning dreams."

"It is, and she is their embodiment."

"It's not like the Greeks and Romans didn't have a half-dozen sleep and dream gods."

"Quite, but some are public-facing and well-known. For our task, we want someone more hidden. Not immediately under suspicion, able to complete the task."

"I see."

Eventually, the dream-attendants called them to the goddess's side. Even awake, Somnia lay propped among pillows. Her outsized canopy bed had filmy curtains, like the coverlet dark-blue and dotted with starry sequins, or possibly tiny stars. Puabi reached out to touch one. It sizzled against her fingertips.

The goddess's attendants brought dream-food—small bites that disappeared immediately as you tasted them, leaving an impression of nothing in your mouth. The drinks were more substantial.

"My lady, we are here on a mission," Puabi said.

"I understood that," Somnia said, yawning.

"You know Yaldabaoth, the Demiurge, with his legions of white-winged angels?"

"Of course. We all know him. Generally I try to ignore him." A flicker of feathers at her back was there and gone again. "I have wings myself."

"Ignoring him is a legitimate tactic," Azazel said. A rolling baritone, his voice still gave Puabi shivers. "We are thinking of taking a stand. To push for our freedom, all we smaller gods and spirits, even humans."

"Oh, are you?" The goddess sat up. "Count me in." She leaned forward over her coverlet. "What would you have me do?"

"Is it possible to broadcast a dream to every human in the world?"

"I believe so. I've never tried." She waved to her attendants. "If I must think, I shall require real food." The nearest two, barely substantial wisps of ghost, looked at one another, confused.

"Roast chicken," Puabi suggested.

Over plates of roast chicken, with glasses of white wine, they talked.

"I can do this," Somnia said. "It would help if the other dream deities amplified the signal. Or at least did not get in my way."

"We avoided the other deities."

"Why so?"

"With some, it is hard to say where their loyalties lie," Azazel said. "Some have a very public face, in a way that might be dangerous. But we have other gods and demons and many dryads and satyrs and volcano and earth folk."

"Not much help with dreams. However, I believe I can make this work. Give me the word when you are ready."

"We shall."

"But first—defeating the Demiurge is in everyone's best interest, of course, but what you ask is a significant expenditure of energy. I will want a trade." She glanced at Azazel under her lashes.

Puabi and Azazel exchanged a look. Azazel's eyelids fluttered.

Puabi-Ekur switched form to male, modeling themself as close to the angel as possible without being rude—sculpted body, long hair with a blue-black sheen. "May I be of service?"

Somnia gave a peal of laughter.

"You're an incubus! You will do quite well."

As Puabi, she lolled on the bed, considering sleep after a long bath. Somnia had provided a workout, and then rapid-fire they'd had one meeting after another.

"I'm not a natural diplomat," she said. "Sometimes I just want to kick them and say, make a decision!" Azazel drank wine in his wing-backed chair.

"Joanie is a natural diplomat. Perhaps we should ask her for help," he said.

"Perhaps so. We can use all the help we can get."

"Though it could be dangerous for her. We wouldn't want that."

"No."

Outside, the palms moved in a light wind. Azazel stared into his wine-cup. Puabi idly watched the weather through the open doorway.

The wind grew stronger. Leaves jostled and twirled. With a

whistle, then a howl, the wind whipped at the leaves. They flew out like flags.

"Azazel—"

A bang sounded like a gunshot.

Azazel leaped to standing, grabbing his sword. His black wings unfurled. Puabi moved behind him, drawing her loose robe around her, poised to change form.

"Azazel," came a voice. "Are you at home?"

Only a few could have come through the vast protections of that realm.

In the tent's curtain doorway, all in gleaming golden armor, stood an angel, a golden sword by his side. He was gorgeously beautiful—big blue eyes, shining golden curls, heavily muscled, well-proportioned. His skin had a glittering hint of gold.

It was Mitzrael, who'd shown Puabi how to find Azazel because she loved him.

"What are you doing here?" Azazel asked.

"I cannot stay long, or I will be traced. Your plot is known. Make ready."

"How can I believe you?"

"I have no way to convince you in the time I have. But it is my nature to be truthful."

The two angels stared at each other.

Mitzrael took a step backward, out of the doorway. With a rushing sound, all the palms bent toward a blue-black hole in the sky, and he was gone.

Puabi slipped forward to Azazel's side.

"Some white-wings must be extremely discontent to merit this visit," he said.

"I guess we're in a hurry now," Puabi said.

"I do not ordinarily do this, but I am going to fold time to round up our last allies. I cannot bring you with me."

"What do you want me to do?"

"Before I do that, let us go to Somnia first. Then I will call you to the battlefield, as we have fought before." She'd fight as General Ekur. "It will seem barely the passage of a moment. Make ready."

~

"Would you like to sleep and get the dream?" Somnia asked. "It will roll out across humanity over the next few weeks. It will take a while to reach some of them, and some may ignore it or forget it."

"I must be away," Azazel said. "Much to do. I thank you." He shot a glance at Puabi-Ekur, asking them to do the honors.

"Sure, why not?"

Servitors led Puabi-Ekur through a loggia, to a canopy bed with filmy black curtains, a wooly black coverlet, and black sheets with a sheen of purple. In a blink of an eye, they were Puabi, enfolded in a nightgown. They lay down among feather pillows and shut their eyes.

A single, impossibly tall white pillar curved to a flat top, where lay a wide-open foyer, a vault of blue sky on three sides. On the fourth side loomed a marble throne two stories tall, decorated in gold with rays that flared behind it. On its seat, a solid white light burned like a star, too bright to look at.

In this space milled white-winged angels, conversing or walking past on errands. One flew in, settling like a bird and folding his wings. To one side, an angelic choir stood, mouths open in song, a harpist accompanying them.

The view of the dream panned downward, down along the pillar to a rocky swath of earth, and below. It led through complex dungeons with black adamantine walls. Iron rods barred cave mouths.

There beings languished, in chains. Some were recognizably angels, with black wings, brown, or white. Some were human, or humanoid. One was a giant lizard. One was a swarm of bees in a golden net. One was a flaming ball of eyes. Some lay as if made of stone; some writhed in their fetters; some shouted or called or sang. Some screamed.

"There is no reason for me to be here!" one angel shrieked. "I have done nothing!"

Farther on were beings in torment: beaten, burned in fire or lava, mauled by black-furred wolves, boiled alive.

"I don't know what I did! At least tell me what I did!"

"I'm just here because I got in your way!"

"I'll do anything you want!"

White-winged angels led the torture, faces impassive.

A mist passed, and scenes of the earth flew by. In deep-dug mines, machines ripped hillsides' flanks; rivers ran slick with oil; trees fell by the thousands. A scene appeared in the mountains, with a look of the Carpathian forest. A rim of dark trees, spruce and fir, circled rough brown grass. Outcrops rose, mica-shining limestone. A coterie of spirits collected, earth spirits and fey, angels, humans, some undefinable.

Small, muscular dwarven-looking men, smeared with dirt, stood beside gnomes with bright red caps, dryads, and rock-beings. Wispy fey fluttered on butterfly wings. Tall people like sticks ranged beside angels of androgynous beauty. One had a full fan of peacock feathers, eight feet tall.

Ragtag humans mustered, all colors. Some were clearly magic workers, draped with ritual robes and necklaces. Some wore office garb, or jeans and t-shirts, hoodies. One woman had dressed for a gala, in a full ballgown shimmering gold, with a long train.

At the center stood an impassioned being—impossible to tell if they were male or female. Human, perhaps, or a race like human, they had coiling black hair and a lanky frame, not tall.

"We deserve better than this!"

The crowd rumbled assent. "Hear, hear!"

"The oligarchs in heaven reflect the oligarchs on earth. We

must return to the old ways, the good ways, where the earth was protected and listened to!"

A wave of cheering rose.

"Will you fight with us?!"

"Yes!"

Louder, the speaker cried, "Will you fight with us?!"

Louder, the crowd replied, "Yes!"

Chapter 42

N

The mortal present

*B*efore the Fourth of July, Gus drove south to a local reservation that sold unregulated fireworks. He brought his purchases to Witch Farm that night.

Twilight fell late in July. They had dinner on the back porch, with early corn on the cob and raspberries from the farm. Jonathan had bartered for salmon and grilled it. Kirk made himself scarce.

To shoot fireworks, they went to the gravel road that passed Witch Farm. The verge and its trees were dense green this time of year, maples rustling, huge leaves the size of dinner plates. The darker fir towered behind them. Cleo set the fireworks off, Jonathan helper and backup—Joanie was no aficionado of anything that went bang.

An explosion upward, a waterfall of sparks, burst again and again. She did enjoy the pretty of it, the colored flame. Cleo and Jonathan smiled and joked. Afterward, they retreated to the back porch.

Jonathan had bought beer. Joanie made herself a gin and tonic. "I'm drinking it ironically. Appropriated from the British."

"As long as that's all you take with you," Cleo said.

"A few other things, maybe. Punk rock." Pete had always identified as a punk. "But I agree with revolting and starting a democracy. Even if it's heading for the rocks now."

"I can agree with the ideals of the country," Jonathan said. "But it was started by slaveholders, and it was based on stolen land. Blood-soaked land. Maybe that always meant it would fall apart."

"Speaking of bad actors," Gus said to Joanie, sitting beside him, "I found out more about who's passing information to Odin's Hunt."

"Who is it?"

"Julia didn't have a name, but she said it had to be one of two people. One was a friend of someone at Witch Farm, which seemed too vague to be useful. The other was one of the women who catered the wedding."

"I can guess who that is. It's that girl with the Othala tattoo." Gus, with his background in Northern paganism, would know Othala—the "blood and soil" rune of the Nazis. "When she hired on, I had a talk with Jeremy about it, but he didn't want to be biased against someone for their beliefs."

"Even white supremacist beliefs?"

"I asked her about it at one point, and she acted like she didn't know what I was talking about. She's been weird to me ever since. She hasn't gotten the tattoo covered up." She fished the lime out of her drink and squeezed it.

"Can you get her fired?"

"I don't think I can get Jeremy to fire her without evidence she was behind the attack. Plus it might not be her."

"True. Either way, we need more information."

"I can talk to Jeremy, though."

The small farmer's co-op recommended Joanie to friends, and Cleo passed her name to a couple of people associated with Northwest Farms of Color. All of a sudden, Joanie's accounting roster was full. She needed to rejigger her work schedule, but Jeremy was both hard to catch and hard to talk to. He loved certain parts of the coffee-shop owner's life—he loved coffee with a passion—but for much of it, he was barely there.

At points he'd considered selling the shop, and Joanie and a couple other folks had talked about making it into a co-op. But he'd changed his mind. He'd talked too about making her general manager, but when he had, she was focused on college. Now she had this offer to make. Anything he hadn't thought of himself, he was inclined to reject.

On her day off, she met him midafternoon at the shop. She got her usual cappuccino and took the back booth. She'd brought her laptop and preparations for a short lecture on Othala, though Jeremy would likely find some way to sidetrack the conversation. Hot sun flooded the shop, but her corner was blessed with shadow.

Jeremy sat down across from her, his usual double espresso in his personal cup. He was a thin, tall, stooped, blond white man who'd only recently stopped wearing his hair long in a ponytail. It still hung nearly to his shoulders, trimmed but floppy, spilling onto a madras shirt thrown over a Grateful Dead t-shirt.

"What's up?" he asked.

"A couple things." With Jeremy, you cut to the chase. "One is, you know Chelsea, who has the Othala tattoo?"

"Excuse me?"

"Remember when we were hiring her, and I said she had a Nazi tattoo, and you gave her the benefit of the doubt? I have a theory, backed up by some evidence, that she told Odin's Hunt about our wedding."

Jeremy's face wrinkled up—he looked ill. He'd been at the wedding, though far away from the bullets shot. "If she's connected to violence against another employee, that's grounds for being fired. I do need evidence, though."

"I understand." No need to discuss runes after all. But if she hadn't had the rune lecture handy, she'd have needed it. "The other thing is, now I'm out of school, my accounting business is picking up. I need to cut back on my hours here. My proposal is, you keep me at half-time, with insurance, doing your accounting for free."

"Hmm. To give you insurance, you'd need to work at least thirty hours a week." She'd expected this answer; this was standard policy.

"My counter-proposal would be that I quit and you set up an accounting contract with me, at my usual rate. I start at sixty dollars an hour, which is cheap for accounting. I'd be cutting you a significant deal." She could get insurance through Cleo's work if she had to.

"Hmm." He sipped his espresso. "I like this new Guatemalan Antigua. Give me a couple days to think about it, okay? I'd hate to see you leave—you're a huge asset to the management team. We may be able to give you a special deal, since you're in a special position."

He was going to take her suggestion, but he didn't want to say that yet, for whatever Jeremy reason.

"I just need to get this settled within the month."

Nora bent over her laptop at the dining room table, emailing a supplier. Joanie sat down next to her, letting the early sun soak into her body. She'd never wanted to be an early riser, but stress and light through thin curtains sometimes made her one.

There was still a hint of cool in the air. Out the window, long grey-blue shadows fell across the nearest garden beds, the scent of grass from someone's mowing drifting in.

"I'm sorry it worked out like that with Kirk," Joanie said. "I really wanted to like him."

She wanted to smooth things over. She wanted to be kind to Nora, and it was a practical impulse too.

Nora opened another email. "There's a lot of good in him. I wish you could have met him when he was a young man. I don't think he understood how he was coming across."

"Probably not." Everyone thinks they're the good guy. "I hope it's not going to hurt yours and my friendship. Who you sleep with is your business. I'm sure you wouldn't approve of all my liaisons." That might become an issue once they started the Inanna shrines, but they didn't have to deal with that now.

"I don't think it has to hurt anything." Nora scanned the message, deleted it, and paused to gaze past her laptop screen toward the garden. The sun picked out an edge of greenhouse plastic, making it gleam. "Kirk's default is being poly, and mine is not. So it's maybe a short-term liaison anyway."

"Would you keep doing ritual with him?"

"I honestly don't know."

Her mother's money helped. Joanie was able to access some immediately. She paid for Carrie-Anne's plane ticket so she could come to a memorial sooner rather than later. For the rest, she planned to set some aside—Cleo had friends who could help her invest responsibly. She'd donate some to Northwest Farms of Color, and like a good accountant open an IRA. With a Realtor, she prepared to fix up and sell her mother's house, and she planned to use some to repair Witch Farm's plumbing.

She worked with her mother's pastor to write a eulogy and put together an obituary. The memorial was simple. The funeral home set up donations to her mother's children's charity, and she festooned the room with flowers, as her mother would have wanted—lilies and roses, white and pastel.

Everyone who cared to speak at the open microphone did. She spoke briefly and didn't break down. Dustin did, but only at the end.

On the way out, in the foyer, by the grey-green wall with a sheaf of yellow canna lilies in a vase, Carrie-Anne gave her a hug. A big woman, usually smiling, dark hair cut short and practical, she'd helped with setup and reserved a dinner spot for afterward.

"It was really beautiful," she said. "Your mom would have loved it."

"Thank you."

What would a true memorial speech have said?

"In the last few years of my mother's life, she made belated apologies for her monstrous oversights during my childhood. She finally accepted my girlfriend becoming my wife. We were just on the cusp of a real relationship, and then she died."

They hadn't gotten the autopsy results yet—it could take months. But no matter what the results said, her mother had been murdered.

Now Joanie sat in a straight chair in Witch Farm's main ritual room before the altar, moved to an antique dressing table with side wings. At right by a statue of Hekate lay the ancestor shrine, draped in black. It held framed photos and a few tokens, the pieces mostly Nora's but some from the roommates. Joanie had tucked the powder-blue urn in back, with a small photo of her mom in college, hair in a ponytail, smiling.

In a month or two, she'd drive to the coast and empty the urn in the ocean. For now, she moved it to the center of the altar. She sat a few moments in meditation, then spoke.

"I can't forgive you fully yet. I'm still angry. You were too lost in your own pain to help me. I'm releasing the anger bit by bit."

But she missed her mother. She missed her hug, her smell. She'd still been Mom.

"I love you. May the goddess guide you."

She cried again a while, reaching a kind of peace.

At the end of July, in the middle of the night, Joanie woke from a dream as if shaken.

A ray of moonlight crossed the bed. White-lit clouds patched the sky, stars hidden by milky light. A wind moved the nearest stand of maples, leaves fluttering. The night seemed restless.

Cleo slept beside her, but after a moment, her eyes opened.

"I had the strangest dream," Joanie said.

"So did I," Cleo said.

"Was it a bad dream?"

"Not really. If it was anything, it was a call to arms."

"So was mine."

"Tell yours first."

"It started out—it was actually a place I've been. Remember when I was in that coma?"

"Um, yeah. How could I forget?"

"I told you, during that time, I went to a place that was the Demiurge's heaven. The place in the dream was exactly like that, a white marble tower in the sky full of white-winged angels."

"Okay." Cleo pushed herself back against the headboard, putting a pillow behind her.

"Then we went down to the hells. Past the one where they kept Azazel, down to where white-winged angels tortured people. It was awful. Then came these scenes of, I guess, desecration of the earth. Mining, cutting down forests. Also awful.

"Then we were on a peak in the mountains somewhere, all fir trees and so on. Humans and angels and fey, all together. Someone was haranguing us that we had to fight the Demiurge."

Cleo nodded, digesting this.

"What was your dream like?"

"It was the same."

"Kind of on the nose."

"But a call to arms."

Next morning, Kirk's last day in the house, clouds lidded the day. Under the overcast hung a feeling of thunder, muggy, the heat oppressive. In the filtered light, the green of the trees showed intensely.

Kirk piled his belongings at the edge of the gravel drive below a big cedar tree. He hadn't much—a couple boxes, two suitcases, and an oversized duffel bag. He dusted off his hands, looked around, and pulled out his phone.

From her bedroom window, Joanie watched, laptop with accounting work perched on her small desk. She could have set up elsewhere, but she had to make sure he left without some last act of spite.

Around ten, a yellow pickup truck with one red door bounced down the rutted drive. The men who climbed out looked like old-fashioned bikers, roughly Kirk's age. One had floppy greying red hair wrapped with a red bandana, his gut hanging out of his blue jeans. The other wore jeans and a black leather motorcycle vest. Was that an Odin's Hunt patch? There was definitely an Othala tattoo on his tanned shoulder.

Nora couldn't know about these friends of Kirk's. She had questionable taste in men, but she wasn't a white supremacist.

It took five minutes for these two, with Kirk's help, to throw his boxes and bags in the back of the pickup. "I thought you'd have more!" one laughed.

"Not this time."

He'd known these guys a while.

Maybe Kirk had been playing the Witch Farm residents all along. Maybe he'd told Odin's Hunt where the wedding was.

About to clamber into the cab, Kirk threw a glare at Joanie's window. She drew back.

The truck drove up the driveway and away.

Setting aside her accounting work, she placed herself in front of her black-velvet-draped altar. She drew deep breaths till her body calmed, put up her shields, and let herself drop into trance.

Puabi-Ekur appeared as a wisp of purple with a woman's face. "Did you get the dream?"

"I guess so." She described her last night's dream.

"That's the one."

"So what should I do?"

"Lend energy to the fight. If it feels right to you."

"Of course. But why didn't you and Azazel ask me to help personally?"

"I think Azazel doesn't want to endanger you."

"But everything is dangerous now. I'd rather be clear about what I'm fighting, and able to fight. If we must fight."

"I think the time for diplomacy with the oligarchs of Heaven is over."

Somehow, all of this was connected, and was her work. Dropping deeper into trance, she called up energy from earth and sky, bound it with her will, and sent it against the oligarchs.

At twilight, distant high-piled clouds flared now and again with lightning. As the evening grew darker, white flashes showed more distinct.

The back porch had a big overhang, so Nora and Joanie didn't worry about the rain. Nora had found a couple more citronella candles, and the air was dense with their scent.

Cleo was getting back from traveling late that night. She'd

wanted to be there for Kirk's move-out—she didn't trust him, didn't know what he'd do—but Northwest Farms of Color was growing its range and short on staff.

"Unusual for Seattle," Joanie said. "Thunderstorms."

"This is a dangerous storm," Nora said. "I don't like the feel of it."

Jonathan stepped out onto the porch. "Mind if I join you?"

"Not at all," Nora said.

Jonathan took the chair to Joanie's far side. He lit his pipe, offered it to Joanie. She shook her head.

Against the dark, fairy lights shone on the far greenhouse, there to keep away wildlife—occasionally bears found the berries interesting or deer helped themselves to growing corn. Thunder rumbled, rolling barrels in a hallway far above. Still the rain didn't fall.

It felt ominous. "How are you for weather magic?" Joanie asked Jonathan.

"Some rain would be good for the corn. It's been a dry summer so far."

Dangerously dry, even—this land north of Seattle was a temperate rain forest, but the mast under the trees crackled under a bare foot now. In places, the firs had gone brown, the maples red.

A first few drops began to pat the grass.

Then with a crash a deluge loosed, as if a bucket were dumped.

"At last," he said.

Nora went in, but Joanie and Jonathan stayed a little longer— the burst of rain backed off to a steady patter.

"Think it'll rain all night?" Joanie asked.

"Hope so. We haven't had nearly enough precipitation this July."

Mist rose from the forest. The air had cooled. A rustling, not just the wind, sounded in the nearer trees beyond the greenhouses.

"What's that?" Joanie asked.

Trespassers were a real possibility. Neighbors had found a burned-out trailer on a hillside only a few miles away—everyone assumed it was a meth lab. Kirk had just exited into the arms of Odin's Hunt.

"Birds?" he asked.

"Too big."

"Deer, probably."

~

She woke to Cleo shaking her. She growled. The first sound sleep she'd had in ages, Kirk finally gone, and Cleo decided to wake her early.

There was a sound of crackling. The air smelled like smoke.

"Get up! The house is on fire!"

Joanie sat up, fuzzy-headed, and shook herself.

Fear kicked in. She fished her nightgown out from the sheets, found her sandals. Cleo threw her a hoodie. Earlier in the year, they'd made go bags, backpacks with essential papers, a change of clothes, shoes, simple trail food, and medical supplies. She stumbled to the closet, grabbed hers, swung it on with her purse.

Ahead of her, in the hallway, Cleo said, "Fuck!"

The front room was burning, the coat stand on fire. The first couple stairs had caught. "Out the window," Cleo said.

In the bedroom, Joanie ripped the curtains apart and threw the window all the way open. Leaning, she dropped her backpack into the dirt.

Cleo paused on the sill, looking at the ground.

No use screaming at her. "Better to break an ankle than burn to death."

"You learned how to fall in martial arts." Cleo hadn't.

"Just fall and roll. You can do it. Do you want me to go first?"

In seconds, their filmy curtains would go up in flames.

Cleo pushed herself out the window.

Joanie climbed onto the sill, caught her breath, and dropped.

She hit with a thump, fell to her knees on the gravel driveway. Pain. Then she stood up, brushing her legs off—shaken, scratched, bruised, but not burning to death.

Nora and Jonathan met them. "I called the fire department," Nora said. "They should be here any minute."

The night hung flat black under cloud, the rain done. Against it fire poured upward.

Rank smoke filled the air. She coughed. She was still muzzy-minded, half-asleep. Sparks rained down in front of them. They backed up.

"Oh, gods. What about the kittens?"

She ran a few steps toward the house, sparks falling all around her. One fell on her hoodie, with the smell of cloth burning.

The roof exploded into flame.

"They're smart little cats," Cleo said. "They'll run into the woods. They came from there."

It was too much. Joanie melted into tears. Cleo put her arms around her.

The house burned like a candle, flames thirty feet high.

In the distance, sirens wailed, closer and closer.

In the middle of the night, bitter fumes of burning plastic in the air, they stood on the driveway facing what was left of the house. Lights from the firetrucks illuminated charred sticks from its frame. Smoke drifted from the wreck.

A police detective had taken statements. Kirk's name had come up. It was too early to determine arson.

One of the firefighters walked up to them, chunky in a thick suit of chartreuse green. "Lucky it rained tonight—probably saved us from a forest fire. You got somewhere to stay?"

Joanie said, "We do." Jonathan raised an eyebrow. "Hannah's happy to have us."

The Realtor was having her mother's house fixed up and repainted. Also she needed company.

Chapter 43

The mortal present

In the morning, they convened in Hannah's tiny wine-red-painted breakfast nook. Beyond it, the kitchen windows stood open to birdsong; maple and alder leaves waved in the breeze. Everyone was bleary-eyed, drinking Hannah's double-strength coffee. Joanie was numb, which was fine. It wouldn't last.

"In the long run, we'll be okay," Nora said. "We have good insurance."

"We pay enough for it," Cleo said.

"I can put some in from the mom fund," Joanie said. "But do you all think Kirk set this? Or his friends?"

"They'd have to be pretty stupid to do that," Cleo said.

"If he has friends in Odin's Hunt, that tracks—they're pretty stupid," Jonathan said.

"What do you think, Nora?" Joanie asked.

Nora sat eyes closed, back against the dark-red wall, looking shattered. Witch Farm was her baby.

"I don't think Kirk would do it. At least I hope not. I had no idea he was hanging out with Odin's Hunt."

"That's hardly a certain thing," Joanie said. "I just saw the tattoo—unfortunately, lots of people have that tattoo."

"We're going to have to be out of the house a while," Nora said. "Maybe as long as six months. Insurance will pay rent for a place to stay."

"I already checked with Hannah," Joanie said. "She's happy to let Cleo and me have the open room."

"I have places I can stay for a minimum of rent," Jonathan said. Cleo raised an eyebrow. He grinned.

"I'd like to stay close to the house if I can," Nora said. "Maybe in the yurt, depending on what that looks like. I'm hoping we can save the gardens and the greenhouse."

"Do you want to go over there?" Joanie asked. "I have the day free." It was the rare Saturday she had the day off. She'd planned a ritual in the yurt for that evening, too, and she wanted to see if it could happen.

"So do I," Cleo said.

"Me too," Jonathan rumbled. Nora nodded.

"It's a plan," Joanie said.

They took Nora's car, the largest, a middle-aged SUV. The drive to Witch Farm through the firs and cedar was more contemplative than usual, though it was a brilliant summer day, hot again. Windows up, they put the air conditioning on. Sky blue, a few drifting clouds, the air had been washed clean by rain.

Joanie's laptop, her most valuable possession, was gone. She'd saved her important data. Other than that, she didn't own much. She'd miss a few clothes, some jewelry she'd inherited from her grandmother.

And the urn. Maybe that was gone—ashes to ashes. But she could hope.

"Do you see that?" Nora asked, from the driver's seat. She pointed upward.

"What?"

"An eagle."

Joanie rolled down her window and craned to look at the sky. A bald eagle circled overhead, gliding on thermals.

"It seems like good luck," Nora said.

"I hope so. We can use some."

They arrived, piled out, gawping at the smoldering pile that had been their house. A few charred wall sections and timbers remained from the frame. The firefighters had said it would be a total loss.

"It's probably too early to go where the house was," Nora said. "I'm here mainly for the gardens."

"I'm going to poke around," Joanie said. "Call the kittens."

"Be careful. It's hot." It was still smoking.

She wandered around. "Jinx, Jareth!" They knew their names, sort of, but they were skittish and they'd had a huge fright.

No kittens appeared.

Biting her lip to hold back tears, she turned toward the remains of the house, walked a little way onto the charred cinders.

She didn't get far—the soles of her sneakers got hot, and she backed out.

"We can come back," Cleo said.

"The insurance sends a professional team. They'll let us go through stuff."

Nora and Jonathan consulted in one of the greenhouses. Flying sparks had damaged one, melting the plastic, but otherwise the gardens were unscathed. They'd need to clean up fallen ash and cinders.

Joanie found a blanket in the yurt, that building also mostly intact. She threw the blanket on the grass.

"You got sunscreen, white girl?"

"Right here." They had plain and fizzy water too.

"They'll be a while, won't they?" Joanie asked.

"Yup."

"You think Kirk did it?"

"You heard someone in the woods that night."

"Jonathan thought it was a deer."

"I'm guessing it's not Kirk but one of his friends. If it really was Odin's Hunt, we're on their list already."

Something rustled in the grass. Joanie's heart leaped in her chest. Odin's Hunt again?

There was a tiny mew.

Two little faces poked through the salal at the edge of the field—Jareth and Jinx.

They ran to Joanie and Cleo on the blanket and jumped on them, purring.

"Oh, my darlings," Joanie said. She picked up Jinx, kissed his face, whuffled the black fur on his tiny side. Cleo petted Jareth's head.

As twilight fell that evening, Joanie and Cleo set up the yurt for ritual. Across the yard, the rubble still smoked faintly. A yellow wheelbarrow stood beside the wreckage, the start of cleanup.

In defiance of the fire, she was going forward. They'd planned this, and now was the time.

She and Cleo lit citronella candles in the torches along the path to the yurt, meeting the other ritualists at the path's end.

"We can get started, if you're ready," Joanie said.

Next to the yurt's outer door stood a carven wooden table, on it a towel and a brass washbowl. Joanie stepped up first and rinsed her hands. Behind her stood Cleo, Kelsey, Hannah, and Nora.

Closing her eyes, she prayed silently.

Lady Inanna, bless our gathering. Our intention is to create ritual for you, the beginning of a series.

Inside, another small table held a vial of cypress oil. Cleo entered, and Joanie anointed her on the forehead. "Blessings of Inanna." Cleo did the same for her. The others followed.

Around the yurt, pink, gold, and magenta saris hung gleaming with gilt thread, moving gently in a breeze from the fan. To the side under a dark-blue throw lay a pile of Nora's things. She planned to stay in the yurt while the house was restored.

The group formed a circle around Joanie, in front of the altar.

"I'll lead you in a grounding," she said. "Take a few deep breaths, in and out, then picture a seed in your center, below and behind your belly button. Let it burst open and a root go down through your body, the floor, into the earth. Let a shoot grow upward, through your body, your head, the yurt ceiling, into the night sky. It becomes a tree, maybe a cypress from the Land Between Two Rivers."

Finishing the grounding, she said, "Now we'll do a brief chant to call Inanna. When I say 'Inanna, I hail,' you respond, 'Inanna, I hail.'" The group murmured assent.

Joanie began: "The pure torch lit in the sky, the heavenly light, the great Queen of Heaven, Inanna I hail!"

The group answered, "Inanna I hail!"

"Her brilliant coming forth in the evening sky, her lighting the sky, a pure torch, Inanna I hail!"

"Inanna I hail!"

Cleo lit a coral-pink candle on the altar in front of the Inanna statue, rounded in form, breasts cupped in her hands.

"This ritual is a chance for everyone to try things out," Joanie said, "to see how it feels to do this work for Inanna. We'll start with a greeting, where everyone turns first to the left and then the right and says one positive thing we appreciate about the person there."

Between Cleo and Nora, Joanie turned to Cleo first. "You know I love you beyond anything."

Cleo grinned. "Me too you."

Across the way, Kelsey giggled. Hannah was whispering in her ear.

To Nora, Joanie said, "Thank you for listening to me. I really value that." Nora nodded. When she let her face rest, it fell into long, sad lines.

It was surprising she'd wanted to do the ritual. It was a stretch for all the farm residents, but Witch Farm was Nora's life.

During the greeting, the yurt had grown dark. Joanie lit a couple of candles in glass on the altar, and Cleo turned on the standing lamp. Warm light fell among blue shadows.

"Next, we'll do massage," Joanie said. "You can choose either erotic or nonerotic. Has anyone here not been part of a conversation about consent?"

"I have, for sure," Kelsey said.

"Just to be clear, you can always say no. You can always change your mind or stop things in the middle. It's not a race or a way to show you're tough or brave. It's about pleasure in the loving arms of the goddess. Pleasure can include keeping yourself to yourself."

"We'll use nitrile gloves for any erotic massage," Cleo said, waggling a box, the gloves rose-colored to match the decor. She and Joanie picked up the massage table, decked in ice-pink Egyptian-cotton sheets, and moved it in front of the altar.

"Who wants to go first?" Joanie asked.

Hannah glanced around the circle. "If no one else wants to, I will."

She pulled off her sundress, and Joanie and Cleo helped her onto the massage table. "Let's start with regular massage, and I'll see how I feel."

They stroked her, rubbing her shoulders, going deep on the long muscles of her thighs. "Maybe I do want erotic massage."

Joanie slipped on gloves and began to stroke Hannah's shaved pubis.

"Do you want insertion?" she asked.

"No, just start lightly. Go slow."

Joanie gave herself to the rhythm, Cleo supporting her, also in rose-colored gloves. Their hands traded and intertwined, slowly building. Cleo bent to kiss Hannah's shoulder.

The feeling caught like gentle fire, spark lighting, building, holy.

Bit by bit, in the warm room touched by the fan's breeze, the momentum built, rose and plateaued and rose again, till Hannah cried out full-throated. Energy surged through the room, bit by bit subsided.

After a time, Hannah sat up.

She nodded to the goddess statue. "Thank you, Inanna." To the women around the table, she said, "Also, thank y'all."

Kelsey was sniffling, tears in her eyes. "That was amazing."

Joanie had wondered, but Kelsey's reaction was real. The goddess had called her.

"I want to go next!" Kelsey said.

Chapter 44

The eternal present

$\mathcal{A}$t the edge of Yaldabaoth's heaven, flanked by stands of cumulus, a rocky outcrop appeared in the endless blue. On it stood a huge doorway—white marble pillars topped by a pediment, sky to either side. It gleamed rosy in an unseen dawn, almost heavenly; it dripped ivy and vines heavy with black grapes. Azazel and Samyaza lounged beside it.

Mitzrael appeared, golden face impassive.

"What brings you here, with your mammoth doorway?"

"It seemed only fair you be offered the opportunity to surrender," Samyaza said.

"The opportunity to reframe the interaction between the Demiurge and what he calls his kingdom," Azazel added. "The opportunity to go through this open door and join us in freedom."

"You have the warriors to enforce this reframing?"

"More than enough," Samyaza said.

"You know that it is past time for this," Azazel said. "You are the angel of submission to just authority. Do you really feel that the Demiurge has dealt with us all justly?"

"Only moments ago, in angel time, you helped release Azazel from one of Yaldabaoth's minions," Samyaza said.

Mitzrael's glance flickered, the tiniest acknowledgement. "That does not mean the Demiurge's rule is unjust."

"He claims omniscience. Thus he sees and approves his followers' acts."

"We play a long game. All come to justice in the end. Some not till the very end."

"Be it noted," Azazel said, "we offered you the chance to avoid this conflict."

"You did," Mitzrael said.

The doorway disappeared.

Angels and allies exploded into action. Swords clanged; slash, grunt, and outcry sounded, in the blue sky by the white tower of heaven. Nergal, the Rabisi, further Mesopotamian forces, the fey and earth-folk joined the fallen angels.

Below, on earth, fey and plant spirits released bursts of out-of-season pollen, green clouds that left towns choking in Brazil, Germany, the US Midwest, China. Kudzu in Tennessee and Virginia sped like film at double speed, covering one small town then another. Locusts hit France, Kenya, and Somalia. Fey lights and illusions blocked traffic from tiny towns in Ireland to the center of Shanghai.

Thunderstorms, tornadoes, and out-of-season tropical storms lashed the ocean and the coasts. A rogue wave hit Honshu Island in Japan. Mountains turned feral. In the Carpathian Mountains, a sinkhole swallowed a village whole. Avalanches took out ski resorts across the Alps and Rockies.

Earthquakes shook seismic zones. In Ecuador's eastern Andes, the stratovolcano Reventador rumbled. Active peaks in Hawaii, Japan, and Indonesia sprang to life. The volcano below Santorini puffed gas, preparing to shoot. Mount Etna in Sicily bled lava. Iru Phutunqu and Lascar in Chile burped spurts of magma. In Iceland, quakes rocked the island and the entire Reykjanes Volcanic Belt blew in a volley, smoke rocketing into the air. Rivers of lava blasted down Fagradalsfjall's slopes and buried the Reykjanes Peninsula in molten rock.

Electrical systems went haywire. Cars collided and detonated—the Autobahn clogged with dead and burning vehicles. Tokyo lost power; New York blacked out completely, worse than 1977. Washington, DC, followed. The Capitol hunkered dark. Trains derailed—the first a bullet train in Japan, then one in Italy, then dozens. Airplanes hurtled from the sky. One military plane narrowly missed pancaking the White House to crater in the South Lawn.

The end times had begun.

$$\overline{}$$

Characters of The
Enlightenment Game

$$\overline{}$$

Humans

Alyssa. A witch in Joanie's coven, a barista at the coffee shop where Joanie works, and Gus's girlfriend.

Bruni, aka Thomas Mueller. A former leader of the white-supremacist heathen group Odin's Hunt.

Celia. A barista at the coffee shop where Joanie works.

Cleo Gleeson. Joanie's fiancée, a witch and devotee of Inanna, and an employee of a nonprofit, Northwest Farms of Color, which supports Black and Indigenous farmers.

Crystal MacEwan. Joanie's mother.

Dustin. Crystal's boyfriend.

Gus. A biology student, a witch in Joanie's coven, and a former member of Odin's Hunt, a white-supremacist heathen group.

Hannah Redstone. High priestess of the witch coven that Joanie belongs to, and Alyssa's and Gus's landlady and housemate.

Jeremy. Joanie's boss at the coffee shop where she works.

Jimbo. A housemate at the house where Gus, Alyssa, and Hannah live.

Joanie MacEwan. Cleo's fiancée, a student finishing a bachelor's degree in accounting, a witch, and a manager at a coffee shop. Joanie identifies as a sacred whore, giving sexual healing in the name of the goddess Inanna.

Jonathan. One of the housemates at Witch Farm, the farm co-op where Joanie and Cleo live.

Julia. A former member of the Odin's Hunt women's auxiliary and Gus's former lover.

Kelsey. A barista at the coffee shop where Joanie works.

Kirk McDonald. Nora's lover, a chemist who creates grey-market hallucinogens.

Mark Walker. A hotelier formerly involved with Odin's Hunt, now dead.

Max Dwyer. A former lover of Gus and leader of Odin's Hunt, now dead.

Mike. A member of Nora's coven.

Nora. The woman who started the farm co-op Witch Farm and a witch high priestess.

Pete Martin. A former lover of Joanie's, now dead, who became an avatar of the Horned God and who protects Witch Farm.

Ray Gleeson. Cleo's father.

Robert Carpenter, aka Rob. An anarchist killed by Odin's Hunt.

Sandy. A member of Nora's coven.

Sharon Gleeson. Ray's wife and Cleo's stepmother.

Thomas Mueller. See Bruni.

Angels and spirits

Alfstein. A member of the Icelandic huldufólk spirits who is an ally of the Watcher angel Samyaza.

Azazel. One of the Watcher angels, brother to Samyaza and former lover to Joanie and Puabi-Ekur. The Watchers are forbears to Joanie's witch lineage, fallen angels who seduced Eve's children.

Berkana. A dryad who is an ally of Samyaza's.

Ishum. A vizier of the Sumerian god Nergal.

Mitzrael. An angel who is a follower of the Demiurge.

Puabi-Ekur. An incubus-succubus, lover to Azazel and Joanie. Puabi-Ekur can shapeshift into Puabi, a dancing girl from ancient Sumerian Uruk, and Ekur, a military general from Uruk.

Rabisi. A group of Sumerian wind spirits.

Samyaza. One of the Watcher angels, brother to Azazel.

Suriyel. An angel formerly allied with the Watchers, now a follower of the Demiurge.

Deities

Dea. A goddess who guards Witch Farm and who can appear in human or bear form.

Demiurge, aka Yaldabaoth. Chief archon of heaven and god of the manifest world.

Ereshkigal. Sumerian goddess of the Great Below, the Sumerian hell, and a lover of Joanie and Puabi-Ekur. Sister to Inanna and wife of Nergal.

Hekate. Greek goddess associated with the crossroads, ghosts, witchcraft, and the moon, and also with keys and liminal spaces.

Horned God. A deity of the woods around Witch Farm. Joanie's former lover Pete is an avatar of this Horned God.

Inanna. Sumerian goddess of love and war, Queen of Heaven, Ereshkigal's sister and Joanie's patroness.

Nergal. Sumerian god of death by battle and plague, husband to Ereshkigal and lover of Joanie and Puabi-Ekur.

Somnia. A Roman goddess of dreams.

Star Goddess. Androgynous deity of primal darkness and all creation, the All That Is as a deity.

Yaldabaoth. See Demiurge.

About the Author

Mary Trepanier writes fantasy, horror, and erotica. You can find her short stories in the *Blood in the Rain* anthologies of vampire erotica, among others. For more of *Tales of the End Times*, check out *The Queen of Heaven's Daughter*, *The Deer Stalker*, *The Way to Witch Farm*, and *The Plague God*.

Connect with Mary through her mailing list, her website (http://marytrepanier.com/), or by finding her on social media. Be the first to learn about each new volume in the *Tales of the End Times* series.

Also by Mary Trepanier

Thank you for reading *The Enlightenment Game,* sixth in the *Tales of the End Times* series. We hope you enjoyed it enough to consider leaving a review.

Did you read the other books in the series? If not, you can purchase the entire series by visiting your favorite bookstore or wherever books are sold online.

Mary Trepanier has also edited four collections of short vampire erotica stories, *Blood in the Rain,* volumes one through four. Also available at your local bookstore or online.

Gillian Bainbridge and Damien Grey narrate the first collection—it can be found on Audible and iTunes.

Look for future releases by signing up for our newsletter at Cwtch Press.

www.ingramcontent.com/pod-product-compliance
Lightning Source LLC
Chambersburg PA
CBHW060650190726
48289CB00002B/346